"Do you understand what you're doing?"

Cain asked.

"Yes," Maggie answered breathlessly.

"Do you understand I have nothing to give you?"

"Yes."

"You can't reform me, you can't save me, you can't own me. I will keep you hostage even after this moment, but I will also definitely let you go once we get to where we're going. You can go your way, I'll go mine. But I am not one of your lost causes, Maggie. I've made my choices, and I'm willing to pay for them. Just don't ask me to pay for yours."

"All right."

"None of that is going to change because of one moment of passion," Cain continued.

"I know," Maggie said, but she thought he was lying. Because this *wasn't* just one moment, and it *would* change everything.

Dear Reader,

By now you've undoubtedly come to realize how special our Intimate Moments Extra titles are, and Maura Seger's *The Perfect Couple* is no exception. The unique narrative structure of this book only highlights the fact that this is indeed a perfect couple—if only they can find their way back together again.

Alicia Scott begins a new miniseries, MAXIMILLIAN'S CHILDREN, with *Maggie's Man*, a genuine page-turner. Beverly Bird's *Compromising Positions* is a twisty story of love and danger. And welcome Carla Cassidy back after a too-long absence, with *Behind Closed Doors*, a book as steamy as its title implies. Margaret Watson offers *The Dark Side of the Moon*, while new author Karen Anders checks in with *Jennifer's Outlaw*.

You won't want to miss a single one. And don't forget to come back next month for more of the best romantic reading around—only from Silhouette Intimate Moments.

Leslie Wainger
Senior Editor and Editorial Coordinator

Please address questions and book requests to:
Silhouette Reader Service
U.S.: 3010 Walden Ave., P.O. Box 1325, Buffalo, NY 14269
Canadian: P.O. Box 609, Fort Erie, Ont. L2A 5X3

MAGGIE'S
MAN

ALICIA
SCOTT

Published by Silhouette Books

America's Publisher of Contemporary Romance

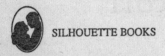

SILHOUETTE BOOKS

ISBN 0-373-07776-9

MAGGIE'S MAN

Copyright © 1997 by Lisa Baumgartner

This edition published by arrangement with Harlequin Books S.A.

® and TM are trademarks of Harlequin Books S.A., used under license. Trademarks indicated with ® are registered in the United States Patent and Trademark Office, the Canadian Trade Marks Office and in other countries.

Printed in U.S.A.

Books by Alicia Scott

ALICIA SCOTT

recently escaped the corporate world to pursue her writing full-time. According to the former consultant, "I've been a writer for as long as I can remember. For me, it's the perfect job, and you can't beat the dress code." Born in Hawaii, she grew up in Oregon before moving to Massachusetts. Now an avid traveler, she spends her time chasing after two feisty felines, watching Val Kilmer movies and eating chocolate when she's not running around the globe.

She is currently at work on her latest project in Boston, where she awaits the discovery of true love or ownership of a chocolate shop—whichever comes first.

Chapter 1

"Don't move."

Maggie Ferringer looked up blankly from her seat on the wooden bench outside the second-floor courtroom. Eight-fifty a.m. and she hadn't had coffee yet. She was tired, disgruntled at being called for jury duty and still preoccupied with how she was going to rearrange all her appointments for the next five days. Plus, one of her cats was sick. She was thinking she'd better take him to the vet.

"Don't move," the prison guard repeated, and this time his voice was very hard.

She blinked rapidly, looking at the man with mild confusion. Strangers were always approaching her. There could be one hundred people on the street and the tourist would stop and ask Maggie for directions. She supposed it was because she was so unassuming. At five feet, she had a slight build and pale skin that only burned, never tanned. Her clothes ran toward the admittedly conservative—she had a weakness for low-slung, hopelessly sensible pumps. Today, she'd matched her favorite pair of beige pumps with a brown plaid wool skirt and simple pink blouse that declared, I am an intelligent, professional woman with really boring taste in clothes.

Last week, her mother—one of those tall, wildly beautiful women who could actually wear leopard-print jumpsuits—had flown into town, greeted Maggie with two fofooey cheek kisses and dramatically exclaimed, "My God, Maggie darling! How did I ever give birth to a creature who will probably marry an accountant?"

And Maggie, who felt the same sting she always felt when trying to understand her exotic, temperamental artist mother, had the sudden urge to toss back her red hair and retort fiercely, "At least an accountant would come home every night for dinner, which was more than I could ever say about you!" She hadn't said any such thing, of course. She was still slightly surprised she'd bothered to think it. After twenty-seven years, she'd come to the realization that Stephanie would always be Stephanie. Getting angry with her immature, self-centered, extremely un-Mom-like behavior was as productive as hating the sun for shining.

"Lady," the guard was now growling tensely, "I said move!"

"Move where?" she asked him politely. As far as she could tell, the second floor of the old courthouse was still deserted. Space should not be a problem for him.

Then Maggie noticed the gun. The big gun. The big black gun pointed right at her, here, in the middle of the vast gray marble hallway of the Multnomah County Courthouse. The hallway was dead quiet, hushed as a courthouse should be hushed—particularly one that had opened its door just five minutes before. But this was only the second story of the building. Just one floor beneath them, she could hear the reassuring hum of people beginning to enter and the parrotlike chirp of the metal detectors as brass business-card holders, chunky gold earrings, key chains and pocket change occasionally triggered the systems guarding the door.

She stared at the gun still held unwaveringly in front of her, blinked several times, then stared at it again.

The prison guard abruptly jabbed her in the ribs with the cold, metal barrel. Oh God, it was real. She was being attacked by a prison guard!

Maggie quietly stopped breathing.

Hello, her mind whispered. *Somebody come up here and do something. Somebody jump out and tell me I'm on "Candid Camera."*

The only person who moved was the prison guard.

"Do exactly what I say," the light-haired man said steadily, his green eyes boring into her. He shifted, positioning his solid body between her and the top of the stairs where the first smartly dressed morning commuter was now appearing. That man was followed by a woman in a paisley-print dress, then another man in a suit.

The guard in front of her shifted again and she lost her view of the top of the stairs completely. One moment she was admiring the grand gray marble staircase with its cast-iron and brass railing, the next her universe was reduced to bulging biceps, a granite chest and a pair of chilling green eyes that told her he was bigger, better and badder than she would ever be in her whole entire life.

She would grant him that. She was one of those people who could never even get the lid off the pickle jar. *C.J., Brandon…help!*

"Listen up and don't make a sound," the "prison guard" murmured. His voice didn't waver, the gun didn't waver, his gaze didn't waver. He exuded one-hundred-percent-focused, honed control. She was a dead woman.

"Okay," she whispered weakly. Her eyes flew from his face to his brown uniform, to the badge on his chest. Then her eyes fell lower and she realized the shirt was too tight across his chest, the pants unbuttoned at his waist, the hems ending a good two inches above his ankles. His feet were squashed awkwardly in the shiny black boots, as if he was forced to walk tiptoe by the constraining leather.

"You're not a prison guard!" she exclaimed softly.

The left corner of his lips twisted up. "Very good, you win the double-jeopardy question. Next time, give your answer in the form of a question. Now stand up and do exactly as I say."

The gun dug into her ribs with clear authority and she jumped to her feet as if it had been a cattle prod. Her oversize beige purse promptly fell off her lap and vomited onto the floor.

"Damn!" her prison guard/captor swore. With a harsh impatient gesture, he planted one broad palm on her thin shoulder and shoved her down. "Grab it and let's go."

"Okay," she said again, her fingers trembling so hard she scrambled three lipstick tubes, a set of house keys, a metal nail file, four throat lozenges, a pocket calculator, two cat rabies tags and her checkbook all over the floor.

"Lady!" he warned.

"I don't know what I'm doing!" she cried out perilously loud. The ringing footsteps of one man's dress heels against the marble floor came to a suspicious halt.

The guard hunched down immediately, the gun sharp against her ribs and his shoulder hard against her body. One sweep of his broad hand and everything was back in her oversize leather purse. He leaned so close she could feel his breath on her lips, smell soap and sweat, and see the burning-green determination of his eyes.

"One more stunt like that," he told her quietly, "and you're dead."

His fingers wrapped around her thin arm. Effortlessly he dragged her to her feet, her body pressed against him as if she were weightless. And all she could think was that her tax dollars had probably paid for the prison barbells that had made him so strong.

Ha, ha. Reform doesn't work. She was going to break into hysterical laughter any time now.

Her tour guide didn't seem to care. With quick, breathless steps he dragged her boldly right to the stairs. Maggie caught the gaze of a startled man in a deep gray suit still watching her. *Run, yell, do something,* she thought. Fingers dug into her upper arm and she smiled at the halted man instead. He politely nodded at her, she nodded back. And he walked away as Attila the Hun dragged her bodily down the rapidly flooding stairs.

They were going against the flow of traffic, but nobody seemed to mind. The stream of humanity split around them without a second glance. Executives in their suits passed so close she could touch them with her fingertips. One judge already in his black robe walked up the broad steps just two feet away. Court clerks in professional, but not *too* professional clothes sipped coffee and chatted about the beautiful spring weather as they moved to one side so an escaped felon could drag her down to the front doors.

Say something, do something, her mind whispered. *Lydia always said your hair marked you as one of the legendary Hathaway Reds, and all the Hathaway Reds were women of great courage and passion. So do something! Just this once, actually do something!*

As if reading her thoughts, the Terminator's fingers dug into her skin, clamping her arm tightly and effectively. She had to half jog to keep up with his long, lean strides, which cut through the stairs like butter. Obviously, the man not only lifted weights but ran on the prison treadmill machine. Did they give convicts StairMasters, as well, so they could climb skyscrapers as modern-day versions of King Kong? She was definitely writing a letter to her state congressman after this. Definitely, definitely, definitely.

They made the turn of the sweeping staircase. The huge bay of glass doors loomed before them, guarded by the standing metal detectors everyone had to walk through. For a minute, Maggie felt the hope soar in her chest. The minute he dragged her through the detectors, his gun would set them off and she'd be home free!

Then she realized the detectors were only for the people

walking in. There were no such protective devices for the people walking out.

His footsteps quickened and she was helpless to stop the momentum.

The security desk was to her left. Three men sat there in uniform. *Look over here, darn it! Hey, hey, someone set down your jelly doughnut and look at me!*

But they only watched the people entering the building.

Maggie rolled her eyes frantically to the right. Phones, the bank of phones. If she could twist away, if she could make it to the phones. Her brother would help her. C.J. had joined the Marines when he'd turned eighteen and taken to it like a seal to water. He even had more medals than their grandpa had gotten in World War II and Korea combined; no one messed with C.J. Or Brandon. Where was he these days? He just hadn't been the same since burying his young wife two years ago, taking off and traveling the world in a manner frighteningly similar to their late, departed father.

She made an instinctive lunge for the phone banks. At least she thought it was a lunge. Her captor glanced at her quizzically as if she'd hiccuped, then proceeded to drag her through the big glass doors like his own personal Raggedy Ann.

She blinked like an owl beneath the sudden harsh glare of sunlight. A part of her was instantly relieved. It was daylight, after all, prime commute time on a bright spring day in downtown Portland; everyone knew bad things only happened after midnight in dark alleyways where stark streetlights reflected off big puddles.

Attila, however, showed no signs of slowing down. He dragged her to the corner, then came to an abrupt halt. She was so unprepared for the stop, she tripped in her low heels and practically flung herself around him like a spider monkey. He caught her hundred-pound body effortlessly, not even swaying from the impact. Strong hands gripped her shoulders and righted her curtly. Again, she did her impression of a blinking owl.

"God, who taught you how to walk?" he muttered, then pinned her with a determined green gaze. "Where's your car?"

"Car?" she asked weakly. They were on Fourth Street, populated pulsing Fourth Street, swamped by morning commuters on foot and in cars. Beautiful wide street, nice clean sidewalks because Portland was a nice, clean city. Wide blue sky, bright spring sun, gentle wafting breeze from the waterfront just four blocks away. Across the street, a simple city park offered a touch of emerald green and a thoughtful memorial to the U.S. Volunteer Infantry. Behind it, she could see the towering white stone building of the Justice Center.

The walk signal's green man lit up, indicating for pedestrians to proceed, and her captor dragged her briskly across the street. Drivers watched them politely, fellow commuters rushed by hurriedly. Abruptly, Attila pushed her into the park, ducking them both behind a four-foot-high hedge. She had time for one gulping gasp of air, then he pinned her between the prickly hedge and his rock-hard frame.

Her hands were captured against his broad chest, her legs clamped between his muscled thighs. She was just a tiny, delicately built woman, and he looked as if he could bench-press a sumo wrestler. She blinked, then blinked again. No matter how many times she did it, he remained standing before her, his steely thighs clamped around her legs.

"P-p-please," she begged weakly. Her body began to tremble, her eyes squeezed shut; she had no pride. She was very scared and she would do anything if this man would just let her go. "D-d-don't hurt me...."

"Look at me," he commanded.

She had no choice. She opened her eyes to find his face looming over hers, those bright green eyes hooded by thick, blond brows. For the first time, she could see the sweat beading on his forehead and upper lips, the smooth texture of his skin. His cheeks held the faded gold stamp of old

sun and the fresh pallor of a man who hadn't been outside
in a long while. His jaw appeared to have been carved from
a mountain, strong, square and absolutely unrelenting. His
neck was so strong she could see corded lines of muscle
from the tense way he held his shoulders.

By God, he didn't look like someone who believed in
compromise. And those lips were only an inch from hers,
the closest any man's lips had been in a long time.

"I don't want to hurt you," he said quietly and without
any trace of warmth. His green eyes scrutinized her, not
cruel, not crazy, but unrelentingly sharp. She imagined sci-
entists used the same gaze on lab rats right before they
conducted the next horrible experiment.

She giggled hysterically; she couldn't help herself. In
response, he jammed the gun against her side so sharply
that she hiccuped.

His eyes narrowed and when he spoke, his tone was all
business. "Any minute now, a half-naked guard is going
to come running out of that courthouse. You don't want
that to happen, because if that happens, you're my insurance. It's going to be you between a convicted murderer
and a corrections officer who doesn't want a black mark
on his record. Understand?"

"Convicted murderer?"

Slowly, coolly, he nodded. His gaze was suddenly
hooded. "After killing the first person, the second is easy."

She flinched reflexively, once more shutting her eyes.
*Faint, Maggie. Just faint and then you'll be no good to him
and he'll leave you alone.*

"Tell me where your car is."

Her face crumpled further, the hysteria rising up in a
sickening mixture of giggles and hiccups. Oh God, she
was incapable of fainting. Whoever would've known? It
wasn't as if she was a particularly strong person. In the violent war that had masqueraded as her parents' marriage, she
had been a heartbroken, seven-year-old diplomat, not a soldier. Nor was she an adventuresome, temperamental wild-

woman like her mother. She lived alone in the suburbs with two cats. These days, buying a new brand of panty hose constituted a major event in her life. Really, she thought she ought to be able to faint.

"Are you listening to me?"

"I don't have a car," she whispered glumly, her eyes opening and gazing at him miserably. "Want a bus pass instead?" She tried for a hopeful smile.

"Damn!" His arms snapped around her upper arm, and suddenly his voice was hot and urgent in her ear. "Start walking. *Fast!*"

Her eyes popped open. Behind her she could hear a sudden commotion. The real prison guard, she thought. He was coming out. And then she remembered what Attila the Hun had told her about her future opportunities when the real prison guard appeared. She started walking *fast,* her captor's hand still clenched tightly around her arm.

"Car," he whispered urgently, his voice hot against her cheek. "We need a car. I'm not lying."

"I don't have one," she whispered back just as intently, then winced as his grip tightened on her arm. "Honest! I took the bus! Don't you know what traffic is like on the Sunset Highway these days?"

"Oh sure. In prison we listen to the traffic reports all the time. It would be such a shame to be caught in rush-hour traffic on our way over the wall."

He dragged her straight down the street, pushing bodily through the morning pedestrian traffic. His hand was so tight around her arm there was no way they looked like lovers casually strolling. But no one gave them a second glance as he pulled her past rapidly filling office buildings, then Starbucks, overflowing with well-dressed caffeine junkies desperate for a fix.

That was big-city life for you, she thought resentfully. Where was a hero when you needed one?

He yanked her abruptly into a public parking garage. "Do you have any money in your purse?"

"What?"

"Do you have money?"

"A...a little."

"Good, you can pay for our parking."

"But we don't have a car."

"We do now." He gestured to the wide concrete expanse of a second floor filled with shiny, gleaming automobiles. Then he turned back to her, his green eyes like hard emeralds. She stared at him with genuine horrified shock until he arched a single blond brow. "Did you really think I was a Boy Scout?"

"But...but stealing is wrong." She smiled tremulously at the blatant banality of her statement, then shrugged. *You're discussing morality with a convicted murderer, Maggie. Why are you discussing the evils of theft with someone who* kills *people?*

"Uh-huh," Attila the Hun said dryly, seeming to agree wholeheartedly with her thoughts. He nodded curtly and then, as if he was tired of waiting for her to make up her mind, jerked his head to the right. "We'll take that van. Let's go."

He dragged her forward, his grip iron-tight around her wrist. She wanted to resist. She'd taken self-defense classes; she knew you should never let them get you into a vehicle. Once in the car, there would be no way to run, no way to break away. She'd be trapped as effectively as a moth pinned to a tray.

He outweighed her by a good hundred pounds. He looked to be in tremendous shape. Those arms... Heavens, he could probably pull a tractor out of the mud single-handedly. Or wrestle an ox or pin a steer. Her footsteps slowed. She tried to dig in her sensible pumps; she yanked back her arm.

He didn't even look at her. His fingers tightened, he murmured, "Don't be an idiot," and dragged her forward without ever missing a beat.

He was definitely going to get her into a vehicle.
My God, Maggie, what are you going to do?

Cain selected an old, beat-up blue Dodge trade van from the late seventies. Unlocked and easy to hot-wire. He'd driven something like this way back when in Idaho. He popped open the door and peered in quickly, still clutching his insurance.

Two front seats and a gutted back that doubled as a bachelor pad. Some kid had built in a bed along one side while old milk crates lined the other, some filled with clothes, some with books. An apartment on wheels. Just the right accessory for the convict on the run.

"I'll take it," he murmured.

He turned back to his captive. She was the scrawniest woman he'd ever seen, composed of ninety percent flaming red hair and ten percent skin and bones. Looking across the hallway, he'd known she was the one. She wore a plaid wool skirt from the eighties, a ruffled pink silk blouse that was even older than that and low-slung beige shoes like his grandma once wore. She didn't even wear much jewelry, just a plain heart-shaped locket around her neck that looked old, varnished and worse for the wear. Mousy court clerk, he determined with a single glance. A woman with the spine of an invertebrate. The perfect accommodating hostage, if she'd stop trembling like a leaf.

"Get in."

Her blue eyes opened wide, peering out from the thick jungle of fiery hair. Her gaze went to the van to him to the van. He tapped his foot impatiently. He didn't want any trouble—that was why he'd selected her. He just needed her to do what she was told. Twenty-four hours and it would all be over. He'd waited six years for this day. He'd taken a big gamble. The only way to make it work was to be willing to play it out all the way.

A man made choices. A man paid for those decisions.

Cain had always believed that and he was willing to live
with the consequences of his actions.

"Get in," he repeated sharply, and this time his lips
thinned dangerously. He didn't want to hurt her, but he was
willing to be forceful.

Wonder Woman cringed at the edge in his voice. Then,
rather than obeying, she peered up at him miserably
through the shiny red veil of her hair.

"We can't take this," she whispered, then promptly
tucked her chin against her chest and hunched her shoulders.

He blinked several times and looked at the spineless
wonder once more. Sirens cut through the air.

"What did you say?"

Her whole body went in a shivering fit. His eyes narrowed fiercely and she shook even more. She licked her lip
nervously, finally dragging her gaze up to his face. She
looked terrified. But somehow, her shoulders had set in a
resilient line that did not bode well.

"We...we *can't*," she stated again, her voice soft, but
dangerously firm.

The sirens sounded closer.

"Get *in* the van," he ordered tightly and followed the
words with an urgent push of his arm.

The sweat was beginning to trickle down his cheek.
More than the moment when he'd actually knocked out his
guard in the isolated corner of microfiche machines in the
fourth-floor Multnomah Law Library, more than the moment when he'd quickly pulled on the guard's uniform before anyone else arrived, he understood that he was committed now. He might have considered himself a victim
once; he might have considered himself wrongly accused.
But he'd just knocked a man unconscious. Then he'd taken
a hostage. He'd crossed that line between passive victim
and aggressive avenger, and if they caught him now, that
was it.

The time for self-doubt and moral quandaries was over.

"But you said I could pick," his captive waif was exclaiming in a rush, her free hand clasping the heart locket she wore as if it were actually a cross filled with divine power. "And this is just some poor kid's van, but not just a van. I mean...look at it. It's probably his home, his life. I bet it's not even insured. Does it look insured to you? You steal this and you've...you've taken someone's whole life—his clothes, his books, everything. You can't do that, it's just...just..."

"Cruel?" he supplied expressionlessly.

She looked at him with huge blue eyes, then slowly nodded. "Can't you...can't you steal a nice insured car? Please?"

He stared at her, then he blinked a few times and stared at her again. She smiled back sickly. She was obviously near hysteria—for God's sake, they could probably hear her knees knocking together in China—but she still didn't look away. And she didn't get into the van.

This woman had just been taken hostage by an armed, escaped felon, and she was worried about some kid's future? Oh good, Cain. You just managed to kidnap the one woman in the courthouse who's mentally unbalanced. Great job.

And the sirens came to a squealing halt just three blocks away. That decided the matter.

"Get into the van or I'll shoot you. Those are your options."

She scrambled into the van, climbing awkwardly over the seats and landing with an uncoordinated plop on the passenger's side. He hefted himself in easily, looking at the gun, then at the ignition he needed to hot-wire. He would need two hands. He would need to move fast.

The police were so close. Keep calm, Cain. Keep moving. Life is nothing more than a game of chess.

He looked in the rearview mirror, rapidly contemplating his next steps. He saw the parking garage, which was still empty. Then his gaze shifted to the makeshift bed and the crates filled with books and clothes in the back of the van.

He'd lived out of a truck once. When he'd first come from Idaho to Oregon, driving into Portland and so determined to make something out of himself. He'd had nothing. Just his old truck and the makeshift bed in the back. He used to eat raw frankfurters for dinner; they were all he could afford. But he hadn't minded; he'd lived his whole life up till then in a plywood shack so he had no expectations of luxury. And the truck meant he was free, that he'd gotten out of the hills, that he had a chance to see the cities his mother used to tell him about, softly, when his father wasn't in the cabin.

If someone had stolen his truck then, what would it have done to him? How much would it have convinced him that maybe his father was right and the whole world was out to get him? How much would it have convinced him there was nothing worth fighting for after all?

Damn. Damn damn *damn*.

"Get out of the van," he ordered crisply and was already climbing down.

His hostage looked at him with unabashed relief. "Maybe there's hope yet," she murmured, then immediately clamped her lips shut when she realized the words had been spoken out loud.

He dragged her from the van, curt and impatient and more than a little bit on edge. He could hear more sirens approaching in the distance. He was playing Good Samaritan and the entire city was being cordoned off. Smart, Cain, smart.

He pulled her bodily to a newer, sleek pickup truck. He'd grown up with trucks and he valued their off-road abilities. If the going got tough, this baby looked like it could take him down the Grand Canyon and back up the other side. Probably insured. He peered in at the gas gauge. Almost full. Perfect.

He popped open the unlocked door. In Portland, people

were still trusting. He didn't want to dwell on that or what it made him. Prison did change a man, even when he swore it wouldn't.

"Get in," he told his captive for the fifth time. She hesitated and he whirled on her abruptly, thrusting the gun beneath her chin as she froze like a pillar of salt. Her eyes widened, her breath sounded loud and labored in the cement drum of the garage. He could feel her terror like a palpable presence. He could see the blue pulse point at the base of her neck pound furiously. Sweat beaded up on her pale, oval face and slowly trickled down.

Don't push her too hard, he thought, but he didn't relent.

"Listen to those sirens," he whispered against her cheek. "They're not playing 'Where's Waldo?' I want you to get into that truck. I want you to do everything I say. If you cooperate, I won't hurt you. You have my word. The decision is yours."

He stepped back, but his eyes remained hard.

"All right," she whispered immediately. Her gaze remained locked on him warily as she turned her body toward the high truck. She tried valiantly to lift her skirt-hampered leg up to the looming step. It wasn't going to happen. She was too short and it was too high. With a burst of impatience, Cain planted his hand firmly on her butt, ignored her squeak of indignation and tossed her up onto the bench seat. She went sprawling, landing with a lewd spread of creamy white thighs. He disregarded the flashing white limbs and climbed in after her, filling the truck doorway.

With another yelp, she scrambled to the opposite side, crossing her legs and pressing her skirt around herself like a mortified nun.

"Don't worry," he said tersely. "I'm trying to escape from jail, not molest a child."

"I'm not a child!" she said, and for a moment sounded wounded.

"Uh-huh." He turned his attention to hot-wiring the truck.

But there was no way he could do that and hold a gun on her. Worse, the sirens continued to wail with increasing fervor just a few blocks away. For one moment, he felt the dark spiraling panic of a man watching events twist out of his control. He squelched the feeling instantly, his fingers drumming on the steering wheel as his mind frantically sought solutions.

He'd never escaped from jail before. He'd never taken a hostage before. He didn't know what he was doing....

Stop it! No panic, no fear. Life is a chess game, and if there was one thing you were very good at, Cain, it was chess.

His hands steadied. The worst that could happen was that he would fail—that his brother would find him and that his brother would kill him. He was willing to take that risk, he was willing to pay that price. There were very few things he believed in anymore. Freedom of choice was one. The absolute value of truth was the second.

You waited six years for this, Cain. Either do it or bow your head and return to your cell.

There was no way he was willingly returning to prison. Besides, it was only a matter of time before the Aryan Brotherhood finally succeeded in having him decommissioned. If he was going to die, he wanted to die as a man, not as prisoner number 542769.

He set the gun between himself and the driver's side door. Then, while the court clerk stared up at him with widening eyes, he pulled out the handcuffs.

"What's your name?"

"M...Maggie. What are you doing?"

"I'm handcuffing us together, Maggie."

"No!" She clutched her hand to her side. "You can't keep doing this. You can't take me hostage. I...I have dependents!"

He actually froze for a minute. "Kids?" he asked slowly. He didn't want to know this. He really didn't want to know this.

"Cats," she whispered.

"What?"

"I have cats," she continued in a rush. "Two cats and I live all alone and there's no one to feed them. One of them has been sick lately. And...and Friday has only three legs—"

"What?"

"She has only three legs. She was born that way—it makes her very high-strung. If you don't feed her at exactly the same time every day she throws these fits. I really wor—"

He reached over, clasped her wrist and slapped the handcuff around it. While looking at her steadily, he slipped the cuff around his wrist. "Maggie, you're now a hostage, not a pet owner."

She stared at him miserably, her eyes welling up.

"Don't!" he said immediately. "Don't do that."

"Do what?" she whispered soggily. Her chin began to tremble.

"No! No crying. I forbid it!"

"Okay," she whispered and a single tear streaked down her cheek. Then another and another. Big, silent tears that tangled in her long, red hair.

He stared at her in stunned silence as she wept soundlessly, turning her head away from him as if she were ashamed of the display. Already her hand was wiping furiously at her cheeks. "Crying is bad," she muttered. "Don't cry, don't cry." Her hand abruptly closed around the old locket around her neck, her fingers fumbling and shaking. She clung to the locket desperately, her face still turned.

Cain's mouth opened. Something twisted deep in his gut. She looked so small, so defenseless. There was something about her, an innocence, he supposed. It had been a long time since he'd encountered innocence; he didn't know how to treat it anymore.

He should let her go. This was a bad idea.

More sirens filled the air. He stared at the windshield. He couldn't let her go. There was no way he was going to make it out of the city without being caught, and if he was caught a hostage was his only bargaining chip. If he let her go, he might as well return to prison now. And if he returned to prison, no one would ever learn the truth about that dark, bloody night six years ago.

A man did what a man had to do. Twenty-four hours from now, he'd let her go and she'd never have to see him again. This event would become a dull memory. She would survive. Her odds, at least, were better than his.

"Move," he said abruptly and popped the truck door open. He started sliding out and since he outweighed her by eighty pounds she had no choice but to follow.

"Where are we going?" She'd composed herself. Her tears were gone, just a faint hoarse edge remained in her voice.

"Back to the van."

"But I thought you weren't going to steal the van."

"Relax. I want his clothes."

He slid back the side door forcefully, hopped in and dragged her with him. She stumbled, of course, tilting them both dangerously off balance. He righted them both quickly and turned his attention to the clothes. Not much time.

He flipped over a milk crate and rapidly perused his options. Shirts, jeans, socks, a pair of worn-out tennis shoes. A black baseball cap with Oregon State University scrawled across the front in orange. Size was feasible, too. A little too large but that was preferable to too small. Good.

He set the gun down on the bed, far out of Maggie's reach. Then he began unbuttoning the ill-fitting guard uniform.

"What are you doing?" she choked.

"Changing."

"You can't do that!"

He looked at her expressionlessly, his fingers moving nimbly down until they reached the last button at his groin.

The shirt opened, revealing his naked chest. And good ol' Maggie blushed six different shades of red.

"Did you grow up in a nunnery?" he asked mildly and shrugged off the shirt. It remained dangling over the handcuffs.

"No." Her voice was so strangled he could barely hear the word.

"Just checking."

He grabbed the cotton-blend uniform where it hung on the chain between their wrists and because he was in a hurry, gave a small yank. The material ripped off like meat falling from a bone.

Maggie's eyes grew round as saucers.

"My tax dollars," she muttered, staring at the torn shirt, then his bare torso, which rippled and flexed like a marble statue.

"Probably." He'd used the one-hour rec time he received every day as a maximum-security inmate to work out. Being surrounded by two-ton murderers and rapists had that effect on a man.

His hands moved purposefully to his waist. Maggie promptly squeezed her eyes shut. For a moment he hesitated, his upbringing warring with his circumstances. The handcuffs, however, limited the amount of distance he could put between the two of them. She cracked open her blue eyes as if to see what was holding him up, looking miserable and forlorn.

"All right," he said abruptly. He acted quickly, before he could debate the wisdom of his decision yet again. With one deft movement, he picked up her wrist, unlocked the metal bracelet and dropped her freed hand to her side. "Move, and I'll shoot you."

"I want to go home," she whispered.

His lips twisted slightly; some of the force went out of his stance. "I know," he said quietly. "I know."

He turned away. Briskly, he peeled off the ill-fitting prison guard pants and kicked them away. Then he pulled up the new pair of jeans. Moving fast, he donned a worn T-shirt with a blue-striped short-sleeved overshirt. With his fingers, he impatiently raked back his blond hair, momentarily revealing the port-wine stain riding high on his forehead that had earned him his name from his father. His mother had tried to argue that Cain was no name for a child, but she never had been a match for her fierce, hard-hearted husband.

Cain pulled the baseball cap low and completed the transformation from state prisoner to prison guard to Joe Blow in fifteen minutes or less.

He picked up the gun, locked the safety and slid it into the waistband of the loose-fitting jeans, the dark pistol covered by the overshirt. Then he retrieved the handcuffs and slapped them into place on their wrists once more.

"All right, Maggie. Now we hot-wire the truck."

Her blue eyes rose silently, no longer desolate but resigned. "When my brothers catch up with you, you'll regret having ever done this," she informed him softly.

"Yeah?" He dragged her out of the van.

"C.J.'s a Marine. Force recon. He's invented new ways of handling men like you."

"Yeah?" They were back at the pickup truck. He held open the door. "After you."

"And Brandon is just plain dangerous. You think he's just a investment banker, but then you see his eyes. He's very focused, very intelligent, and knows exactly how to get what he wants. He'll have you in line for lethal injection by morning."

Cain looked at her silently. "My brother Abraham cut his teeth on a Remington 12-gauge shotgun, Maggie. With a crossbow, he can shoot a hole through the middle of a quarter from forty yards. He also believes the numbers on the back of the road signs are to help the Zionist Occupational Government—ZOG—someday herd all dissidents into forty-three concentration camps and that Gurkha troops are being secretly trained in Montana to attack and disarm

God-fearing Americans such as himself. If he finds us, Maggie, he'll kill us both.'' His lips twisted, but the expression couldn't be called a smile.

"Concentration camps?'' she whispered sickly.

"Welcome to Paranoia-R-Us. Or in Idaho, another name for the militias. Up you go.'' He slid his hands beneath her arms, intent on hefting her up into the cab and hearing her drag in another sharp hiss of outrage. She shifted to get away from him, but only succeeded in pressing one small breast against his palm. Firm breast, apple shaped. Soft. Beautifully, delicately soft. Definitely the breast of a woman and not a child.

His breath held. Her breath held. Her eyes widened in terror and very slowly, she edged back. His breath came out hard and low.

"Maggie,'' he said in a low, measured tone, "I haven't had sex in six years. Don't do that again unless you mean it.''

"Okay,'' she squeaked.

He smiled, cursing his body, her shyness and the whole situation. Next time he escaped from prison, he was kidnapping a prostitute or a very eager widow.

With a sudden, deft movement, he tossed Maggie up into the truck, away from his hand and the swelling that was becoming almost painful against his jeans. The binding link of the chain, however, forced him to follow her up awkwardly.

He grabbed the gun and vented his frustration by using the handle to break open the ignition. Sixty seconds later, the truck roared to life with the sleek growl of an expensive lion.

Thank God for misspent youths. The tension began to dissolve. He was going to do this. He was going to get away. It would all work out if he just kept thinking.

"Sit next to me, Maggie.''

"No.''

He smiled and with a negligent yank of his sinew-roped

forearm, dragged her against him. "Sit here, sweetheart," he murmured. "Look at me affectionately, place your hand on my thigh. And when the police look over at us to check for an escaped con in a prison guard's uniform, smile at them sweetly and say you have no idea but you'll certainly keep your eyes open. It'll be very easy, very simple. And in no time at all, I'll return you unharmed and untouched to your three-legged cat."

She stared at him, her eyes unexpectedly mutinous, her cheeks flushed. Her red hair tangled wildly around her pale features, and her full, petal-pink lips parted with stubborn defiance.

She looked suddenly vital and stunning.

He figured six years was definitely too long to go without a woman if he thought a thin scrap of female like her was stunning.

"What are you thinking, Maggie?" he whispered. "What can you really do against someone like me?"

Her mouth abruptly shut. The light died in her eyes. She slumped beside him, and that quickly she was the mousy clerk again. It was as if a switch had been thrown and the woman simply turned off.

"Okay," she said.

He gazed at her a minute longer. She didn't look up, and there were no more signs of life in her face. He nodded finally. It was better this way.

He shifted the truck into gear and backed out of the lot. Casual and easy, that was the ticket. If they appeared calm, no one would ever guess they had something to hide.

"Where are we going?" she asked at last, her blue eyes fastened on the dash.

"To Idaho," he said lightly. "We're going to find my brother, Ham. Then, I'm probably going to have to kill him."

Chapter 2

"Ticket, please."

"Ticket?" her esteemed colleague repeated absently. He was peering up three blocks to the mass of blue and red flashing lights and dark-uniformed police officers. His eyes were narrowed intently and his fingers drummed rhythmically against the wheel as if he was lost in great thought.

Maggie risked a look over his shoulder at the parking lot attendant. Because of the considerable height of the truck, she gazed down at him. He appeared amazingly small next to Attila the Hun's broad shoulder, and his face was covered with pimples. Probably barely a day older than eighteen and his width hadn't caught up with his height.

Not exactly Superman material. She sent him desperate thought waves anyway. *Hey! Hey you! Look at me. Just look underneath Godzilla's arm and spot me for one moment.*

"Your *parking* ticket, sir." The young man's voice cracked with the impatience. He stared at them both glumly

as if to say, I spent four years in high school and all I got
was a lousy parking-attendant job.

"Parking ticket?" her captor repeated, focusing on the
attendant for the first time. He gazed around the cab then
straight at her. "Do you see a parking ticket?"

"No," she whispered. She looked up the street. She
could see blinking lights and the blue-clad police officers
scurrying around like ants. She counted eight of them. Eight
cops. So close.

*Honk the horn, Maggie. Hit him in the ribs. Do some-
thing bold and courageous. This man is planning to commit
another murder!*

But she couldn't move. She'd never liked loud noises,
she lived in fear of making a scene. She still vividly remembered her mother throwing Waterford crystal across
the parlor and screaming at her father that he was nothing
but a philandering rat. And she remembered the very late
nights, when the house was finally dark and quiet—sometimes not until 4:00 a.m.—when she would creep downstairs just to sit in the parlor and listen to the silence. Once,
she'd found her father there, sitting in the dark, still and
brooding. Then he'd finally reached over and picked up the
phone, speaking in a hushed, murmuring voice. She'd remained in the hallway, curled up on the Persian runner,
listening to his deep, velvety baritone wash over her like a
soothing wave.

She had loved him so much and then he was just gone,
off to visit one of his other families where Maggie was sure
the mother didn't scream or throw crystal across the room.
Then he was more than gone—his plane crashed—and all
Maggie had left was the locket he'd once given her, and
memories of a midnight phone conversation she'd never
told anyone about. That secret was the only piece of her
father, the infamous Maxmillian the Chameleon, that was
solely hers.

Abruptly, her captor leaned over, violating her small
space and interrupting her thoughts. His lips halted right

next to the corner of her mouth, the way a lover's might, while his keen eyes fired to life. Maggie's whole body went rigid. She stopped breathing and curled up inside of herself while the masculine scent of soap and sweat washed over her cheeks and flared her nostrils.

"Wh-what?" she asked unsteadily, unable to breathe, unable to move. Should a felon's eyes be so green? And so…intelligent, steady, composed? She thought murderers had beady eyes, black beady eyes that were always darting to and fro. That way you knew they were trouble.

He said, "Ten dollars."

"Huh?"

"The attendant claims we have to pay ten dollars," he repeated. He leaned back, his fingers drumming against the wheel as his gaze returned to the police lights blinking up the street. "Expensive," he murmured absently.

She could only stare at him, then belatedly at the purse beside her. The car behind them impatiently honked its horn.

The Terminator's attention pivoted back to her immediately. "Come on, Maggie," he said tersely, his voice so low only she could hear it. "No games now. There are a lot of people who could get hurt."

"I know," she whispered. "I know." Frustration and humiliation thickened her throat, but she still couldn't think of anything to do. If she tried to raise a fuss, she'd probably get everyone killed. Maybe if she just humored him for now. She would cooperate, they could get beyond the city limits where no one else would suffer if she did anything rash…. She took a deep breath. Okay, she'd get through this. Just one moment at a time.

She grabbed her purse and managed to retrieve a ten-dollar bill with trembling fingers.

Mr. Escaped Con promptly handed over the money to the impatient, thin-shouldered attendant. "Sorry about that," he said politely and beamed a perfectly charming smile.

Maggie's teeth set painfully as she watched the black-and-white-striped gate swing up. In front of the police, the pedestrians and God, the truck pulled out into traffic.

She peered back. Two cops had stopped to watch them, no doubt watching all vehicles. If she could just raise her left hand a little, enough for them to see the handcuffs. Or maybe a sign. Didn't those cardboard shades people placed behind their windshields during the summer say Help! Call the Police on one side? She gazed around the cab, easing away from her captor.

"Good idea," he said so abruptly that she flinched. "Look and see what we have to work with."

"Work with?"

"What's in the glove compartment? Any maps, spare change, anything?"

"Wasn't stealing the truck enough?" she muttered, then glanced at him nervously to see how he'd handle that remark. His hands were tight on the steering wheel, and for the first time she noticed the beads of sweat trickling down his cheeks. So he wasn't as calm and cool as he pretended. Even as she watched, his gaze darted to the rearview mirror, then his hands tightened on the wheel.

As if sensing her gaze upon him, he turned to her tersely. "Look in the glove compartment, Maggie. *Now!*"

She hastily opened the glove compartment. She had a feeling not too many people argued with him when he used that tone of voice. She certainly couldn't.

"One map of the northwestern states, one map of Portland, the vehicle registration, a flashlight, four packets of ketchup, two straws and six unpaid parking tickets," she rattled off. "Why is it nobody ever pays their parking tickets? It really is a shame." She glanced outside. They were at the waterfront now. Traffic was still sluggish with morning commuters. She spotted one cop parked on the driveway of the Alexis Restaurant, scrutinizing all traffic through mirrored sunglasses.

Look over here, she begged him, her teeth sinking into her lower lip. *For God's sake, look over here.*

"Maggie," Attila's voice said quietly. "Fasten your seat belt."

She looked at him abruptly, then the rearview mirror. A cop had pulled in behind them. Even as she watched, he picked up his radio and spoke into it.

"He heard me. Finally, somebody heard me," she whispered triumphantly.

"Don't break out the champagne yet," the Terminator muttered. He downshifted the truck as if preparing for a mighty leap forward.

"You can't outrace an entire city full of cops!" she cried instantly.

"Watch me."

"No!" Before she could stop to think about it, she reached over and latched her hands on to the wheel. She stared up at him as fiercely as she could, though her body was trembling again. "There are pedestrians out there. Innocent people crossing the streets and strolling down sidewalks. They could be killed! Don't you understand that? Don't you care just a little bit?"

His green gaze slid over her, dark and glittering, his square jaw set so rigidly she could see a muscle flinch. "Let go, Maggie. Now."

She gritted her teeth, prayed her knees would stop knocking together and kept her fingers wrapped stubbornly around the wheel. Behind them, the police officer made no moves. He didn't speed up, he didn't turn on his lights, nor did he change lanes. Did he understand this was a dangerous area for high-speed pursuit? Or did he think they were simply lovers snuggling up on the bench seat of the pickup truck?

She took a deep breath. "I'm not letting go. I can't. Too many people could get hurt."

"Starting with you."

"Trying to evade the police here is stupid and you know

it!'' she exclaimed desperately. He appeared an intelligent man.

He frowned abruptly, and she had the faint satisfaction of knowing that she'd reached him. The light in front of them turned red. The cop was still driving patiently behind them.

"Damn!" Attila swore. He looked at her darkly, but his foot finally pressed on the brake and the truck slowed to an easy stop.

Okay, Maggie. You got him calm. Point one for the good guys. What was she supposed to do now? It had been a long time since her abnormal psych days. Okay, keep the psychotic from dehumanizing things. That's right. Remind him everyone's a person, she's a person, he's a person, the cops are people, too.

She was going to be sick.

"What...what's your name?" she whispered at last, having to moisten her lips to speak.

"Prisoner number 542769." His gaze remained on the rearview mirror. "But you can call me Pris for short."

She swallowed a hysterical giggle and practiced deep breathing. Remember, there must be a human being in there somewhere, no doubt just hiding really darn well behind those cold, cold, eyes.

"Your real name?" she tried again, then added weakly, "Not that Pris isn't cool."

His face remained frozen for a moment, then abruptly his full, well-shaped lips twisted. "Cain," he said levelly, "my father named me Cain. He said God had given him the gift of sight." His face didn't change but she paled.

"How apropos," she murmured at last. A long harsh tremor shuddered through her body. His thigh was pressed against hers, his shoulder hard against her chest. She shuddered again, and he didn't even flinch.

The light turned green. He pressed down lightly on the gas. The police car remained right behind them. Then, several blocks back, she saw a second cop turn into the traffic flow.

"Cain," she forced herself to say, "Cain, don't do this. You can't win this way, don't you see that? It's a nice truck, but they have cars and guns and helicopters. The minute that policeman turns on his sirens…if you run for it, you'll only hurt all these nice, innocent people, people with spouses and children and parents and…and even three-legged cats."

She stared up at him with her most pleading blue gaze. C.J. had once told her no sane man could say no to such big blue eyes. Of course, C.J. was a flirt and Maggie was the one whose love life had entered the ice age sometime around the age of sixteen and never unthawed.

"You're right," Cain said abruptly.

"What?"

"You're right." His gaze left hers, focusing on the road while his hands flexed on the wheel. Green eyes darted to the rearview mirror, then back to the road signs. "I can't win in a high-speed chase. I'm spending too much time on tactics and not enough on strategy." He seemed to be talking to himself more than her. She didn't mind that. His voice was steady and soft, the voice of a man contemplating life versus plunging rashly ahead. *Keep him calm, Maggie. That's good.* She might not be a fighter, but she was good at soothing people. Though her mother routinely dismissed Maggie's job as being too prosaic, Maggie was one of the best marriage counselors in the field.

Cain glanced at her. "Ever play chess, Maggie?"

She shook her head.

"It's a good game," he said absently, his fingernails drumming on the steering wheel as he peered back at the cop. "It's based primarily on mathematics, you know. People like Sir Isaac Newton and Benjamin Franklin used to write formulas for perfect Knight Tours. The chessboard is eight by eight, and originally the number system was base eight. It's why computers can be programmed to play chess as well. Really, it's simply a matter of rapidly computing and calculating all the different scenarios. Quite logical."

Maggie stared at him. "Oh," she said at last. It was the only syllable she could get out of her mouth. For an escaped felon, he seemed surprisingly intelligent, lucid even. Not a raving, insane bone in his body. Was that good or bad?

"Strategy," he muttered now. "It's all about strategy. I'm spending too much time on tactics and not enough on strategy."

"What?"

"Get the map," he said abruptly.

"Why?" she risked countering.

He turned and looked at her, his face composed and his startling green eyes steady. "I'm following your advice, Maggie. You're going to plot us an escape route that will take us away from all these cars and pedestrians. Something rural would be ideal."

"But...but..." But she would be helping him. She couldn't help him, that would be wrong. And though she wasn't exactly superwoman material, she didn't want to do anything that might hurt other people. "I...I can't," she said at last.

He arched a single brow and she continued in a frantic rush. "To...to...to get the map I'd...have to take my hands off the wheel." Aha! "And then you might do something rash and that would be bad."

Her captor looked at her levelly. "What do you weigh? One hundred, one hundred and five pounds?" Her lips thinned, then finally she nodded. "I bench-press twice your weight, Maggie. Do you really think you can stop me from controlling the wheel?"

No, no, she didn't, and they both know it. Her face fell, her shoulders hunching. She was a lousy excuse for a heroine.

She felt his gaze on her face. For one moment, it almost seemed to relent. "You do try," he said abruptly, his tone indecipherable. "I'll give you points for that. Now plot out an escape route, Maggie. We have to get off these main drags. There's no place to go here, and there are too many cars. We need some good, twisty side streets, something small and unknown." He was back to staring at the cop. "And Maggie, get the damn seat belt on."

"Sure," she whispered, giving in and retrieving the map. "Heaven forbid I should get killed in a high-speed car chase. Then who would you have to shoot?"

His lips curved. For a moment, she was startled to see that his green eyes held a glint of humor. "Very good. Ever think of becoming a hostage professionally?"

"They're going to catch you," she retorted with a small spark of rebellion. "And when they do, I'm going to dance on your prison cell."

She fastened her seat belt with as much dignity as possible and opened the map. Then she stared once more at the cop in the side mirror. Why wasn't the police car doing anything? Did she forget to send out engraved invitations to rescue her? They were almost on top of the I-5 exit, where a large percentage of the traffic would turn off. Was that what the police were waiting for?

"The map, Maggie."

"Oh, hold your horses! Shoot! Get into the right lane. Now, now!"

"I can't evade the damn police by getting in a car accident. Damn. Get over here, I need two hands."

He'd put on the blinker and was looking frantically over his shoulders. She could see the lines creasing the corners of his eyes and the thin set of his lips. He looked desperate and, for a moment, almost afraid. If she hadn't been his hostage, she might have felt sorry for him. Clearly, he was a man grasping at straws.

But he was also an armed, escaped murderer, something that was a little hard to overlook.

"Maggie, now!"

She fumbled with her seat belt, sliding over awkwardly

so he could place his right hand on the wheel and swing the huge truck over to the next lane. The fit was so tight she squeezed her eyes shut and hunched her shoulders down, waiting for the crunch of metal. But the car in back, a nice polite driver, had put on his brakes so the murderer could switch lanes.

"Now, Mr. Cop," she muttered. "There's no time like the present!"

But even as she watched, the cop car drove right on by them, signaled a left turn and disappeared down the side street leading to I-5.

"No," she whispered. "No, no, no."

"Don't take it so badly," Cain told her. "At least no innocent people are at risk."

"Except for me!" she cried, and then because she was too disappointed to care, she walloped his shoulder with her free hand. It was like hitting concrete. She popped three of her knuckles and he didn't even grunt. His green eyes looked at her steadily, hooded and unreadable beneath the black brim of the OSU baseball cap. For a moment, he seemed strangely sympathetic.

"Sucks to be you, doesn't it?" he said quietly.

"Yes!" she agreed fiercely and picked up the map again, having to blink away the tears in her eyes.

He looked at her a minute longer, then turned away.

Front Avenue turned into Barbur Boulevard, four lanes of curving road winding around strip malls and way too many traffic lights. Portland was now behind them; they were southbound, heading toward Tigard. Cain didn't feel any relief, though. With every minute, the risks became greater and greater.

Had the original owner of the blue truck returned to the parking garage yet? Maybe he'd already sounded the alarm, having his choice of police officers to notify. The cops would put two and two together, and within minutes an

APB would be issued on the stolen truck. The next cop to pull in behind Cain wouldn't be turning away.

Or maybe the owner had parked his truck in the garage because he planned on being gone all day. Maybe he worked downtown. Maybe he was serving jury duty in the courthouse and would be tied up all day. Maybe the truck was the perfect escape vehicle because the cops were looking for a lone man on foot in a prison guard's uniform, not a Western-looking fellow casually driving his brand-new truck with his girlfriend.

Or the owner of the truck had thought he would be gone all day, but he'd been dismissed from the jury. Or he'd realized he'd forgotten something at home and needed to go back. Or he'd found the item he was shopping for in the first store he entered and there was no reason to go to any others.

So many variables and Cain couldn't anticipate nor control any of them. His life had just become a case study in chaos theory. Somewhere in Tokyo, a butterfly would flap its wings and Cain Cannon would be arrested five miles outside of Portland.

He looked over at his hostage, yet another variable he couldn't control. She was hunched over the map, quiet and still, her face obscured by a thick waterfall of deep red hair. He'd thought she would be perfectly submissive, but that wasn't quite the case. Maybe the red hair should've been a giveaway; she seemed to harbor a stubborn streak as wide as any he'd ever met.

And she cared an inordinate amount for others. It was disconcerting, given the company he'd been keeping for the past six years. But then, it was also something he could use against her.

Use against her? When had he started thinking like that?

If a man lived among pigs for too many years, could he really keep himself from becoming a swine?

He didn't know anymore. And suddenly he was thinking of that first day, walking through the gates of the prison one gateway at a time. You entered the first passage, doors locked behind you, new doors opened in front of you. And so on and so forth, as you sank deeper and deeper into the labyrinth, sunlight and freedom not one door away, but four gateways removed, as if you'd just entered the bowels of the earth and there was no going back.

Entering prisoners started out in the intake section, getting full medical and psychiatric evaluations while the corrections department decided what to do with them. Cain didn't remember the tests much. He'd been too busy staring at the walls like a dazed man, trying to understand how his life had come to this. Then at the end of the second week, when they'd determined to put him in the medium-security wing as he'd been convicted of second-degree murder, not first, they'd turned him loose like a stunned deer in the middle of the general population. His nostrils, raised on fresh air, mountain streams and endless horizons, had recoiled at the sharp, astringent odor of overly harsh detergents thinly masking the deeper, darker scent of too many men and too much fear.

He hadn't known what to do or where to go, and for a moment he'd been afraid. He wasn't sure he'd ever been afraid before. Wasn't sure he'd ever really understood what people meant by that. He'd been born with a rifle in his hand and the brain of mathematician in his head; there had never been anything he couldn't do.

A man had walked up to him, a white guy, looking like a grain of rice against the backdrop of predominantly Mexican and black inmates.

"I hearda you," the guy had said, his voice thick with mountains.

"I don't know you," Cain had replied, but he'd been lying. He'd looked at the man's shaved head and bright blue eyes and overpumped, swastika-tattooed arms, and had instantly recognized the man's type. This man could've been his father or his brother or any number of the men who'd stopped by his family's one-bedroom wooden shack when he was growing up.

"Y'got a choice, man," the guy had continued. He'd held out a pack of cigarettes, a friendly gesture that Cain had known better than to accept. "In here now, in here the True Man is the minority. Here, here in this hellhole, they think we're nothin', bro. Y'can't have 'em thinkin' that. Can't let 'em think that."

"I'm not interested."

"Sure you are. Bright guy like you? Bet y'are. Look around, buddy. You see individuals? Ain't no individuals in prison, bro. They are four families, that's it. And we're your family, the only family yer gonna find here as a True Man."

"I'm not interested."

The man finally smirked. "Buddy, they told me you were bright, some computer-bright guy. But, man, you sure are slow. Where do you think the democracy is? Huh? Didn't that shakedown teach you nothin'? When they were poking and proddin' your body, didn't that teach you anythin'? Like I said, you got a choice. We're it. We protect you, we look out for the True Man. And you join. We got outside connections, you know. We got contacts who are mighty interested in a computer-bright True Man. You ever surf this Internet thing? Shoot, I don't even understand the keyboards, but they say you're scary bright. They say you already belong to us, born into us. Your brother, he's a legend. And now here's you. They say you killed a Jew. Brother, we salute you."

And Cain had moved, faster than the man had expected, faster than Cain had expected. Suddenly he was rage and fury, and the months of brooding, the months of wondering how his brother could've done such a thing were simply gone. He was angry, angrier than he'd ever been, and he shoved the skinhead against the wall so loud the crack silenced the room. Heads turned.

"I'll say it once, then we're through here," Cain stated

quietly, his arm pressed against the man's Adam's apple, pinning him to the wall. "I am not my brother. I am not interested in you. I am an innocent man. But if I catch any of you 'saluting' Kathy's death, that may change."

He'd abruptly released the smaller man, who slid down to the floor. The guy hadn't fallen. He'd been wiry, compact and made from sturdy stock that was used to taking a few beatings. He'd shaken himself out, then had merely grinned at Cain's dark, fierce expression.

"We're all innocent in here," the guy had mocked. He'd squared his shoulders. "But buddy, boy did you handle that poor. We'll cut you slack, being it's day one and all. Next time someone offers you a cigarette, though, buddy, you'd better take it. You a geeky man, a white-collar sissy boy. Mess with us, and that is war. College boys can't afford war, not in here, mister. Not in here."

But the guy had been wrong about that, though maybe not as wrong as Cain would've liked.

Six years, six years... God, he suddenly felt so old.

They approached another red traffic light and he slowed to a halt.

"I'll make a deal with you," he said at last.

Maggie looked at him sideways, her blue eyes barely discernible through her hair. "What?" she asked, her voice clearly wary.

His finger tapped the steering wheel twice. "Despite what you may think, Maggie, I don't want anyone to get hurt. I have to get to Idaho—everyone's going to have to accept that—but I'd like to do it as quietly as possible." He paused to make sure he had her attention. The light turned green so he started driving again, careful to observe the speed limit.

"Yes?" she prodded after a minute.

"Let's think about this logically. We're in Portland, in a state with one of the lowest tax rates. The counties and cities have constrained budgets—"

"Thanks for the political commentary."

"It's relevant, Maggie. Consider the chief of police right now. He has one escaped felon and limited manpower. If you have limited manpower, how do you deploy it? It's all about tactics—how you position yourself in the short term. He has tactics. I have tactics to try to outmaneuver his tactics. What I really need, however, is strategy—a plan for winning the game."

"What did you do before...well, before?" she interrupted curiously.

"Computer programming." His hands tightened reflexively on the wheel. But that had been six years ago. He hadn't been on a machine since then. The World Wide Web, home pages, web sites, were all things he'd only read about, when he thirsted so desperately to know, to play, to understand, to do. He'd missed everything, because it was either that or build an Aryan Brotherhood home page to help with recruitment. He'd preferred to do nothing.

Cain took a deep breath. "Back to the chief of police. He can move cars into the immediate vicinity in hopes they can catch me holed up somewhere. They probably figure I'm on foot, or I've stolen a car—"

"They don't think you had an accomplice for a prison break? A friend?"

His stomach tightened, and something old and sad twisted in him again. For no good reason at all, he saw his mother standing at the window of the old log cabin, watching the rain dance in the evergreens and reaching out her hand wistfully, as if she'd like to catch the rain on her palm. As a child, he'd never understood that look on her face. Now, he understood it a lot.

He kept his gaze on the windshield, though his knuckles had whitened with the force of his grip on the wheel. "No."

"But they don't know that," she pointed out. "They'll still check with your friends."

"I don't have any friends."

Her eyes blinked several times. "Of course you do. Everyone has friends."

He glanced at her at last. "I'm a convicted murderer, Maggie. Just whose Christmas list do you think I'm still on?"

"Oh," she said weakly. For a moment, she looked almost sorry for him. He didn't want that. He didn't need that. "Family?" she suggested at last. "Siblings? I mean...uh...other than this brother you don't like."

"No."

"Oh. Well, your father then."

"He hasn't spoken to me since the day I left Idaho."

"Mother?" she asked faintly.

"Died when I was twelve."

"Wife?"

"Never married."

"Not even a girlfriend?"

"I had a girlfriend," he granted her at last. He turned long enough to gaze at her squarely. "She's the one they say I murdered."

Sapphire-blue eyes widened. She drew in her breath so fast it hissed. She simply stared at him, obviously too appalled to speak.

"Oh," she said at last.

Maggie's gaze swept down to the vinyl seat. He returned his attention to the road and for that she was grateful. She couldn't think, she couldn't move. She was handcuffed to a man who'd murdered his girlfriend. And from the sound of it, he was the classic loner, intellectual type. Probably obsessive, maybe paranoid as well. And armed. Don't forget armed.

She was going to die, killed by a man with a deep, soothing baritone, and she'd always placed a lot of stock in someone's voice. Had his girlfriend thought the same?

Her free hand clenched and unclenched on her lap, fidgeting nervously with the hem of her skirt. Her grandmother Lydia, her father's mother, who'd insisted that Maggie, C.J.

and Brandon spend each summer together on her dairy farm because otherwise the half siblings would never see one another, had always told Maggie that she had the famous Hathaway Red hair, which meant she had the famous Hathaway Red spirit. Someday, Maggie would add to the legend with a story of incomparable courage and passion just like her great-great-great-grandmother Margaret for whom she was named.

Lydia had obviously inhaled too much fertilizer. Maggie had no Hathaway spirit. She was a genetic mutant and she wanted to go home now.

She stared at the handcuff morosely, then at the gun tucked in the small of his back. How to get out of the handcuffs. Or maybe grab the gun. She didn't know anything about guns. Just the noise was enough to send her running. She chewed her lower lip. No immediate plans flared to life in her mind. She risked another glance at Cain.

He didn't look immediately dangerous. His fingers were thrumming against the wheel, his brow furrowed as if he was lost in great thought. Prison break probably did require a certain amount of concentration. Or maybe murder did.

"Do you...have you...killed a lot of women?" she ventured after a bit.

"Women? No. According to the prosecution, I murdered Kathy because she was sleeping with my brother. They called it a crime of passion." His lips twisted ironically, his fingers drumming slightly faster on the wheel.

"Was she?"

"What?"

"Sleeping with your...your brother."

There was a small pause. His face was perfectly expressionless, not hard, not scowling, not angry, not anything. "Yes," he said finally. "She was."

"Oh." Her gaze slid from his face to his hands. His fingers had stopped tapping the wheel. Now he clenched the wheel tightly and his knuckles had gone white. So he wasn't as calm as he sounded. So he wasn't so cold. She glanced at him again, wanting to understand more though she had a feeling she shouldn't.

"And that's why...that's why you think you have to kill your brother," she finished for him.

He glanced at her, his expression not obsessive or maniacal. In fact, he looked abruptly tired and worn. "I don't want to kill him," he said. "I just think it may be the only way."

Maggie didn't know what to say to that and a strained silence filled the cab.

"You can't imagine it, can you?" he asked suddenly. "I must sound so insane to you."

"I don't think murder is particularly sane," she admitted. "It sounds as if your brother and girlfriend made a mistake. Well, okay, so they betrayed you, and well, that must have hurt a great deal. But by seeking revenge, you're only prolonging your own pain and denying yourself a fresh, new future."

"Well said, Maggie, well said."

She risked a brave smile. "So you'll abandon your quest?"

"No."

"Oh."

He smiled abruptly; she had the strange sensation that he was toying with her. "Of course, you wouldn't understand sibling rivalry, would you, Maggie? It sounds as if your brothers are knights in shining armor who are already riding to your rescue as we speak."

"They'll help," she stated with absolute confidence. "We're actually half siblings, related through our father. He disappeared in a plane crash when we were still children, so our grandmother invited us to her dairy farm in Tillamook for the summer. We'd never even met until then. C.J. lived in L.A., Brandon lived in London and I lived in Lake Oswego, Oregon. Our paths never would've crossed—my grandmother is a very wise woman. By the end of the summer, we'd become so close we took a vow to always be there for one another. 'One for all, all for one,' that kind of thing. We've always held to it."

"My brother will come after us, too," Cain said at last, his gaze riveted on the windshield. "But not with quite the same intent."

Cain backtracked abruptly. "But we were talking about the chief of police." Maggie thought his voice was rough, but he cleared his throat and when he spoke again, the tones were the cool, determined tones she'd come to expect. She shook her head, slightly bewildered by the change in topic. "The chief of police has limited resources," Cain continued unperturbed. "He can't barricade the entire city—it would require too much manpower. So the state police start patrolling I-5 and the city police scour Portland. Where else do they go, Maggie?"

"I...I don't know."

"Sure you do, it's common sense. Next they check out logical places for me to go. I have no real supplies or money. It's not like I had a fancy or sophisticated prison break. I simply insisted on representing myself for the appeals process. While the prison legal department handles filing all the affidavits for prisoners, they can't represent me at trial, only I can. So for my new hearing, I was allowed to go to the courthouse with just one guard—I was shackled, of course—but for some reason he only did the leg shackles. Then there came this moment...this completely unplanned, random moment, when in the corner of the law library where I was doing last-minute research, the guard decided to bend down and pick up someone else's trash. I suppose he didn't like litterers. But there he was, bent over, and there I was, hands free above him. And so I...I hit him. I knocked him out cold."

Maggie stared at him, aghast. "That's awful!"

"Yes. Yes it is," he murmured. For a moment, he looked troubled.

"They'll check in with my old employer," he continued abruptly, his tone brisk. "That's Beaverton. We're not headed toward Beaverton, so we should be fine. Next they might try my old apartment building, but after six years that's a long shot. Which leaves us with…''

"Your family," she filled in glumly. "And you are going to Idaho."

"Exactly. You see the problem, Maggie, and why I took a hostage? On the one hand, I'm escaping. On the other hand, I'm doing exactly what they expect me to do. Not good strategy on my part."

"It's hopeless then. Give yourself up and let me go." She smiled at him hopefully.

"I can't."

"You can't?"

"No. I have to get to Idaho. And you're going to help me do it."

"I am?"

"Yes. You have the map. Think of it, Maggie. From Portland what's the fastest route to Boise? Head due east on I-84."

She nodded, and suddenly she realized how much she was helping him.

"But we didn't do that," she intoned dully. "We headed south because I said so. But it was purely accidental on my part! I don't *want* to help you escape."

He shrugged, seeming to think that part was inconsequential. It probably was to him; he had a gun. "Sure, but heading south was a good idea, Maggie. I think we'll do it a bit longer. A lot longer. I think we'll head all the way to Salem, then cut through the Cascades there. Go through Bend. There will be fewer cops covering a much larger area, increasing our odds of escape."

"But that will take all day!"

"At least."

"I have cats!" she wailed.

"They'll make it a few days."

"*A few days!*"

"Maggie, it's an important trip. Besides—" he smiled

at her grimly "—once my brother, Abraham, learns I've escaped, he'll probably come looking for me on his own. Maybe he'll save us both time and meet us in the middle."

Her face went ashen. She gripped the door handle, needing something solid. This had gone too far. She had to do something. He was a murderer, and even if he had a good voice, she could not help a murderer! She had to do something.

Just once in your life, Maggie, do something.

She glanced at the handcuff, she glanced at the door handle. Even if she popped open the door, she couldn't go anyplace handcuffed to his wrist. She had to get rid of the handcuff.

"I have to go to the bathroom," she said abruptly.

"What?"

"You heard me. It's a basic biological function and when I'm scared out of my mind—like now—it's a fairly demanding one." She raised her chin and forced herself to meet his gaze.

He shook his head. "Hold it."

"Hold it? *Hold it?* Do you know that women who try to do such things have a much higher incidence of incontinence later on in life?"

"First we have to get through the next twenty-four hours. Then we'll worry about later in life."

"I can't hold it all the way to *Idaho.*"

He frowned at her. Then he scowled. Obviously he hadn't thought about that. It made her smile smugly. She wasn't so bad at this after all.

"I hadn't considered all the logistical details," he muttered.

Her gaze brightened. "There's no good way to do it. You'll just have to let me go. I'm too big of a liability."

His frown deepened. She had the sense he was struggling with something inside of himself. "I can't do that," he said abruptly.

"Yes, you can," she hastily assured him.

"Maggie, without a hostage how can I *get* to Idaho?"

"You just won't be able to kill your brother," she agreed. "Sorry."

He shook his head and looked tired. "It's not that simple and even if I explained it to you, there's no reason for you to believe me. You're just going to have to trust me on this, Maggie. We're going to Idaho. Come hell or high water, we're getting there. The more you cooperate, the faster the trip."

"But you're a murderer! I don't want to help a murderer!"

Cain didn't reply. Instead, his eyes had gone to the rearview mirror. A cop had turned in from a side street not too far back. "Maggie," he said calmly, "Maggie, look at the map again. Find us a safe route to Salem. I want back roads, I want small, side routes. Do that, find us safe passage, and no one will get hurt."

But he was already too late.

The cop turned on his sirens.

And it began.

Chapter 3

"Turn yourself in, it's your only chance!"

"Like hell!" His foot slammed the pedal to the floor and the truck leaped forward like a jungle cat freed from its cage.

"You can't outrun them!" she cried. He didn't answer, his face remote and grim as his hand hit the horn and stayed there. A car slowed for a red light. He whipped around it so fast, Maggie fell against the door like a rag doll and whapped her head against the window.

"Hang on!" he said curtly. "This is going to get rough."

He floored it through the four-way intersection, red light and all. Cars screamed and squealed. More horns added to the cacophony and a crash of metal sounded the crescendo. Police sirens and shouting pedestrians. Screeching tires and the hoarse cry of her own protest. Maggie had arrived in hell and it was even louder than she'd expected.

"No, no, no!"

"Shut up!"

A road appeared to the right, narrow and snaking straight

up into the hillside. Maggie grabbed the dash, already knowing what he would do. His left hand tightened on the wheel. He spared her one glance, and the stark despair in his eyes sliced through her bleakly.

His gaze returned to the road. At the last possible moment, when she was so sure he'd pass it by, he slammed on the brakes, cranked the wheel with one hand and mouthed a silent prayer. The half-ton truck slid, bucking to escape. His arm bulged, fighting for control. The moment suspended and man fought machine with no clear stakes for the winner.

Veins popped up on Cain's forearm, a muscle jumped in his jaw. With a herculean effort he brutally forced the two-hundred-horsepower engine to his bidding. Wheels caught. The truck fired up the residential hillside of private, luxurious homes.

And behind them Maggie heard the sharp squeal of the police car following suit.

"Get over here," he bit out tersely. "I need both hands on the wheel."

Her hands shook so hard she could barely get them around the metal clasp of her seat belt. She'd just pressed down on the release button when the first blind corner of the narrow road appeared. He didn't slow, he didn't pause. He hit it hard, and Maggie screamed as she tumbled across the seat onto his lap.

The truck fishtailed on the way back out of the turn, almost on two wheels but still too heavy to give up so much ground. It bobbled then straightened once more.

Maggie planted her hands on Cain's rock-hard thighs and pushed herself back as fast as she could. Her hair was tangled across her face and she brushed it away, disoriented and terrified as her eyes found the road.

Another sharp corner loomed.

"Stop, stop, you're going to kill us both!"

"Hang on." His right hand landed on the steering wheel and around they went. This time she grabbed the wheel as well, needing support as she was buffeted across the cab. She could feel the tension of the vehicle, the battle of man against torque. And as they came around the corner she saw a black-trimmed white sign announcing, Caution: Children at Play.

"Oh, God," she moaned. "Oh, God."

Cain's eyes glanced to the rearview mirror. The police car was still behind them, its powerful engine keeping pace. Blind drives and children-at-play signs. He hadn't meant to pick a residential area. He did not want a residential area. Damn, damn, damn.

Another sharp turn appeared. Beside him, his dainty captive moaned with sheer, unadulterated terror. And all he could do was tighten his grip on the wheel.

The truck squealed. He no longer noticed the sound. His arms hurt with the strain of the past five minutes. He absently noted the pain. Mostly, his mind, his keen logical mind, raced frantically for a new plan, some way out. Tactics, tactics. He needed better tactics, for God's sake.

"Look out!" Maggie screamed.

He returned his attention to the road in time to see two women appear, dressed in silk jogging suits and pushing baby carriages down the narrow, shoulderless road. Their mouths opened in shock. He could almost hear their screams.

He yanked on the wheel as he'd never yanked before. He would not kill children! He would not kill children!

The truck slid helplessly across the pavement, tires having lost traction, and now headed straight for the ditch.

"Grab the wheel!" he yelled at Maggie.

"The police car!" she screamed, releasing the wheel in horror.

He glanced at the rearview mirror at the last minute, seeing the police car appear like a rocket, spot the two women, who'd come to a frozen halt, and then swerve faster than a drunken hound dog.

"Maggie, help me!"

Belatedly she refastened her hands upon the wheel. He clenched his teeth. The sweat rolled down his cheeks and he fought with everything he had.

"Crank it the other way, crank it *into* the fishtail!"

Her teeth sank into her lower lip, and she did her best to comply. He grunted and with a mighty groan finally wrenched the wheel around. The truck swiveled in the other direction immediately, losing momentum from the steep grade of the hillside and helping him regain control. Behind them came a mighty crunch, and they glanced in the rearview mirror simultaneously to see the police car plunge into the shallow ditch, right-side wheels still spinning, lights whirling with a dull whimper.

He got the truck in line and they shot ahead.

Maggie let go of the wheel as if she'd been scorched. When she looked at him at last, her blue eyes were saucer-wide in her face. "You crashed a police car!"

"I'm surely going to hell," he agreed.

With the immediate threat gone, his foot relented on the gas. But his mind refused to stop. The truck was blown. Everyone knew about the truck. The police car had most certainly called for backup. How long did he have? One minute? Two minutes? Thirty seconds?

Cain, what are you going to do now?

He reached the top of the hill, the ground suddenly opening up to reveal broad, gently undulating fields. He could see long private drives winding to towering houses that boasted three stories of windows with fantastic views of snowcapped Mount Hood. He saw smaller homes clutched together like refugees, not as grand as the mansions but stealing the same impressive view.

Houses, houses, everywhere, but not a single side road.

"Where are we?" He glanced at her fiercely.

"How the hell would I know?" his terrified captive shot back. Then threw in mutinously, "You could've killed everyone!"

"But I didn't."

"It wasn't for lack of trying!"

He took his gaze off the road long enough to give her his most impressive frown. She glared right back at him, her face flushed furiously, her eyes sparkling like blue daggers. So much for the meek and humble act. This woman looked ready to chew him up and spit him back out as a dollop of Silly Putty.

The color was good for her cheeks, the fire good for her eyes. She was tougher than she looked, he respected that. But he didn't have time for it given the circumstances.

"Find where we are," he ordered curtly. "And get us the hell out of here before I'm forced to repeat that pleasure ride."

"You—you—you reprobate!"

"Get the map, Maggie."

She snatched it up with such force it crackled in the silence, then snapped it open for the finishing touch. He returned his attention to the road, fingers tapping out an impatient, restless beat.

"I don't know where we are," she muttered a minute later. "I think we're lost."

"Look harder."

"I did," she insisted, still in a fine display of temper. "This is a small road and the map doesn't show minor roads. So there! Next time you decide to run from the cops, at least pick a road that's on the map!"

"I'll be sure to remember that." He arched a single brow.

She glared back pugnaciously. "You are not a nice person!" she announced.

That fired up his second brow. "Surely you can do better than that for a comeback. Come on, try."

Her cheeks flushed. "Unlike *some* people," she said stiffly, "I do not go around regularly insulting others. I don't believe violence or yelling is the answer to anything. People yell too much. It's very destructive and doesn't solve anything."

"Of course."

"I'm serious. Exchanging insults is childish and immature. True conflict resolution requires two people communicating as intelligent, rational adults, sensitively in tune with the feelings of the other party—"

"What are you talking about?"

"Let's try it," she said abruptly, turning sideways in the cab and pinning him with eyes that were more than slightly desperate. "I'll tell you how I feel and then you tell me how you feel, and once we understand each other you will feel secure enough to let me go." She smiled at him brightly, but it strained the corners of her mouth.

"Have you been watching too many TV talk shows?"

That smile grew real strained. "No, I'm trying to tell you that I'm intimidated by you. I'm scared out of my mind but I understand your desperation. I'm sensitive enough to your fear of being caught that if you let me go, I won't tell anyone."

"Because you don't want to hurt my feelings?"

"Exactly!" She beamed at him with wholehearted approval.

"Maggie, what do you *do* for a living?"

The smile faded. She appeared puzzled and perturbed. "I'm a marriage counselor—"

"*What?* I thought you were a court clerk."

"A court clerk? Why would I be a court clerk? I'm a marriage counselor."

He groaned, his dismay palpable. He shook his head, and his disgust was sketched all over his face. "Of all the people in that courthouse, I kidnapped a *shrink*."

"I beg your pardon!" Her chin came up lightning fast, her eyes blazing to life. She looked a trifle indignant and more than a little hurt. "I will not be belittled by a term like 'shrink.' Do you have any idea how important marriage counselors are? Do you have any idea of just how difficult it is? What it's like to spend your days listening to people say how much they love each other and their children, and then proceed to scream at each other over everything from how she spends all the money on furniture to how he always leaves the toilet seat up? It's... it's...*hard.*'' Abruptly, her voice broke. She looked away, appalled by how much her voice had risen, how much her chin was trembling.

She could feel the sting of tears in her eyes and the telltale thickness in her voice. Nerves, she told herself. Delayed shock and extreme fear. But she knew, of course, that it was much deeper than that.

She'd been very weepy lately and for no reason that she could understand. She hated crying. Crying didn't solve anything, as her father had always told her. But for some reason, she found herself on the verge of tears a lot these days. Once, she'd been in her office, listening to a young couple explain that they really did want to save their marriage because while they knew they had their differences, they *did* agree that they loved their children more than anything and they would do everything in their power to maintain their family for their kids.

And all of a sudden, Maggie had had to ask them to excuse her for a moment because she knew she was going to cry. She'd hustled the startled people back into the waiting room, barely getting her door closed in time, and then she'd just stood in the middle of her office and bawled like a baby. She was twenty-seven years old and all she could think was had her parents ever talked about her like that? Had they ever loved her, had they ever thought of her first? Had they ever spoken of her with pride or affection? Stephanie had never once said, "I love you." Neither had her father.

And sometimes late at night, she found herself holding the heart pendant around her neck and thinking of her dad. Maxmillian. Maxmillian the chameleon. Even after all these years, she knew so little about him. Even Lydia hadn't understood her son. When she spoke of him, she recalled his high school days as class president, Eagle Scout and student voted most likely to succeed. No one understood the man he'd become. Why he'd loved the women he'd loved, why he'd traveled like he'd traveled. He'd been, and then he was gone, and sometimes Maggie felt this huge, gaping hole she just couldn't fill.

All she had left was a cheap gold locket and a silly little girl's secret she'd still never divulged because it was the only part of her father's life that was uniquely hers.

One night, she'd found her hand on the phone, already dialing C.J. in Sedona. Not to talk, not for anything. But just to see if he was still there, to make sure he hadn't disappeared as well. She wanted to do the same thing with Lydia and Brandon, except she already knew Brandon wouldn't pick up. He was traveling the world. He had become as distant and enigmatic as Max even though he'd sworn to be there for her forever.

People just came and went in her life. She didn't know how to make them stay. She didn't know how to make anyone stay.

"Hello. *Shopping!*" Cain abruptly announced. He turned to her with a triumphant smile that abruptly faded away. "Are you…are you all right?"

She gazed at him helplessly, pinned by those peering green eyes. *Don't look at me like that, don't ask me that kind of question.* She glanced away sharply, blinking her eyes against the tears and clutching the door handle as if that would give her strength. She couldn't look at him and she couldn't bear to cry twice in one day. "I've…I've just been kidnapped," she whispered at last. "How all right should I be?"

"Of…of course." But she could still feel his gaze upon her back. The silence stretched in the tiny cab. She didn't know why he didn't snarl or growl, why he didn't act a little more mean. She didn't know why he kept looking at her like that and she wished he would stop.

Finally, he turned away. She heard a small sound as he

cleared his throat and could almost picture his hands flexing and unflexing on the wheel.

Another moment passed in silence, then she realized that Cain was now pulling over the truck. She glanced up to see a row of mud-splattered cars and pickup trucks, and the bright orange Caterpillars of a work crew excavating a broad space for a new housing development.

"What?" she asked, bewildered.

"New truck."

"No!"

"Yes." He turned their truck in at the beginning of the line of vehicles. She glanced toward the construction crew, waiting for one of them to notice. They were intent upon their work.

Cain opened the door and hopped out, yanking her with him. She tumbled out behind him with less grace.

"You can't do this," she whispered urgently, tugging in vain on her half of the handcuffs. "Stealing the first truck was bad enough."

"Keep your head down."

"Are you listening to me?"

"Of course I am. Stealing is wrong, bad, evil. I've broken one of the commandments and I'm not a nice person. Did I miss anything?" His gaze was sardonic, and because he outweighed her by one hundred pounds, he slowly and methodically dragged her toward his intended prey.

"Haven't you looked at the construction crew?" she continued desperately. "These people are hard at work to earn paychecks to support their families. You can't steal their only vehicle while they try to earn a living like that. It's just...just—"

Cain whirled on her abruptly and the cold, hard look in his eyes killed the words in her throat. Oh, she'd gotten to him all right, and now she wished she'd never opened her mouth. He bent down over her, huge and imposing, and she bent back as far as she was able. Even then, she felt his breath against her cheek.

"Shut up," he whispered with deceptive softness, his eyes pinning her into place. "I know what I'm doing, Maggie. Don't ever think I don't know it's wrong. Don't ever think I don't have regrets. But I'm ready to live with them and you're just along for the ride. Got it?"

Weakly, she nodded her head, still unable to breathe. Her stomach was suddenly tight. Her limbs quivered with an emotion she didn't completely understand. He seemed fierce enough to tear up the world and strong enough to do it.

He straightened abruptly, looking suddenly uncomfortable. Then with another scowl, he turned back to the trucks. Very slowly, she drew in a ragged breath.

He popped open the door of a little blue Toyota truck. "Ladies first."

He turned back toward her. His eyes no longer glowed with a feral gleam. Now they were perfectly expressionless, merely waiting. "Come on, Maggie," he said and she caught the edge of warning in his voice.

She stepped forward without another word and slid into the vehicle.

With the gun tucked into the waistband of his jeans, Cain lowered his head beneath the dash and got on with the business of hot-wiring a car. The car roared to life in under sixty seconds. The man was amazing. She couldn't even program her VCR and he made stealing a car look as simple as turning on a flashlight.

"Here we go," he announced grimly and swung the truck back onto the road.

The orange Caterpillar froze. The men glanced over, then one of them did a double take. Maggie didn't have to roll down her window to hear the man cry, "Hey, that's my truck!"

Cain said nothing, but his face was grim. He floored the gas pedal and they zipped away. She glanced back at the poor construction crew, the men waving their arms frantically for the vehicle to stop. The men quickly disappeared, lost in the distance. In addition to hot-wiring cars, Cain seemed to have a penchant for driving them *fast*. Where did men learn that kind of thing, anyway?

She looked at him with open reproach. "Do you think this vehicle is insured?"

"I don't know." His voice was clipped.

"I hope it was insured. I don't think that man has much money."

Cain's grip tightened on the wheel.

"It must be very hard, working like that to support your family," she continued relentlessly, "and then through no fault of your own, having your truck stolen. What do you think he'll tell his wife?"

"You don't even know if he has a wife."

"He looks like he has a wife. Probably two kids, too. Cute little kids who used to like to ride in the back of the truck with the sun on their cheeks."

"All right!" Cain threw up his hands and cracked as thoroughly as any suspect under intense interrogation. "He'll get it back!" he exclaimed harshly. "We won't hurt the vehicle, we won't take it far. End of day, he can still drive his truck home to his wife and two kids and one hound dog. My God, you are like the Betty Crocker version of the Gestapo!"

Maggie finally relaxed. "Yes, but it's expensive to replace an automobile."

Cain appeared to grind his teeth, his gaze locked on the road with almost grim determination. "You know," he said abruptly. "I'm not as big a cad as you think, Maggie." He glanced at her briefly. His tone was stiff. "I've gone hungry. Where I grew up, dinner was what you could shoot or pick off a bush."

She looked at him expectantly but he didn't say anything more on the subject. His attention focused one hundred percent on the road.

"Look for a map," he ordered curtly.

But then it became unnecessary. Like a miracle, a road

appeared on his left, forking out. He didn't ask, he didn't debate. He seized it as a gift from God and picked up the pace. That road led to another, then another. If something appeared, he took it, and soon they were so lost they couldn't even find themselves, let alone anyone in high pursuit. He settled down to drive and the fields took on a green blur around him.

Cain had been eighteen when he'd first met Kathy. Eighteen and fresh from Idaho, a hillbilly former survivalist who wanted desperately to join mainstream society. Kathy hadn't laughed at him or made him feel self-conscious. Instead, she'd seemed genuinely intrigued by his blunt statements and matter-of-fact approach to life. If people wanted platitudes, they didn't hang out with Cain.

They'd been just friends in the beginning, Cain too preoccupied with carving out a life to think of anything more. But then things had slowly slid into place. He'd enrolled in Portland State and discovered that the formulas, theories and music that so often haunted his mind suddenly had meaning. His professors didn't greet him with raised brows or dismissive gestures as his father had done. Instead their eyes widened and they demanded to hear more.

Cain had always known he was different. Most people thought in words; he had a tendency to think in numbers or notes. He was most intrigued by the number eight, of course. It was the basis for everything. Chess, mathematics, music, even the periodic table. Nature had recurring themes—life truly seemed to favor the cycle—and inevitably, the basis of such cycles was the number eight. He'd once tried to speak to his father about it. Zechariah had said harshly, "Chess isn't about numbers, boy. Who cares about numbers? Chess is all about killing the king, that's what you should care about. We are the last of the Minutemen, the last of the true patriots. We must safeguard freedom against the ZOG and don't you forget it."

Cain had never had anything in common with his father.

But at Portland State, he'd suddenly belonged. He'd made friends for the first time. At least he'd thought they were friends. Later, he'd had cause to question everything.

He'd made it through college in three years, taking classes year-round and discovering his true calling. Graduation had given him more job offers than he'd known what to do with and suddenly life had been on track.

And somehow, he and Kathy had become more than friends. He didn't remember the exact moment, anymore. He didn't remember the first date. He remembered other things instead. For his twenty-third birthday, she'd given him a marble chess set and challenged him to a game of strip chess. For each piece you lost, you had to remove a piece of clothing. Kathy had been lousy at chess and he'd had her naked and laughing in no time. He remembered the time she'd served him French toast wearing nothing but a pair of red high heels.

She'd been a generous woman, warm, intelligent and funny. She'd made a small home for him and given him laughter when he hadn't laughed since his mother had died.

He wished sometimes he'd had something to give her in return. Maybe it was the way he thought. Maybe it was because he'd spent so much time alone after his mother's death, but he didn't fit like other people fit. Even in the middle of a room filled with people, he was somehow separate, apart, isolated. Kathy complained that he didn't seem to need her. He'd answered that he didn't understand why she would want that. People should be with each other out of choice, not need.

She'd become more distant after that, veering toward little games and petty displays he didn't know how to respond to. He couldn't play the jealous type, he couldn't pour out his soul as she seemed to want. If she didn't want to be with him anymore, he accepted that. It was her choice to move on, and he honestly wished her well.

He would miss her, but that was life—cause and effect, choice and consequence. He accepted that. He valued his independence. And if he lived alone and died alone because of it, he was willing to pay that price. Choice and consequence.

When Abraham had abruptly appeared in Portland and instantly swept Kathy off her feet, Cain had figured it was for the best. Kathy had seemed happy. She'd always liked men with an edge and Ham certainly had that. But Ham had also seemed to have turned over a new leaf. He'd claimed that he'd left the militia movement and their father's racism behind. Cain had figured that must be the case for Kathy was Jewish, something that Ham never would have tolerated before.

Cain had never suspected a thing. Down to the last moment, he'd never suspected the truth about his brother.

I knew you were many things, Ham. But a murderer? A murderer?

God, how could he have not seen that coming? How could he have let Kathy pay for his mistakes with his family? For not realizing just how deep Ham's hatred ran, just how dangerous Ham had become?

He'd tried to tell everyone at the trial. He'd testified on his own behalf, telling the judge, the jury and Kathy's family what Ham had done. But the weapon was Cain's hunting knife with Cain's fingerprints. Then Ham got on the stand, calmly swore on the Bible he held sacred and proceeded to tell the room how he'd witnessed Cain's attack on Kathy in a jealous rage. And Cain had no alibi to back up his version of events.

It had been over after that. No one believed him. Not even Kathy's brother Joel, whom he'd considered a good friend, not his boss, not his co-workers, not anyone. Cain had no proof on his side and no one was willing to listen to him otherwise. They all just said they never had felt very close to him, they never had felt as if they truly knew him. No one believed in him at all.

He stood alone. He went to jail alone. He held the truth alone.

And the first six months in prison, he'd listened to the cell doors slamming shut every night, *kchnk, kchnk, kchnk,* and dreamed of Kathy calling his name.

"Cain?"

He was so disoriented, it took him a moment to realize the voice wasn't in his head.

"Cain?"

He forced himself back to reality, blinking his eyes and peering belatedly at his passenger. She was chewing her lower lip and staring at the gauges. "I think we get to walk soon," she said.

His gaze swung to the gas gauge. It already rested on Empty. "I am having such a bad day," he muttered at last.

"Really?" Maggie chimed. "Mine's been rather nice." She smiled glumly.

"Try to locate us on the map again. We either find civilization or take up hiking."

Maggie retrieved the map, her mind moving quickly. She thought they were still heading toward Tigard and Tualatin. What if they did run out of gas? Then they'd walk. Could she run for it? Somehow, she didn't think he'd unhandcuff her to walk. Most likely, she'd be glued to his side. But what if someone came along in a car? He wouldn't want to arouse suspicion by having someone see them handcuffed together. Maybe he'd undo the handcuffs then.

She could try running for it. She wasn't exactly dressed for the occasion, but maybe a car would spot her and offer help.

Or maybe Cain would pull out his gun, shoot the other person and steal yet another vehicle. He hadn't actually done anything violent yet, but he'd gone to prison for murdering his girlfriend. That seemed to suggest he could be lethal when provoked.

Oh God. She started searching in earnest for their road on the map.

"Okay," she said after a moment. "I think we're almost in Tualatin."

She directed him across another few streets, down 99W, across another few back roads and then they were in Tualatin, right off I-5. The library, Safeway, and K mart was on their left. Fred Meyers appeared on their right. Banks and liquor stores. Surely there had to be a gas station somewhere.

"We're ditching this vehicle," Cain said and whipped them into the long strip mall with K mart.

"And stealing another," she filled in morosely.

"I promised the last person would get his car back and Idaho is a long walk."

"I don't think returning someone's stolen car is considered a good deed if you just turn around and steal another."

"Any better ideas?"

"Turn yourself in? Let me go?" She smiled hopefully. "I'm just going to slow you down, I've never been particularly fond of Idaho, and you still don't know how to manage the bathroom breaks."

He turned into the parking lot, shut off the engine and looked at her. "True. Let's think about this." He gazed at her steadily, his green eyes sharp. After a moment, he nodded to himself. That worried her.

"How much money do you have?" he quizzed.

She instinctively clutched her purse against her.

"Now, Maggie, we've come this far together, don't back out on me now."

"I'm not exactly rich," she half lied, hoping that might sway him.

"Consider it a loan." Cain wiggled his fingers impatiently. "How much?"

She reluctantly opened her purse and took out her billfold. At least she never carried much cash on her. "Five dollars and...sixty-seven cents."

"Five dollars?" he said incredulously. "*Five dollars!* You're walking around with only five dollars on you? How are we going to outrun the entire state police force with five dollars?''

"I didn't 'walk around' with only five dollars in my purse," she said stiffly. "I had fifteen dollars. You already spent ten.''

"Maggie, you can barely fill a gas tank with fifteen bucks.''

"I know. And I took the bus." She smiled grimly, her hands folded on her lap very prim and proper. "Besides, it's not safe for a lone woman to travel with too much cash." And then her blue eyes did flash piercing flames at him.

He glared at her a minute longer, then shook his head. "Of all the people in the world," he muttered, "how did I manage to kidnap a poverty-stricken shrink?''

"I don't know. Why don't you return me and try again?''

He scowled, contemplating her for another moment. He was starting to feel strung too tight, and that would get him nowhere. If there was ever a situation that required logic and rationality, this was it. It was only his freedom, his life at stake. *And now that you've kidnapped her, is her life at stake as well? Do you think Ham would hesitate to harm her?*

The thought came out of nowhere and floored him. For a minute, he could only sit there and blink. He stole another glance at her. She sat quietly, her hands folded on her lap as if she didn't want to draw any attention to herself. Her tangled red hair was torched by the bright spring sun, shimmering a deep burning red. Her skin was alabaster perfect and her lips a rose petal pink. She was beautiful in her own way. If he'd met her under any other circumstances, he might have nodded politely at her, but he still would have walked away.

He preferred sophisticated and experienced women, ones who wouldn't expect things from him he couldn't give. Ones who considered great sex to be its own reward. This woman before him...she looked as if she still slept curled in a ball, her hands clutching the satin edge of a thick blanket, her dreams searching for a happily-ever-after that had never quite found her.

A marriage counselor. A woman hell-bent on saving the world when God knows she didn't look as if she could even save herself.

He glanced at her again, and her bright blue eyes seemed vulnerable.

You got her into this, Cain. What do you do now?

Nothing, he decided resolutely. Just a few more hours of her assistance and he'd be in Idaho. Once out of the immediate range of the Oregon state police, he'd let her go. She'd call her brothers. She would be safe. If Ham did hunt her down and ask questions, she certainly wouldn't tell any stories. As far as she was concerned Cain was a murderer, and he was best off to keep it that way. As long as she thought the worst of him, she was safe from Ham. Cain owed her that much, and if there ever came a day when he was a free man, he would find her and thank her for the small part she played in helping him uncover the truth.

Cain didn't know if he ever would be a free man, though. The cops would hunt him until he cleared his name, and to clear his name he needed to confront Ham. Confronting Ham would probably lead to his own death, or possibly to Ham's. Which would finally make Cain guilty of one murder though convicted of another. Either way, Cain's future didn't look very encouraging, and for all his brilliance, he couldn't quite crack this riddle. Cain's conundrum, he called it.

First things first: He had to make it to Idaho.

"Do you have a cash card?" he asked Maggie abruptly.

"Y-yes."

"All right." His voice was deliberately hard. "This is what we'll do. We're going to walk across the street to the other mall. I'm going to remove the handcuffs for the occasion, so don't do anything that will make me make you regret it. Got it?"

She nodded, but her brow was furrowed into a rebellious scowl.

"At the mall," he continued relentlessly, "you'll withdraw as much as you can. Then, we'll steal another car and head for Salem. With any luck, it will take them a while to notice the vehicle is gone."

She opened her mouth as if to protest, then abruptly shut it again. She hunched her shoulders a little more. Finally, in a faint voice, she asked, "Are you ever going to let me go?"

"When we get to Idaho...if you cooperate."

He followed up the statement with a dispassionate stare. And she peered back at him from beneath the long, tangled locks of her red hair, looking like someone who'd gotten too many hard knocks and not enough pick-me-ups. Her lashes swept down abruptly, brushing her pale cheeks delicately and hiding her eyes. Her fingers knit together on her lap, as if seeking to comfort one another.

He forced himself to watch and remain impassive.

"All right," she agreed.

"We use your ATM card. We steal another car," he repeated.

"I cooperate. You don't hurt anyone," she repeated.

"We have ourselves a deal."

He reached across the bench seat and briskly grabbed her handcuffed hand, releasing the metal bracelet. He folded the cuffs in his back pocket, beneath the cover of his overshirt.

"I still have a loaded gun," he reminded her softly.

"Who could forget?"

He opened the truck door, peered around for cops and drew her half out of the vehicle. "We walk, nothing fancy. Let's take the map with us."

She obediently retrieved the map and handed it to him.

She was silent for a moment. Then, she expelled in a rush, "You don't have to do this. Running from the law, stealing cars, it's no way to live. If you'd let me call my brother Brandon, he's very smart, you've never talked to anyone as smart as him. He could help you, I just know he could. You seem like you're quite intelligent. I mean…surely you must want more from life than to spend your days running from the police. What kind of future is that?"

"It's not much of one."

"My family could help you—"

"Maggie," he interjected quietly. "Enough."

He turned and walked away, and the motion of his arm forced her to follow.

Chapter 4

She cast a surreptitious glance at her captor as he led her across the parking lot.

His steps were long, forceful and not at all furtive. His green gaze was hard and level and never ducked guiltily to the pavement. In the faded blue shirt, worn T-shirt and work-softened jeans, he looked like anyone, any random man who might work with his hands and know what he was about. Solid shoulders, lean flanks, muscled forearms. A few women gave him a second glance before spotting Maggie.

He'd been a computer programmer? She never would have guessed that. She thought computer programmers were supposed to be like accountants, nice, bland men with innocuous smiles and rapidly blinking eyes. In jeans and T-shirt, Cain looked more like the dairy farmers she'd spend her summers with in Tillamook. She could see him striding along in the field, shirtsleeves rolled up to reveal tanned forearms, and bright August sun torching his golden hair as he wrapped his gloved hands around baling wire

and hefted bales of sweet alfalfa effortlessly onto the flatbed. Heave-ho, heave-ho. From the time of the summer of
'78 on Lydia's farm, she'd spent all her summers watching
that ritual, driving the tractor that pulled the flatbed through
the fields and feeling her heart beat in rhythm to the con-
stant, sweaty motion of heave-ho, heave-ho.

Her mouth was suddenly dry. Her shoulder was pressed
against his rib cage, her hand still firmly tucked in his, and
shivers abruptly raced up her spine.

Oh, God, Maggie, you have finally gone and lost your
ever-lovin' mind.

"ATM machine," Cain exclaimed briskly as they arrived on the other side of the four-lane intersection. "This
way."

He pulled her to the left and she trotted along blankly
like a well-heeled puppy dog.

Do something, you ninny!

She looked at him again. His face was determined and
composed. His intelligent gaze had locked on target, and
he led them to the machine with rapid, precise steps, as if
he had no care in the world and he would escape from an
entire state's police force through sheer force of will.

That was the problem. She knew that look. She'd seen
it on Brandon's face more times than she could count. The
oldest of them, he'd had the opportunity to know Max the
best, and he'd been the first to watch their father simply
walk out the door one day and never come back. He could
have hated her and C.J., particularly C.J., for while Maxmillian had married Brandon's mother for her inheritance,
he kept returning to C.J.'s mother in L.A. out of love. But
Brandon had been the first to realize that C.J.'s fierce ex-
terior hid a scared, angry little boy who'd lost the father he
considered an idol. And in those rough beginning weeks,
Brandon was the one who would calmly and firmly say,
"It's all right, C.J. Everything is going to be all right."
Then he would look at both C.J. and Maggie with a gaze
just like Cain's, cool, composed and magnetic, as if through

sheer force of will, he'd keep them safe. After ten days, C.J. and Maggie would have followed him anywhere, they trusted him that much.

At the time he was solid and reliable, everything their father hadn't been. And now? Ever since his wife's death, Brandon had been jetting around the globe, unreachable and unpredictable. Even C.J. had edgily growled last week, "What the hell does he think he's proving? That he can disappear like Max?"

Maggie couldn't answer. She just knew in some deep part of her heart that Brandon would never return, just as Max never returned, just as her mother had always threatened to never return.

"All right. Proceed, Maggie."

Cain came to an abrupt halt, turning briskly. She stared at him blankly, her hand tucked into his, her shoulder against his chest. She felt very small, all of a sudden. Lost in her thoughts and the emptiness that sometimes consumed her from the inside out.

"Woolgathering?"

She could only nod. He looked big, she thought abruptly. He looked big and strong and capable. Even on the run, he appeared composed and in control, as if he didn't doubt one iota his ability to succeed. She couldn't imagine being that sure. She couldn't imagine not lying in bed at night, wondering if she would ever fall in love, wondering if anyone would ever hold her close and love her enough to stay.

That had to be love: staying forever.

"Maggie?" Cain prodded. "Dreaming of being rescued by a dashing young man?"

She shook her head, keeping her eyes down, fixed on his sternum and the nubby fabric of his T-shirt. "Just take the money," she told him. Her voice was faint, faint and meek. She hated that. Abruptly she swallowed and the emptiness was gone, and instead she was just angry, angry and frustrated and furious with herself because she sounded like such a mouse, acted like such a mouse, and what had it ever gotten her?

"Take the money," she demanded more harshly now. "Take it and kidnap me and get this show on the road. We have to go to Idaho. You have to kill your brother. I suppose if you let me live I can write up the events and option them for a Sunday night movie. Robert Redford can be you. Do you think Sandra Bullock would mind playing me?"

Cain was silent, then he frowned. "You say the damnedest things, Maggie."

"Yes," she agreed curtly and suddenly she was the one pushing ahead to the ATM machine, already digging for her card. "I'm the odd one, the quiet one, the timid one. I'm never any trouble, just ask anyone. Good, sweet little Maggie." She yanked her cash card out of her purse with more vehemence than necessary and jammed it into the machine. "So," she stated aggressively, "how much money does an escaped felon need these days?"

"Two hundred," he said quietly. His eyes were still on her face. "You know, you're not that passive, Maggie. You've already argued with me several times and I'm carrying a gun."

"Oh goody, so I am developing. I've gone from passive-aggressive to suicidal. Give me a decade, I'm sure I can hit manic-depressive."

She fairly snatched the money from the machine's mouth.

"Self-pity, Maggie?"

"Yes, it's the next step of the hostage trauma process. First denial, then self-pity." She jammed her ATM card into the pocket of her skirt, then stuffed the wad of twenties into his hand. "Here's your allowance. Don't spend it all in one place."

He still wasn't moving. "Maggie, I won't hurt you," he said quietly. "Help me get to Idaho and you'll live to see your three-legged cat. I promise."

"And I'm supposed to trust the word of a convicted murderer?"

"I'd ask you to trust the word of the pope, Maggie, but he's not currently available." Abruptly, he pulled her against his body. His eyes were no longer so calm or expressionless. They burned, the tension radiating from him like waves. He looked frustrated, too, frustrated and angry and edgy. She could feel his thighs pressed against hers, and was suddenly painfully aware of her small breasts pushing against his chest. Her nipples were hard and sensitive. She wondered if he could feel that, too, and then her cheeks flushed with pure mortification at the thought.

She blinked several times rapidly, then in a small rush of anger she planted her hands against his concrete chest and pushed away vehemently. His grip on her hand kept her from going too far, but she could at least tilt back her head and stare at him mutinously.

"Stop it," she demanded. "If you're going to kidnap me, you're going to kidnap me. You're bigger than I am, stronger and armed, so I suppose I don't have much say in the matter. But don't mess with my mind. Don't tell me what my problems are. You're a murderer, for God's sake. You're trying to kill your brother. What do you know about happy, healthy life-styles?"

A muscle twitched in his jaw. He flinched as if she might have actually hurt him, but she wasn't so big of a fool that she believed that.

His eyes remained hooded, dark. His face appeared carved from a mountain. The silence stretched out, grew taut. Behind them, she could hear the random sounds of chattering pedestrians and roaring cars. The simple, everyday sounds of a busy mall. Bright, pinging noises that still couldn't break the tension between them.

Abruptly, Cain nodded. His shoulders came down, his face grew smooth and expressionless, impenetrable. "You're right," he said. "You're absolutely right."

Then without another word, he turned and started pulling

her toward the parking lot. "Come on, Maggie. We have
another car to steal."

They walked across the huge parking lot of Fred Meyers
twice, peering in windows to see which doors were unlocked and how much gas prospective vehicles had. Cain
preferred trucks for their powerful engines and off-road ca-
pability. Besides, he'd driven trucks all his life and felt less
conspicuous in one than in a sedan. He finally narrowed
down the selection to two trucks located at the back of the
lot, both big and relatively new.

"They're both probably insured," he declared dryly.

Maggie lifted her chin. "Good."

"Is there a color you prefer?"

"Oh no, I'm not going to have anything to do with this.
If you're going to steal another truck, then you steal another
truck. For the record, I think we should take the bus."

He glanced at her. "Oh yes, the special program Trimet
started just for escaped murderers. I'd forgotten about
that."

"I hear it's very good." She played right along with him.

"Let's take the blue truck, Maggie. I've always liked
blue."

"Buses might be blue."

He granted her a small smile. "You really do try, Maggie. You really do try."

"It's never too late to change."

He didn't say anything, but as a silent rebuttal, opened
the truck door for her, one hand already reaching out to
assist her.

She batted it away with more force than necessary, holding herself perfectly rigid. "I can get in all by myself, thank
you."

"Yes, but this way is faster." And while she was still
opening her mouth for another rebuke, he clasped his hands
around her supple waist and tossed her up into the king-
size cab. With a startled cry, she grabbed the dash to keep

from sliding on the floor, then with another gasp, hastily rearranged her skirt to cover her thighs. She gave him a look of pure indignation, but he simply smiled.

"I think we're getting the hang of this," he murmured and swung himself into the cab. Quick glance in the rearview mirror revealed no one else around. He got to work.

Maggie was glancing at her watch as the truck roared to life. "Forty-two seconds," she muttered. "I don't know how you do that."

"Lots of practice."

"As a computer programmer?" She raised a skeptical brow.

"As a minuteman who would someday have to rise up and protect the last frontier from the ever-encroaching, ever-devious ZOG."

That widened her eyes and shut her up in a hurry. He enjoyed the effect so much he continued talking casually as he swung the vehicle out of the parking lot. "Didn't you know that ZOG is out to stupefy the American people?"

She shook her head.

"Public water supplies are contaminated, secret troops are being trained. The World Bank and the United Nations are actually ZOG puppets ready to take over the world once the government crushes the last of the U.S. resistance. It will be like the apocalypse, that's what my father always said. 'We are in a state of war, son. A state of *war!*'"

His voice trailed off. Maggie's face was pale now; he could hear the wheels turning in her mind. *The patient appears to be suffering from paranoid delusions, perhaps even acute schizophrenia.*

"Can you open up our loyal map?" he said lightly, his gaze on the road. "We need a course for Salem."

She muttered something under her breath but complied. The woman was obviously scared of him, but the meek act was certainly dropping away in a hurry. In its place she was...he didn't know who she was. But she could certainly flash those blue eyes like nobody's business. And her stubborn streak might be even wider than he'd previously estimated.

Interesting, in a woman who seemed so humbled at first glance. Who had taught her to look like that, to think so little of herself? She cared so much about others, why hadn't someone thought to give a little more care to her? He had the impression sometimes, from a fleeting, wistful, look in her eyes, that she was a woman who was very lonely. And when he saw that look…

He shut off the thought with a curt shake of his head. It was none of his business, dammit. She had been absolutely on target back there. It was bad enough he was taking her hostage; he certainly had no right to mess with her mind.

For his purposes, all that mattered was that she seemed to have a remarkably level head, she held up under pressure, and she could navigate. Yes, she was a serious candidate for the hostage-of-the-year award.

"Okay," she said after a moment. "I've found us on the map."

"All right, Sulu, lay in a course for Salem, sticking to back roads."

"Sulu?"

"'Star Trek.'"

"Oh." She glanced over at him narrowly, then shook her head. "Geek."

He simply smiled.

Mile turned into miles. They left Portland's suburbs and whizzed through the lush, green fields of places like Molalla and Wilhoit. Mount Hood rose up behind them, old and wise with its snowcapped head. The mountains ringed them in, green and distant as they circled the valley like ancient forefathers keeping a benevolent watch. They passed farmers out working their fields, dogs leaping and racing along the side of the road as if on this bright spring day they could outrun even a metal animal. Red grain silos rose, silver domes winking in the sunlight. Two fields of tulips spread out, offering a dazzling feast of color, then slowly faded away to be replaced by young, earnest ears of corn struggling to break ground and push triumphantly to the sky.

After a bit, Maggie glanced over at Cain, then decided on her own she was willing to risk the act of rolling down her window. The scent of fresh-mowed grass filled the cab. The wind caught her hair, lifting the red strands to the sun and streaming them back away from her face.

They drove in silence and the sky remained blue and vast and beautiful.

They passed through Silverton and came to I-5 just north of Salem. Three miles, that was all they had to spend on the interstate. Three miles, then the welcome exit for 22 would whisk them off the highway and lead them to mountains. Three miles through the thick of Salem, four lanes of traffic and even more spots for state troopers to sit in wait for an escaped felon.

Cain's knuckles were white on the wheel. The tendons stood out in rigid relief on his exposed forearms. He kept the speedometer at a diligent fifty-five, the appropriate speed for passing through city limits.

Wordlessly, Maggie rolled up her window and her hair died on her shoulders.

"It's not that far," she said quietly.

"It doesn't take much to spot a stolen truck."

A cop car was pulled over on the right. It had been a long time, but even after six years, Cain recognized the spot. Cops always waited there to catch the anxious speeder who hadn't wanted to slow from the interstate's speed limit of sixty-five miles per hour to fifty-five in Salem. At least habits hadn't changed while Cain was behind bars.

He kept his gaze straight ahead and his hand on the wheel. Would Maggie try anything? One tap on the window, one frantic wave, and with the news of an escaped murderer posted all over the radio, the cop would pull out and blare his sirens without a second thought.

Sweat trickled down Cain's hairline. He didn't even risk the motion of wiping it away.

Maggie remained silent and still and he swallowed harshly. She didn't realize, of course, the full power that she wielded, that in fact, she held his life in her hands and not the other way around. One earnest attempt on her part and the pawn would checkmate the king. He couldn't even blame her for it. She had the right to fight for her life, to run from a convicted murderer. He, on the other hand, had gotten an innocent involved in a drama that might leave her dead. She had just cause on her side.

It was more than anyone could say about him.

The exit for 22 approached. He released a breath he hadn't known he'd been holding. He turned onto 22 and the Cascades rose up verdant and promising before them. They picked up speed.

Beside him, Maggie rolled down the window once more and let the spring-filled wind whip through her long red hair.

The mountains were beautiful this time of year. Sunlight dappled deep green firs and lighter-colored maple. Ferns and moss formed thick dark carpeting and ran all the way to babbling brooks and, in some cases, cheery waterfalls. The sky here seemed endless and the air tasted as good as it smelled, clean and fresh and the way Mother Nature intended.

Maggie admired it as they wove along the winding highway, climbing higher and higher until they finally traversed Santiam Pass. They broke through to the other side of the Pacific Crest, and suddenly snowcapped mountains beckoned on all sides. Mount Washington was to their right, Mount Jefferson as well. Three-Fingered Jack waved frosted digits on the left, while way out on the horizon, the Three Sisters flirted with the faded blue sky.

It was beautiful, stunningly so. Maggie didn't pass this way often and she tried to appreciate it, because she always remembered the stories her grandmother had told her of how all this had looked to straggling pioneers after months and months of plodding across the country. How they'd taken one look at the lush, bursting greenness, and realized they'd found home.

Of course, right now Maggie was having a hard time appreciating that sentiment. She uncrossed and crossed her legs for the fifth time in twenty minutes, then gave up.

"Time for a pit stop," she suggested, wanting to sound firm, ending up sounding desperate.

Cain frowned and finally glanced at her. "Really?" He didn't sound happy.

That brought her chin up. "It's been four hours. I know time flies when you're having fun—and stealing cars—but don't you think one bathroom break is at least in order?"

As if reading her mind, the road produced a sign advertising that a rest stop was available in one mile. She looked at him levelly. "Well?"

"We have to cross this bridge sometime," he murmured. Lines creased his forehead. His finger began tapping the wheel. Maggie swallowed the groan building in her throat as she read the signs—he was thinking, and generally his thinking led to diabolical plans or at the very least, grand theft auto.

"You're not going to dump this truck and take some poor soul's only means of transportation, are you?"

He looked genuinely startled. "No, I wasn't. But it's not a half-bad suggestion."

"I'm sorry I brought it up." She clenched her teeth. He slowed for the exit. At least that was something.

He pulled into the parking lot. There were two cars and one big vacation vehicle present. Next to the small wooden shack offering rest rooms, a family of four sat at a picnic table in full sunlight. They were eating sandwiches, passing around a thermos and chattering with the merry glee of a family on vacation.

Maggie thought, if I walked right to them and quietly

informed them I'd been kidnapped by a homicidal maniac, would they help me or look at me as if I'd just stepped off the planet Mars?

As if reading her mind, Cain said, "Don't do anything stupid, Maggie."

Her bladder hurt; she was no longer amused. She looked at her evil jailer crossly and said, "Define stupid."

That deepened the lines creasing his brow. His fingers began tapping the wheel again. Heaven help her.

"All right," he said at last, in a tone of voice that declared he'd found the magic answer, "this is the deal."

"Deal?"

"I'll let you out of the truck unescorted—"

She perked up at that.

"But, Maggie," he said quietly, "if you run, I'll just turn around and take another poor innocent woman hostage in your place. As we've already discussed, I need a hostage."

She opened her mouth, she closed her mouth. She stared at him dumbstruck, and then when she finally found her voice she cried in the most virulent tone she could, "You despicable cad!"

The left corner of his mouth twisted up. "I thought you'd like that."

"You...you...!" She couldn't think of a vile enough word. "You just made everyone my responsibility. You kidnap some other poor woman, and somehow it's my fault. You can't just make everything my fault!"

"I didn't," he said levelly. "You did. You and your Mother Teresa complex."

"How..." Her lips pressed together so tightly they turned white. She glared at him as harshly as she could. He appeared completely unmoved. "You're not a paranoid schizophrenic, are you?" she quizzed vehemently. "You're a pure psychopath instead!"

"Possibly." He cocked his head toward the rest rooms, his green eyes steady and unyielding. "Those are the terms,

Maggie. You can run away if you like. But I will kidnap another woman. Just so you know.''

''I hate you!'' she declared miserably.

''I know, but do you still need to use the rest rooms?''

Oh, how she wished she was C.J. at that moment. And not to run, either, but so she would know some really creative and painful ways to kill this man. She settled for stamping her feet against the floor, and when that just reminded her of how badly she did need to use the facilities, she gripped the door handle.

''Fine,'' she said, her blue eyes shooting daggers.

''You do have a temper,'' he observed.

''Only when you're around!''

''Then I have my uses after all,'' he murmured.

For her response, she popped open her door and slid out from the truck as fast as she was able. Her shoulders rigid, her head held high, she stormed toward the single hut containing the men's and women's rest rooms.

After a minute, Cain pulled the baseball cap lower on his forehead and followed.

''Christ, Cain,'' he muttered to himself. ''And you thought she was spineless?''

Once inside the questionable sanctity of the tiny women's room, Maggie stamped around in a small circle. Two stalls, the ripe odor only a rest stop could offer and no paper towels. In her current state, she scoured the concrete floor and wooden walls for possible weapons. She could find only one feminine hygiene dispenser. Great, next time Attila the Hun pulled out his gun, she could counterattack with a tampon.

She grew so angry she actually saw spots. Spots! Meek, humble Maggie so ticked off she couldn't even speak. She stopped long enough to take a deep, steadying breath and allowed one moment to marvel at her own temper. Maybe she was a true Hathaway Red after all. But what good was it doing her?

She hated rest stops. She hated long drives. She hated everything about this hostage business. And she still had no idea what to do about it.

She used the facilities; she washed her hands. And then, because the room hardly offered an instant-escape kit, she walked back out into the sunshine. The family was still eating—she could hear the low murmur of their voices. Cain was nowhere to be seen.

Walk over to them right now, Maggie. Walk right up to them and tell them everything.

And put four innocent lives at risk? Her mouth went dry at the mere thought.

But you can't do nothing, Maggie! All your life you've done nothing. You watched your father come and go as he pleased, accepting whatever scrap he tossed you. You sat quietly as Stephanie threw all her tantrums, then simply helped the maid clean up the mess later on. You are nothing more than a bureaucrat, never taking sides, never making a stand, never putting anything at risk. The world has enough bureaucrats. It needs more foot soldiers.

Her gaze came to rest on the pay phone.

Her breath held. She glanced from side to side. Cain was still nowhere to be seen. What about money? She could call collect.

Do it, Maggie. Do it.

Her feet moved on their own. She didn't remember consciously willing them to action, but they moved anyway, carrying her toward the phone. She arrived. She clutched the receiver for dear life and suffered one last shuddering pang of anxiety.

For one moment, she saw the bleak look on Cain's face as he cranked the truck up the hillside to escape from the police. So much raw determination in his bulging arm, so much desperation in those intelligent green eyes.

For crying out loud, Maggie, you sympathize and protect everyone but yourself. Can't you at least draw the line at empathizing with a murderer? Use the darn phone!

With one quick punch, she dialed the operator, and since no one ever knew where Brandon was these days, she gave the woman the number of C.J.'s bar. A ponderous moment passed, then abruptly ringing filled her ear. Once, twice.

In Sedona, Arizona, the phone was picked up and the warm, smoky sounds of a lively bar filled her ear. Eric Clapton music and laughing conversations. Fizzy drinks and pouring beer.

"Gus's Mortuary," C.J. announced cheerily in his deep baritone. "You stab 'em, we bag 'em."

And suddenly Maggie was eight years old again, seeing C.J. for the first time at the beginning of the Great Experiment. His hands were scrunched in his pockets, his shoulders up around his ears. He was wearing a full-fledged scowl and looking at her and Brandon with deep resentment.

"My mother was the one he loved!" he declared hotly. "He married yours for money, but mine he loved."

And then he looked away and a tremor shook his small, wiry frame. Maggie thought he was going to cry and she'd never seen a little boy cry before. But then he pulled himself together, digging his chin into his chest.

"His mother died last year," Brandon explained quietly. "He's actually been living with Max for a year. Can you imagine, Maxmillian actually taking in one of his children?"

"Don't talk about my father like that," C.J. muttered, but Maggie could tell that he was still very sad. He hadn't lost just one parent, he'd lost both. And though her mommy wasn't very nice, Maggie was glad she had her just to have someone to have. Without thinking, she stepped forward. And though C.J. tensed, though he howled and muttered a vehement protest, she wrapped her arms around him anyway. And then abruptly he sagged against her and she knew he was crying though he didn't make a sound and she knew she was crying without making a sound, because that was what Maxmillian had taught his children—never make any demands, never make any sound.

Never need him.

"Sure I'll accept the charges." C.J.'s voice, adult and assured, resonated across the phone lines. She saw him as he would be standing now, one hip cocked against the bar, the phone tucked between his ear and shoulder, and his hands busy pouring the next beer while a quick, easy grin split his face. "Maggie...Maggie, how the hell are you?"

"C.J.," she whispered. Her hands tightened on the phone. For a minute, she didn't know what to say. "C.J.... C.J., I need you."

"Maggie? Maggie, what's wrong?"

"I went to jury duty," she cried. "And the—"

The phone went click. She stared at the receiver incredulously. And then slowly, her gaze drifted up to the single, callused finger holding the button down.

Her gaze rose farther and finally encountered the chilling green eyes of a man who looked fit to kill.

Chapter 5

"What the hell do you think you're doing?"

She cringed instinctively, only to become trapped by the cool, hard feel of the metal pay phone. Cain's eyes glowed with almost demonic rage from beneath the brim of the baseball cap. In contrast, his grim jaw was set and his face perfectly expressionless. He looked like a murderer, and at that moment she was more terrified than all the previous moments put together.

"I didn't run away," she offered weakly, then winced as his eyes narrowed dangerously. In one quick, forceful move, he planted his hands on either side of her head and clasped her legs between muscle-hardened thighs. She couldn't move, she couldn't twist away. She was caught as effectively as a fly in the spider's web, and she was unbearably aware of the heat of Cain's body, the soft feel of his cotton shirtsleeves against her cheeks, and the scent of deodorant soap flaring her nostrils.

"Who did you call?"

She moistened her lips nervously with the tip of her

tongue. That only brought his gaze homing in on her mouth
with single-minded focus. She stopped moistening in a
hurry. "N...no one?" she tried.

He bent over her so fast she didn't have time to breathe.
One moment she was simply trapped, the next she was
consumed by his body, his hands, his mouth. She felt him
touch her lips with his—surely that was his mouth there.
Her whole body cried out for escape, to run, to hide, to
cringe. But there was only the cold phone bank and his
heated torso. Only the unyielding sharp corners of the
phone hurting her back, and the smooth, sculpted lines of
his biceps bracing her cheeks.

Her hands were wrapped in his overshirt, handfuls of
blue chambray fisted between her fingers. Her breath held
and caught. The emotions thundering through her blood
made her dizzy. He was not kissing her—that thought took
a minute to penetrate. He was not even hurting her—that
thought took a minute more.

"Who did you call?" Each word was enunciated clearly.
Each syllable brushed his lips over hers, violating her space
intimately, ravishing her with his control and determination.

She could feel the frustration and rage crackling around
him. Beneath it was the fine-wire tension of his fear, the
hair-raising prickle of panic running up his own spine. So
many emotions. So much power held tautly in check
through the force of his will, the grit of his jaw. He could
hurt her a hundred ways, but he still didn't move. He just
stood there, hard and powerful and charged.

Her belly contracted. Her breath held. She didn't fight
him; she didn't pull away. She stood on the tingling edge
of his war, and the hair prickled up her arms and up to her
shoulders. She could still feel his anger, and she could still
feel the thin layer of steely control holding it in check.

And for one suspended beat of time, she realized that
she wanted to rip away that barrier. She wanted to strip
him raw. She wanted to wrap her arms tight around his
corded neck and see what happened.

"What the hell are you doing?" he demanded hoarsely.

She looked at him blankly, unaware of the deep, mesmerizing hunger blooming in her large, round eyes. "Wh-what?"

"God," he said, and his green eyes darkened a fraction more. His gaze fell to her lips, and suddenly, she was aware that he wanted her, too. He wanted her fiercely. He wanted her as a man wanted a woman, with passion and fire and thunderbolts. Holy smoke—no man had ever looked at her like that before.

She *liked* it.

"No," he declared abruptly, harshly. "Dammit, no." He twisted away so fast she had no time to prepare herself. The cool spring air hit her like a slap in the face, and she was so stunned that for a dangerous moment tears stung her eyes.

Cain backpedaled fiercely, his steps short and jerky. His hand came up, knocked off the baseball cap and raked through his hair so vehemently he should have pulled all the strands out by the roots. Then he did it again. Then he took a deep breath.

He whirled back again, and the tight look in his face made her suck in air all over again.

"What the hell was that?" he demanded angrily. His eyes had darkened to a midnight forest that had never seen the sun. His chest rose and fell in rapid, bone-deep fury.

She just stared at him, opening and closing her mouth and not finding any words. She'd wanted to kiss him. Oh God, she still wanted to kiss him. And she wanted him to kiss her. She wanted...oh, Lord, she wanted, she wanted, she wanted.

That was it. She was damned. Twenty-seven years of clean, boring existence wiped out in a mere heartbeat. She would never be able to look her grandmother in the eye again.

Her gaze fell miserably to his chest. She saw his collarbone, exposed, broad, and strong. She saw the pounding beat of his pulse at the base of his neck. And she wanted to press her lips right there and taste his skin.

She squeezed her eyes shut and prayed for the earth to open up and swallow her whole.

"Oh, no, you don't," Cain whispered lowly. Abruptly his rough fingers were beneath her chin, forcing up her head. "We're beyond the blushing virgin stage," he said crisply. "If you think you can use your 'feminine wiles' to turn me into a blithering idiot, think again, Maggie. One more inviting look like that and I'll throw you on the ground and take what you're offering. But I won't let you go afterward and nothing will be changed. Do you understand that?"

The blush started at the base of her throat and crept all the way up to the roots of her hair, then darkened four degrees and set her skin on fire. She would gladly have curled into a ball and hidden until nightfall, but his green eyes wouldn't let her escape and his fingers were still rough and insistent beneath her chin. She took a deep breath. "Uh…yes. I understand."

"Is that what you want? Are you one of those women attracted to dangerous men?"

"Oh no," she said most hastily. "That's not what I want. I…I…I don't do the dangerous man thing." Or any man thing. Oh God, how had she gotten herself into this?

He seemed to relax a fraction, but his gaze was still hard. "I believe in the power of choice," he stated firmly. "We make our decisions, we pay for them. If you come on to me again, don't believe that afterward I'll shoulder the blame or accept any guilt. I've told you what you're getting into. You choose to play this dangerous game, then you get the consequences."

She smiled weakly. "Not much for pillow talk, are you?"

"Do you really need more platitudes in your life, Maggie?"

Her breath caught, then she released it with a smile that

was old and wise for her. "No," she admitted honestly. "I don't need any more platitudes."

"Good." His fingers released her chin, but he didn't step back. "Now tell me who you called."

"My brother." It didn't occur to her to lie.

"The Marine Force recon, the one who's invented new ways for me to die?"

"Yes."

"Did you tell him where we are? Did you tell him you were a hostage?"

She shook her head. "I didn't have time. I just said I...I needed him."

Cain's gaze went flat. "Where does he live, Maggie? Where is he?"

Her chin came up defiantly, her nostrils flaring. They both knew he was wasting his breath. Maggie would fold if he so much as plucked a hair from her head, but she'd fall willingly into her own grave rather than hurt someone else. Her blue eyes stared back at him mutinously, and finally he swore.

"He'll find us," he said curtly. "It shouldn't take a rocket scientist to put all the pieces together. Damn."

His fingers curled abruptly around her arm, hard enough to bruise. "Get in the truck, Maggie. We have a lot of ground to cover now, thanks to you."

He sounded furious, but he also sounded tired, and that fast the spirit left her. Her shoulders slumped. She followed the pull of his arm without protest. He didn't say another word. He didn't have to. The disappointment and stress were obvious in his green gaze, and she curled up inside herself just looking at him.

It was illogical, she knew, to feel as if she'd failed her captor, but her parents had trained her well. Or maybe she'd trained herself well. She didn't know anymore. She just knew she'd disappointed Cain, and logically or not, there was nothing she couldn't stand as much as disappointing someone.

Once inside the cabin of the truck, Cain produced the handcuffs.

She held out her wrist without protest, and the sound of the metal cuff closing in the silence rang in her ears.

In Sedona, C.J. didn't waste any time. He dialed Maggie's office and learned from her secretary that she was supposedly on jury duty downtown. Then he dialed Maggie's home just to be sure she wasn't there. Finally, he dialed their grandmother, Lydia, in Tillamook.

After a brief discussion, he thought he knew what was going on. According to Lydia, Maggie had reported for jury duty at the Multnomah County Courthouse just that morning. And now according to news bulletins, a murderer had escaped from that building.

C.J. didn't bother with shock or denial. He had some practice in this sort of thing. And nobody, but nobody was going to hurt his baby sister. He gave Lydia her instructions. Then he called and left a succinct message with Brandon's answering service.

Ten minutes later, C.J. had a bag swung over his shoulder and was striding out of his bar. "Gus," he thought to call over his shoulder at the last minute, "you're in charge now."

Gus didn't even look up from drying the freshly washed beer mugs. C.J.'s "other job" as a bounty hunter had made his spontaneous exits for places unknown for times undetermined fairly commonplace.

C.J. was whistling beneath his breath as he shouldered open the door. "Hang on, Maggie. The cavalry's coming."

Cain wasn't speaking to her anymore.

Hunched up on her side of the truck, her arm laid out across the bench seat thanks to the handcuff, Maggie stared miserably out the window and told herself that silence was a good thing. What kind of pathetic prisoner longed to make idle conversation with her captor anyway?

She was obviously already suffering from Stockholm syndrome, a phenomenon where a hostage bonded with her jailers and began to sympathize with their plight. Why not? Maggie had always been too sensitive for her own darn good. And now she was insane as well.

She sneaked another glance at Cain. The baseball cap was off, and his window was rolled down two inches. The cool spring wind tousled his light blond hair, every now and then raising the strands high enough to reveal the port-wine stain at his hairline. So his father had named him Cain due to that birthmark. What would it be like to go through life named Cain?

She had a feeling that indicated less than desirable family dynamics. Was that why he became a killer? It sounded as if his family was violent and steeped in paranoia. Maybe he'd never had a chance. If he'd been raised in more idyllic surroundings, he and his brother would have suffered from simple sibling rivalry instead of a homicidal need for revenge.

What are you going to do, Maggie, reform him on the road? She was idealistic to the point of hopelessness. Even as she called herself a dim-witted fool, she found herself saying hesitantly, "Are you still angry with me?"

She risked a second glance at him. His forehead had creased into long lines. His hands flexed on the wheel of the truck, then slowly curled around the grip. "I'm not angry," he said abruptly, "I'm frustrated." He turned toward her briefly. "And why does it matter if I'm angry with you?"

"Well…you do have a gun."

He finally nodded as if to say that was a valid point. She sat up a little straighter. "You must be getting tired," she said after a moment.

He didn't respond one way or another, but her stomach growled. She flushed and his lips twitched suspiciously close to a smile. "I must be getting hungry, too," he suggested.

"Perfect," she said with false cheeriness. "I'm starved!"

"When we get to Bend."

"Bend? That's another fifty miles!"

"So it is."

"Why do we have to wait so long? We haven't seen a cop since Salem."

"And I'd like to keep it that way. Plus, we now have this brother of yours to deal with."

She managed to bite her lower lip right before she blurted out that C.J. couldn't possibly be on their tail yet since he had to come all the way from Arizona. She might be naive, but she was trying not to be a complete idiot.

"And your other brother," Cain continued levelly, slanting another glance toward her. "I suppose your other brother will join him?"

"Ah...yes," she declared.

Cain was so impressed he arched a droll blond eyebrow. "Is he a Marine, too?"

"Brandon? No, he's an investment banker."

"Wonderful. So one brother can shoot at me and the other can sell me short. Any shotgun-toting father I should be concerned about as well?"

"No, my father's dead. His plane went down in Indonesia when I was seven." She stated this matter-of-factly. "They never found his body. After a year, we had a memorial service and buried an empty casket, as if that made sense of it all."

"Oh." The conversation drifted. Finally, he shifted restlessly on the seat. "Well, what about your mother, then? Will she come after me with knives? A man needs to know his opponents."

Maggie, having seen her mother wield steak knives before, was not amused by the picture. "My mother is a little wild," she conceded, unconsciously scowling. "She likes to break things, but only expensive things. If they won't be missed, then they aren't worth breaking, that's her motto."

"Sounds nice."

"Oh yeah. She's the life of the party." Maggie didn't want to talk about Stephanie anymore. Supposedly she was somewhere in the Mediterranean now with some man she'd met on some yacht in some sea. Stephanie was never without a man. Maggie had no idea how she and her mother could even be remotely related. "You know who you should be genuinely terrified of?" she suggested at last, switching from her mother to a much more pleasant topic of conversation.

"Do tell."

"My grandmother!"

"Your grandmother?" If his eyebrows had climbed any higher he would have lost them.

"Yes, absolutely. My grandmother is a Hathaway of the famed Hathaways who used to be incredibly beautiful Southern belles." He looked even more skeptical—which hurt—but she'd long ago come to terms with the fact that she hadn't inherited her ancestors' looks. "The Hathaways," she continued unperturbed, "fell on hard times after the Civil War. My great-great-great-grandfather decided plantation life was over so he packed up the whole family and they headed west to Texas and got into cattle rustling."

"Rustling? As in stealing?"

"Absolutely. No one said my great-great-great-grandfather was honorable. Actually, we consider him the first real entrepreneur in the family."

"I see."

"His wife was my great-great-great-grandmother Margaret, who was renowned for her flaming-red hair."

"Ah. Now I get the connection."

Maggie beamed at him as if he were a very good student. "Yes, my grandmother, Lydia, named me after the first Margaret, but I'm afraid red hair is the only thing we have in common. She wasn't exactly a marriage counselor. I gather she could ride and shoot like nobody's business, and she and Harold pretty much ran amok as outlaws in Texas.''

"Ran amok?''

"My grandmother's phrasing, not mine.''

"Of course.''

"At any rate, Harold was finally captured by a posse formed by one of the more powerful landowners, and sentenced to hang in the morning as an example to all cattle rustlers. My great-great-great-grandmother was so distraught at the news that she approached the land baron dressed in only a black lace shawl and her flaming-red hair.''

Both of Cain's eyebrows climbed to the ceiling again. "The plot thickens," he murmured.

"Oh, yes. She strode into the hacienda, her noble head held high, her bare feet padding against the cool tiles, her red hair shimmering around her shoulders, and in front of all the slack-jawed, lusting cowboys, she told the land baron that if he would let her husband go, she would give him a night like no other.''

"She said this, half-naked in front of a bunch of hired guns?" Cain quizzed dubiously.

Maggie leveled him with an impatient stare. "She was a very brave woman.''

"And a good candidate for gang rape," he exclaimed.

"Hey!" Maggie hit his shoulder so hard she startled both of them. "Don't talk about my great-great-great-grandmother that way!''

Cain blinked, looked at her stubborn features and blinked again. "My apologies," he said at last, his voice perfectly sober.

"Well," Maggie said, instantly relaunching into her story, "since the land baron apparently didn't have a mind as filthy as yours, he didn't toss her to the rabble. Instead, he agreed to her offer. If she could make him unconscious with satiated lust by morning, Harold would go free.''

"Hmm," Cain said and shifted a bit in his seat. He wasn't sure this was a good story for a man of six years' abstinence to hear, but on the other hand, he certainly didn't want to interrupt. "So did she conquer the man with passion?"

Maggie looked at him triumphantly. "Of course not! My great-great-great-grandmother was a one-man woman. She was also incredibly devious. She took a thick lotion, added arsenic and rubbed it all over the evil land baron's body, telling him it was a Far Eastern aphrodisiac. When he was still blubbering about how this was going to be the best night of his life, she pulled out his own gun from his holster and turned it on him. He tried to fight, of course, but by then he was too sick to move. She calmly put on his clothes, pulled his hat low over her head and grabbing the keys to the prison, marched right out to the shed, freed her husband, stole the land baron's two best horses and rode off into the sunset! Ta-da!"

She grinned at him, her cheeks flushed and her eyes brilliant with vicarious triumph.

"Happily ever after," he filled in, amused in spite of himself.

"More or less." Then on a more serious note, she concluded, "Unfortunately Harold wasn't as good a rider as Margaret and broke his neck falling off his horse a year later. But Margaret lived to be eighty-five years old, outliving her own children, and at the age of seventy-two she still lived by herself and protected her land by pulling out her false teeth and chasing warring braves from her log cabin with the chattering dentures."

"That must have been a sight to behold," he concurred.

"Yes." Then abruptly she jabbed her finger in the air at him. "And my grandmother comes from that stock, and she doesn't take any garbage from anyone, let me tell you. If you have a choice about whether to get captured by my brother C.J. or my grandmother, pick C.J. He's only a trained Marine. My grandmother is a Hathaway woman!"

"I'll remember that," Cain promised soberly, having a hard time taking his eyes off Maggie's face. Flushed and triumphant, she was something else. His ever-uncontrollable mind took in her old, dowdy clothes and replaced them with a simple, black lace shawl. His hands tightened instantly on the wheel and he swallowed two times really fast, then made his brain promise never to do that again. Six years, Cain. Six years, and she looked at you like she wanted to inhale your lungs. God give him strength.

When he trusted himself enough to speak, he said as carefully as possible, "You're a Hathaway woman."

It must not have been the right thing to say. Maggie seemed to simply wilt beside him. Her shoulders hunched. Her gaze fell to her lap and her fingers picked restlessly at her wool skirt. Then she gave up on her skirt and toyed with the old locket around her neck. He wasn't even sure she was aware she was doing that. "I suppose," she said at last, but the doubt was evident in her voice. Finally, she simply shrugged. "All gene pools get a mutant sooner or later."

His forehead creased and though it wasn't his business, he was insulted for her. "Who told you that?"

Her head came up and she peered at him curiously. "No one told me that," she said clearly. "But it's fairly obvious. I mean, just…look at me." Her hands came up, doing a little motion as if to say, This is it and don't I know it.

Cain's frown deepened to a full-fledged scowl, and he hated scowling. His fingers flexed and unflexed on the wheel again. Then he found himself saying abruptly, "Don't sell yourself so short, Maggie. Maybe you just need to meet the right Harold, or get into cattle rustling."

She smiled softly, but he could tell from her expression that she didn't believe him. She shrugged and that was the end of the matter. "And *your* parents?" she asked lightly. "Were they cattle rustlers?"

"I don't know. They're not storytellers like your family."

"What did you do at night?"

"Read from the Bible."

"Oh."

He offered her a crooked grin. "From the little I know, my mother came from well-to-do people back East. I don't know how she met my father, but she fell in love with him for reasons that escape the rest of us, and he convinced her that cities were too dangerous for raising a family. So they moved from Newark to the untamed mountains of northern Idaho, for it is said, 'On the mountain of the Lord, it will be provided.'"

Maggie nodded wordlessly. The phrase sounded familiar—she went to church every Sunday with her grandparents—but she couldn't quite place it.

"I don't think my mother understood what she was getting into," Cain said abruptly, his hands tightening on the wheel, his eyes narrowing unconsciously. "People have a tendency to mistake fanaticism for stupidity and that's not the case—fanaticism is very clever, very insidious in its own way. You don't ask new members to promptly walk up to the Cliff of Reason and leap off. You lead them down it one step at a time, slowly and surely. Was my mother a good Christian woman? Yes. Was she concerned about the environment? Definitely. Did the disintegrating social fabric of the U.S. culture worry her? A great deal. Did the growing number of fractured families scare her? Did schools seem overcrowded and hotbeds for gangs, violence and drugs? Did she worry about the future for her children? Of course.

"And so she found herself living on ten isolated acres of Idaho, educating the children at home to protect their values and their minds. But my father had read in some pamphlet that children could also be contaminated by poisoned public water supplies, so the next thing she knew she was digging wells and pumping her own water. Taxes were no longer being paid because my father pointed out that the white race is God's chosen people and God stated, 'The earth is mine,' and thus why should the white race pay taxes on 'His Land'? Which soon meant disregarding social security cards, driver's licenses, insurance, vehicle registration, hunting licenses, all that stuff, because those are 'man-made laws,' ZOG laws, and we have only to follow the words of the Almighty God.

"The militias haven't 'sprung' from the earth as everyone seems to think. They've grown slowly and carefully over time, fertilized by the fear of our decay, and as with most movements, powered by a deeply buried kernel of truth."

He paused, realizing suddenly everything that was pouring out and wondering if he'd said too much. His hands loosened on the wheel. He forced his shoulders straight. For six years, in the oppressive solitude of his jail cell, he'd turned over these issues in his mind, replaying his childhood like a movie reel that should have lost its color, as he sought to understand what of his upbringing he could accept and what he had to reject. He'd thought it would be a simple matter. He hadn't realized how easily and tightly natural fears and rampant paranoia could mesh.

Now, Cain forced his voice to sound light. "Well, at any rate. My mother found herself married to a husband who'd transformed himself from Bob the accountant to Zechariah the sermonizing militia leader, and she spent the rest of her days in a one-room cabin, hand-pumping water from a well and dressing fresh-killed deer." And she'd grown old too fast, worn too fast. The only time he'd ever seen her faded eyes light up was when his father was gone and Abraham out. Then she'd sit down Cain, and tell him her one good story—the time she'd gone to Boise before he was born. Then her face would become animated once more as she described the wonders of the city, the crush of the people, the flavor of the streets. She only shared this story with him. It was their little secret, this quiet longing to leave the mountains and see what else was out there. To maybe live a little bit more.

"Oh," Maggie said. Her face had paled again. "That...that must have been...very interesting."

He smiled and forced himself back to attention. "You're a lousy liar, Maggie."

She nodded readily. Then as if following his lead for light conversation, offered, "It's the fresh-killed deer thing. I don't like blood. I can't even buy hamburger from the grocery store because it makes me too sad."

"*Hamburger* makes you sad?"

"Yes. Haven't you ever seen a cow?"

"I've seen a cow," he agreed slowly and with something akin to fatalism.

"But have you ever really looked at one?" She leaned forward earnestly, peering at him with those soulful blue eyes, and he had a hell of a time keeping his attention on the road. "They're such gentle creatures, you know. You can scratch them behind the ears, they love to lick salt off your fingers. And their eyes...they have such huge, liquid brown eyes and they are so trusting. Can you imagine turning that into hamburger?"

"Ah..." he said weakly, "no."

She sat back with a sigh. "Exactly my point. But please, don't tell my grandmother I said all that. She's a farmer. She doesn't really approve of overromanticizing animals. I once took one of the beautiful Swiss heifers for a pet—Maple—and the year she went dry, Grandma sent her out to get butchered along with the other dry cows. It didn't matter that she had a name, it didn't matter that I trained her to come when I called—"

"She trotted over whenever you called her name?"

"Oh yes. Just like Lassie."

"Of course."

"But then they butchered her." Her face had gone pale with just the memory and she looked at him with troubled eyes. "Can you believe they had Maple one night for dinner?"

"No," he said, honestly feeling a little queasy at the mere thought—and he was a man who appreciated a good steak. "But I'm beginning to understand how you ended up with a three-legged cat."

"Exactly," she said and slapped her knee. "Would you believe no one would give her a home just because she was missing her hind leg? I mean, she was born without it and she didn't seem to miss it. If she could be so well-adjusted about it, why couldn't the rest of us?"

"Of course," he murmured and suddenly had this image of himself being slowly and methodically snowed under. "Why couldn't the rest of us?"

"You're not just humoring me, are you?" she asked abruptly, her voice suspicious.

"Maggie," he said sincerely, "I wouldn't do that."

She relaxed again, and appeared satisfied, her gaze going back out to the windows and the verdant line of towering trees.

He stifled a yawn, then another, then figured he would have to bring it up sooner or later. "I have a project for you, Maggie," he said lightly in the companionable silence.

"What's that?"

"I'm getting very tired and it's too dangerous to risk encountering my brother exhausted. We need to stop for the night so I can sleep. How should we manage that?"

"Night? Sleep?" she asked weakly. "Ah!"

"Exactly."

Chapter 6

Brandon stood in the middle of the luxurious suite in the Waldorf Hotel looking conspicuously out of place in his ripped-up jeans, battered wool sweater, filthy T-shirt and boot-encased feet. He hadn't shaved in two weeks. He hadn't bathed in four days—sunken bathtubs were a little hard to find when hiking around the volcanoes of Indonesia. As a result, the concierge maintained a careful distance of ten feet and even then wrinkled his nose at the pervasive odor of sulfur.

Brandon didn't blame him. He'd hiked the live volcanoes for nearly a month, the steaming ground pulsing and popping beneath his feet, and if he never smelled sulfur or ate a fried banana and hard-boiled egg sandwich again, he wouldn't be sorry. Now he tipped the concierge generously, closed the door behind the man and started stripping off his clothes where he stood.

He'd never been out of shape or slovenly, but even so he barely recognized his body anymore. Whatever executive softness had existed had disappeared in the past two years, melting away slowly and surely as he hiked the complete length of the Appalachian Trail, scuba dived in Samui, went snowboarding in the Alps. He'd also rearranged a few joints and limbs along the way. Maybe men who grew up in private boarding schools weren't meant to be rough and rugged after all.

He padded naked into the huge, gold-marbled bathroom and filled the tub. A suite was incredibly extravagant and just the right thing for a man bound and determined to lose money. Then again, he would gladly have paid a million dollars just for the deep, jet-propelled bathtub. With a groan and a grimace, he eased his aching body down, sinking into the wonderful heat, closing his eyes and letting the steam seep into his pores.

You're back in New York, Brandon. What are you going to do now?

He'd avoided the city for two years. He'd thought it would be too much, that every place would remind him of her, that though he'd survived a freak blizzard on the AT and a startled encounter with two poisonous snakes in Samui, Central Park might still break him. Even now, through the rising sulfur-soaked steam, he thought he smelled his wife's perfume and it was as beautiful and god-awful as ever. She'd loved cheap fragrances. She'd loved anything cheap and tacky. He'd proposed with a diamond, but she would have been just as thrilled with a paste ring from a gum ball machine.

He was right after all. New York still hurt.

He got out of the tub, dried off his whip-lean body and, knowing there was no point of returning to civilization without at least contacting it, called in to his answering service with the white bath towel roped around his bronzed flanks.

The first message was from his broker. The stock he'd bought in a failing company had just doubled—some white knight had come in unexpectedly and bailed the company out. Industry experts were thrilled, and Brandon, who had dedicated himself to losing his money, had just made fifty grand.

"Damn."

The next message was from his mother, wanting to know why she had received only a lousy postcard for Mother's Day and not a phone call. And where was he anyway and why was he so hard to get hold of? He was just as cold and insensitive and unfeeling as his father....

Brandon skipped over the rest of the message.

The last message was from C.J. Brandon replayed it twice, then calmly recradled the phone and got dressed while he buzzed the concierge. Two minutes later, there was a knock on the door. Brandon was already prepared.

"I'm leaving," he announced without preamble. "Please take my bags downstairs and hail a cab."

"But sir, you just arrived—"

"Don't worry, it's nothing personal—the suite is as beautiful and overpriced as always." He picked up his briefcase. "I reserved the whole week. Bill me for it."

"That won't be nece—"

"No, no, I insist." Brandon smiled grimly, already striding out the door. "After all, it's only money."

They came down the other side of the mountain, catching up with the river and running alongside like its mate. Cain rolled down the window all the way, resting his arm on top of the door and feeling the fresh spring sun soak into his prison-white skin. The trees were greener than he remembered, the sky even more blue. The river fascinated him, looking like a mischievous child as it raced gleefully over stone boulders and fern-lined banks. Sometimes it plunged into full-fledged lakes, sometimes it thinned down to a babbling brook, but it never gave up completely, and Cain admired that a great deal.

The red-laced granite cliffs soaring up on his left, the snowcapped mountains beckoning out front, the blue, crisp water racing on his right. White and yellow daisies waved merrily from the protective shade of trees, and deep pink foxgloves rose up regal and serene above them, nodding in the wind like approving matrons supervising young, impetuous charges. Golden dandelions swept beneath it all, adding dazzling touches of sunlight to a pulsing, populated forest floor.

After six years of concrete walls, concrete floors and iron bars, the lush grandeur of the Cascades was almost enough to make him pull over the truck and roll in the carpet of moss, pine needles and wildflowers just to make sure it was real.

He'd been born in the mountains, then left them for the city. He'd been lying to himself all along. The trees were in his blood. He didn't want to leave them again.

And his fertile mind ran away from him that quickly, drawing vast, impressive images of a two-story log cabin with towering panes of glass to let in the sky and two layers of decks for barbecue, and a four-wheel-drive vehicle for the winters and two German shepherds for company. He saw himself fishing along the riverbank, hunting deep in the forests, and skiing along the mountaintops.

He cut off the pictures before they grew roots and planted too firmly in his mind. The future was a luxury for innocent men. He had the police behind him and Ham ahead of him.

If you make it to Idaho, Cain, if you do find Ham, what will you do then?

Shoot him? Or get shot? And how do either of those options help you?

"Are you woolgathering?" Maggie asked at last, her gaze curious on his face.

"No. Playing chess."

The Cascades surrendered to central Oregon. The sun grew fierce, the air unbearably dry. Moist greens gave way to a resilient brush of straggling pines and tumbling sagebrush. Red dust swirled along the side of the road, and while green rolling hills and white-topped mountains lined the horizon, they might have been just a mirage compared to the immediacy of red dirt and sun-bleached grass.

Cain's eyes became dirty and gritty. He'd driven almost two hundred miles under intense stress and strain, and he was beginning to feel each moment as an oppressive heaviness pushing his body deeper and deeper into the seat. He approached Sisters, and the stark red landscape gave way to vast, cultivated fields where white, brown, and black llamas poised prettily with the snowcapped North and Middle Sisters mountains behind them. Next came the stables, with wooden corrals and sturdy Thoroughbreds already waiting at posts in Indian blankets and Western saddles. Finally came the town itself, small and charming with a single main street lined by Old-West storefronts. Ice cream parlors. Saloons. Indian jewelry.

In a blink of an eye, Sisters was gone and the red, endless brush took over once more. Cain rubbed his weary eyes and knew he'd had enough. Bend loomed ahead of them, large, modern and easy to get lost in.

It was good enough for him.

"We're stopping," he said thirty minutes later when the outskirts of the city abruptly burst out of the land.

"Lunch?" Maggie asked hopefully, but her voice was already wary.

"Bed."

Her face paled instantly. "It's only four. The sun is still out."

"Good. Then we can get up and drive again during the night."

"But...but...my cats."

"Are doing just fine. It's one night, Maggie. You can handle it."

She smiled weakly and flattened against her side of the truck.

Cain drove through the outskirts of town and finally selected a hotel that was close to the center, a long, two-story wooden structure tucked off the road alongside the river. It seemed to do plenty of business, the kind of place where two new people could pass unnoticed.

After turning off the ignition, he contemplated his options. Leave Maggie in the car handcuffed to the steering wheel, or take her in with him to get the room? He glanced over at her. She looked nervous and wary once more, as if she'd give anything to disappear. It would be too dangerous to leave her in the truck, he decided, let alone inhumane.

He produced the key and wordlessly took off the handcuffs. If anything, Maggie looked even warier. Slowly, she massaged her slim wrist. "Now what?"

"We go into the lobby and reserve a room."

"One room?" Her voice was so faint he could barely hear it.

"One room, two beds."

"Gee, thanks." She squeezed her eyes shut and a small shudder rippled through her.

He reached over and picked up her hand. "Just a little bit longer," he said steadily. "Think of it as your first Hathaway Red big adventure."

"Harold wasn't a convicted murderer," she muttered.

Cain just smiled.

He popped open the door. She followed glumly, her head lowered and her red hair cascading down his arm. It felt cool and silky, but the color promised deeper fires. He turned his mind quickly from that direction. This woman and her fires or lack thereof were not his concern. Remember that, Cain. Remember that.

He led her to the lobby, his grip firm on her wrist.

"How many rooms, sir?" the attendant asked politely.

"One," Cain said, not taking his eyes off Maggie. Her blue eyes had latched on the dark green carpet. Now they swept up slowly, steadily homing in on the attendant. Cain's body tensed. Was she going to try something? Unconsciously, he gripped her hand more tightly. Immediately, her gaze plummeted to the floor.

"Smoking or nonsmoking, sir?"

"Nonsmoking."

"A king-size bed, sir?"

"Two beds."

"Twin-size or queen?"

"Would you just give me a damn room!" The explosion of temper made Maggie jump and the attendant blanch. For a minute, Cain just stood there, unable to think. He'd never lost his cool before. He couldn't afford to lose his cool. Stay in control just a few minutes longer, dammit. Don't do anything stupid now.

He took a deep breath and released it slowly. His left hand slid into his pocket and pulled out the cash. That got the attendant's attention. "Sorry," Cain forced out more calmly. "It's been a long day. We'd like one room, with two beds, whatever size you have available."

The attendant stared at his screen for a minute, then braved another direct glance at Cain. "We have one room, nonsmoking, two queen-size beds overlooking the river."

"The river? Perfect."

The attendant rattled off the price and Cain began peeling off bills. He needed some sleep. A long, hot shower, and a deep, deep slumber.

"Look," he said five minutes later with forced bravado, "two beds, just like the man said."

Maggie nodded with the stricken expression of a woman dancing on a tightrope. She half walked, half tiptoed into the blue-and-beige-colored room, looking like a skittish colt and careful to keep at least five feet between them at any given time.

Taking a deep breath, he sat down on the edge of the bed closest to the door. That made her dance back five more steps. "Maggie," he said at last, his tone a bit dry, "I'm a murderer, not a rapist."

"Oh goody. I'd forgotten."

"Are you becoming hysterical?"

"Why would I do a thing like that?" She was definitely becoming hysterical.

There was no good way of doing this. If he'd been a compassionate man, he would have just let her go. But he couldn't do that. Not just yet. Sooner or later, when Ham was closer, the decisions would become more difficult. For now, the immediate danger was the police, and she was his only bargaining chip. In chess, maneuvering was critical, but so was the strategic sacrifice of key pieces.

He rose off the bed and picked up the handcuffs. Her blue eyes widened. "What are you going to do?"

"Don't worry, it's only for a short bit."

"Wh-what?" She was already too late. He slipped the handcuff over her wrist, then with one deft move, attached the other end to the bedpost.

"I have to go run some errands," he said calmly. "I'll try to be back as soon as possible."

"You can't just leave me like this!"

He picked up the remote control and handed it to her. "Entertainment." His lips twisted. "Welcome to prison life."

She simply stared at him. "You are so cold."

"Yes. What would you like for dinner, fried chicken, pizza or hamburger? You can choose." He tried smiling, but it felt weak and dispirited on his face.

"Dinner?" she whispered. "You handcuff me to the bed and then you ask me about dinner?"

He couldn't help himself. He reached out and touched her cheek with his thumb. She cringed instantly and he accepted that. It was the least he deserved.

"I'll be back in one hour."

"Is that a promise or a threat?" she cried miserably. Her eyes were accusing. He understood that. One hour before, she'd been telling him the stories of her family. He'd even told her some of the stories of his family. For a woman like her, that had probably seemed like something. Friendship, maybe. A mutual understanding. She'd lost her father, he'd lost his mother. Both came from families where they didn't feel they belonged. When he was still a boy, he used to lie in bed at night and wonder why his father hated him so much. He used to wonder, if he was smarter, a better chess player, a faster shot, would that make the difference. By the time his mother died, he'd come to terms with the fact he and his father would never bridge the gap. He'd even chosen his own path, as a boy must to become a man. But sometimes, he still remembered those nights and the hollowness in his stomach, the rusty taste of despair.

He'd never told anyone that—that little Cain had once honestly loved his father and wished that his father would love him back.

He thought if he told that to Maggie now, she would understand. More than anyone, she would understand.

Stop it, Cain. You're growing maudlin, and you're never maudlin. You are exhausted and under incredible stress. You're not thinking clearly. She is the hostage. You are the escaped felon. Now get out of this room and attend to matters before Ham does it for you.

"I'll bring you dinner," he said quietly and turned away from the image of her sinking down on the edge of the bed, shoulders hunched and face forlorn.

He picked up the baseball cap on his way out and was very careful not to look back. She didn't make a sound as he closed the door, but he could feel her betrayed gaze on his back anyway.

It was still daylight. Cool, with the wind blowing off the mountains, but the sun was warm on his face and the clear blue sky endless. Cain stopped without really meaning to, standing like an idiot in the middle of the parking lot and simply inhaling deeply. The air tasted better than the finest wine or the sweetest woman. His lungs seemed to expand fully for the first time in six years.

In the beginning, he'd been allowed out into the prison yard with the general population. In medium security, in-

mates received both a morning and afternoon break. But
the Aryan Brotherhood agent hadn't lied to Cain. Prisoners
comprised four gangs—the Bloods for the blacks, the Mexican Mafia and Nuestra Familia for Hispanics, and the Aryan Brotherhood for the whites. The invitation process was
mandatory. Unless you were deranged, weak or a religious
fruitcake, the gangs *demanded* your participation.

Once Cain made his rejection clear, life began to quickly
unravel. First there were the drugs found in a hole punched
in his wall and plastered over with toothpaste. The first
guard who'd followed procedure and skimmed the wall
with his fingertips had found the stash and disciplined Cain.
Then there were the razor blades slipped into his pillow-
case. Finally, the antifreeze added to his coffee. Cain hadn't
drunk the whole cup, but he'd consumed enough to spend
five days in the infirmary wishing that he had died.

After that, the prison officials agreed his life was in jeop-
ardy. They moved him to protective custody, where the
rapists, child molesters and prison narcs were kept. The
"snitches and bitches" section, they called it. Cain got a
new room with a roommate serving fifteen years for touching small children.

Cain didn't like that arrangement much. After careful
analysis of his situation, he'd seen only one option. He
became a discipline problem, a true big-D problem. He put
razor blades beneath his bunk so that the first guard stupid
enough to check the bed rim for drugs with his fingertips
and not a mirror got his fingers sliced up. Then he missed
roll call and stopped observing lights-out. One day in a
stroke of pure genius, he'd added plaster of Paris from the
infirmary to the morning pancakes. The prison warden had
so loved pancakes.

Cain got what he wanted—solitary confinement. The
Discipline Board reviewed his case and put him in solitary.
Cast in the maximum-security wing, he finally had his own
cell where no one came in and no one could touch him. He
roomed alone, he ate alone, he lived alone, a mountain man

reduced to a six-by-eight-foot existence—concrete, concrete, concrete. In the beginning, he thought he might go nuts. His one hour outside came and went so fast, five minutes lost just to the luxury of showering. He had to learn to forget the mountains of Idaho and the waterfront of Portland. He had to learn to forget the misty mornings, lying in the trail, bone cold and hunting-focused, inhaling the grass, inhaling the mist. Sinking into the ground and becoming part of the forest, squeezing down his breathing and heartbeat until he was no more than a blade of grass, lying on the ground, waiting for the deer to appear.

He gave up all that. He learned to live in his mind. He learned to play chess in the black and white spaces of his memory. He learned to be the trapped animal and not gnaw off his own limb to ease the pain.

So much he'd learned, forced himself to understand. And now he was in the big vast open again, the sky bluer than he'd realized, the dirt redder, the air sweeter. God, it was good and it was overwhelming. He wanted to spread his arms and embrace it. He wanted to wrap his arms around his head and curl up in a ball because outside was so big and suddenly he felt so small.

Prison did strange things to a man. Made it so he didn't even know himself anymore.

Cain shrugged away the sensation, the vague fear. He had to know himself. Certainly no one else ever had.

He forced his feet to move and willed the agoraphobia away.

He drove the truck to the cinema a few blocks away from the hotel. There, he parked the big blue machine in the middle of the other vehicles, toward the front. It blended in nicely, as Bend boasted almost more trucks than people. Since it was toward the front, maybe late at night the police would assume it belonged to someone working in the theater.

That mission accomplished, Cain found a drugstore for supplies. One heavy-duty flashlight, one roll of duct tape and one bungee cord, because those things always came in handy. Next he bought a water canteen, a pack of small chocolate pieces for instant energy, then a backpack for everything to go in. He spent fifteen minutes contemplating hair dyes, had a beautiful young salesclerk offer him blushing advice and then gave up on the whole dyeing concept. He bought disposable razors and shaving cream instead.

Then he visited a gun and ammunition store.

Bend saw its fair share of hunters and the rifle selection made him pause. But you had to have a license and a permit to buy a gun, so Cain settled for simply buying more ammunition for the .357 Magnum tucked in the waistband of his jeans. The .357 wouldn't be enough if Abraham found him, but it was all he had to work with.

Next, he cashed in five dollars for change at the pharmacy. Then he began plugging the pay phone. His father's cabin didn't used to have a phone. But then a cell site was installed in the area. The other hunters started carrying cell phones in case of emergency. Zechariah decided maybe he should have one, too. In case of trouble, in case anyone ever ambushed his place. Lines of communication were important in war.

The phone started ringing. Was it sitting on the old, hand-carved table? Suddenly Cain could picture the cabin of his childhood too clearly. The receiver trembled in his hands.

"I knew you would call."

Cain paused. For a minute, his knuckles whitened on the phone and his mouth went dry and he felt a little dizzy. Nearly ten years since he'd heard that voice. Ten years of wanting to forget and not quite being able to. Ten years of trying to figure out where that voice ended and Cain began, what beliefs that voice had that Cain could accept, and what beliefs that voice had that Cain must reject.

"Hello, Zechariah," Cain said at last to his father. He raised his wrist and glanced at his watch. No more than sixty seconds, for the call might be traced.

Remain in control, Cain.

"You brought them here," Zech accused, his rusty voice low and vehement. "The hills and the valley are crawling with state troopers and federal sheriffs like the locusts in Egypt. Years they've been waiting for any sort of excuse to invade our land. And you gave it to them. *You* gave it to them!"

Cain felt his lips twist in spite of himself. Cool Cain. Rational Cain. Don't get lost in the hatred. He's never understood your beliefs any more than you've understood his hate. Cain said anyway, "Happy to be of service."

And his father hissed with outrage in his ear.

"Has Ham left already?" Cain continued levelly, trying to get the conversation back on line, though the shortened name generally raised his family's hackles. Ham's full name was Abraham, but Cain had nicknamed his white supremacist brother Ham after one of Noah's sons—the one biblical scholars believed was the forefather of the black race.

"You are a traitor."

"And Kathy? What sin had Kathy committed to deserve the slaughter?" He wanted to recall the words the moment they were spoken. He didn't have time for accusations and emotion. He knew why Abraham had killed Kathy. Dear God, he knew. And found himself stating from someplace deep inside his gut, "I don't want to kill him…Dad. He is my brother. But he murdered her and if it comes down to that…if it comes down to that then I guess I'm no better than either of you after all, because I will pull the trigger."

"When God asked Abraham to take his only son, Isaac, to the mountains of Moriah and sacrifice him there as a burnt offering, did Abraham ask why?" Zechariah sermonized in a vibrant baritone. "Did Abraham say, 'Why should I believe in you, Lord? Why should I accept your command and why should I do as you bid?' Did Abraham say, 'But it isn't logical'? You have no faith, Cain. You have no belief—"

"I only asked for a reason to hate—" Forty-five seconds.

"But your brother has faith," Zechariah continued as if he hadn't heard his youngest son. "Abraham accepts God's bidding and the Lord shall guide his hand."

Five seconds remaining. Cain said quietly, "Then I hope Mom will guide mine."

He hung up the phone, cutting off his father's outraged gasp. Cain stood there for a moment, his forehead pressed against the cold metal pay phone, the sun hammering down on his back. Somewhere inside himself, he felt like a little kid again, standing on the mountain, being told God had created such beauty, but only for the chosen few to enjoy. By right of birth, Cain was one of those chosen.

And instead of being grateful, instead of being filled with divine rapture over his Aryan birthright, Cain had turned to his father and asked, "Why?"

His father hadn't answered his questions; he'd beaten him instead.

Cain took a deep breath. He glanced at his watch. Four forty-five. He was tired now. Very tired. He turned, attended to the last errand, then walked back to the hotel.

She was sleeping soundly, not even stirring as he shut the door quietly behind him. The remote control had been placed on the floor. Now she was curled up into a ball, sleeping in the only position the handcuffs made feasible.

He placed the pizza on the dresser. She still didn't stir. He sat on the edge of the bed across from her. She remained sleeping.

Funny how he'd thought she was meek and invisible when he'd first kidnapped her. He'd glanced over once and seen a wallflower, a red-haired shadow. Now he found his gaze lingering on her full lips, on her unblemished cheek as white as virgin snowfall. Her hair framed her lushly, deep red satin pooling around her face.

He wanted to touch her. He knew he shouldn't. He fisted his hand to keep it on his knee.

She was beautiful, he could see that now. Beautiful in a

special way few women could achieve. She was strong, she just didn't know it. If you put her in a burning building, she wouldn't scream, she wouldn't cower. She'd seek out other people and save them. She cared in a way he hadn't thought people bothered to care anymore. In this day and age, it seemed like everyone was a cynic, everyone was tough enough.

Except Maggie. She tried, she bruised, she tried again anyway. And when she asked him questions, her gaze was open and curious, as if she truly did want to understand, as if she truly wanted to see the best in him.

If a tree falls in the wilderness and there's no one to hear, does it make a sound?

If a man says he's innocent and there's no one who believes him...?

He found himself reaching out and brushing a single strand of her hair from her cheek. She stirred in her sleep, murmured a single, soft syllable of nonsense, then snuggled down deeper into the pillow. He touched her cheek, then her lips. His thumb traced her chin.

And her lips gently parted. Her breath came out with a sigh. Her eyes fluttered open, revealing deep, sleep-soaked pools.

He was lost. So lost. Control slipped.

He bent down and kissed her.

The sensation was soft, featherlight, like rose petals tickling her lips. She opened them wider, seeking the heat of something she couldn't name. And then his tongue slid between her lips, filling her, consuming her, and she groaned low in her throat with the pure delight of it.

The pressure increased. Her stomach contracted. Dimly she was aware of the assault on her senses. Sandpapery beard rasped her cheek, callused fingers stroked her hair. Soap and pine tingled her nose. He murmured soft noises and angled her head to deepen the kiss.

Fire exploded in her belly.

Suddenly it wasn't soft anymore. She arched back her own neck and she demanded him. She feasted on his tongue, grappled with his shirt with her free hand. He was hot and solid, masculine and overwhelming and she wanted to consume him, she wanted to draw him so deeply inside her he would become part of her, fill her, hold her, need her.

She wanted, she wanted, she wanted. The kiss became huge, two tongues dueling and desperate for more. His fingers bracketed her head, pinning her into place so he could gnaw her chin and ravage her lips.

It still wasn't enough. She whimpered low in her throat with the frustration.

And then it was just over.

Cain spun away. From far away, she could hear his low, vehement curse, then the hard sound of his foot slamming against the floor. She blinked twice and the world slowly came into focus.

She was still lying on the bed. Her hand was cuffed to the headboard. Her senses were filled with him.

He'd kissed her. She'd kissed him.

Oh my! She bolted upright, the bind of the handcuff promptly yanking her off balance. With a little yelp, she fell off the edge of the bed onto the brown carpet, landing in a little puddle with her arm suspended over her head.

"Are you all right?" Cain inquired, coming over immediately. He didn't reach a hand down though. He had them both pushed safely into his pockets.

Belatedly, she realized her skirt was now bunched around her waist and that her lips were still bruised from one highly enthusiastic kiss. Holy smoke, she'd practically rearranged his mouth! Blushing three shades of red, she popped back up, then swayed as the blood left her head too fast and made her dizzy. Instantly, Cain's hand was beneath her elbow.

"Easy," he said. "Just take it one step at a time."

He guided her into a sitting position on the edge of her

bed, then whisked back his hand as if she'd burned him. The silence stretched out taut and awkward. He shoved his hand back into his pocket. Then he pivoted away from her and began pacing.

"I didn't mean to do that," he said abruptly. "I had no right. I'm sorry."

"I…" She didn't know what to say.

He pivoted sharply and met her gaze. "I want you to know that I would never force you," he said bluntly. "I want you to know you don't have to fear that from me. I wouldn't do that to you, Maggie. I know given the circumstances that's hard to believe, but for what it's worth, I give you my word."

"It's…it's… I believe you," she said abruptly. Maybe that made her a fool, but she did believe him. He was strong, he was powerful, but to date he hadn't harmed her and God knew she'd given him a few excuses. She couldn't imagine him forcing a woman—he didn't seem that petty or cruel. Of course, she couldn't imagine him killing anyone either. It just…didn't seem to fit. Not for a man with so much control and so much…restraint, she supposed. He had a lot of restraint.

"Here," he said. He crossed close enough to produce the key. She was surprised to see that his hand was trembling slightly. He swallowed, then went about unlocking the cuff. He pulled it off gently. Her wrist sported an angry red welt.

"Do you mind?" he asked.

"No," she whispered.

He massaged her wrist tenderly. It was amazing to her that fingers so strong, so big, could move over her skin like that, soft and smooth. His thumb rubbed small circles and for one moment, she allowed her eyes to drift shut.

She wasn't exactly sure when he stopped. Her eyes took longer to open.

He was standing before her once more and she could see

fresh tension in his stance. His jaw was clenched, his fingers fisted. He didn't move.

"I...uh...I brought you a pizza."

"A pizza?" Sure enough, she inhaled deeply and the
scent of **sizz**ling cheese pervaded her senses. Pizza, hot
pizza. Her stomach rumbled on cue. "That's perfect!"

"I'll get you a slice." He crossed the room quickly. "I
had them put mushrooms and green peppers on it. Vegetables don't make you sad, do they?"

"I like vegetables." She looked at him speculatively, her
head cocked to the side. A vegetarian pizza after she'd told
him that hamburger made her cry. "You're very consid-
erate for a kidnapper," she pointed out softly.

His lips simply twisted, his composure obviously returning. "Dinner is served." He delivered one generously cut
slice, then tossed a pile of napkins at her. "There are no
plates or silverware, but plenty of extra napkins."

He picked up a small bag and shook out more napkins.
She heard the clink of glass.

"Beer?" she asked, her voice sharper than she intended,
her hand pressed unconsciously against her stomach. What
if he was an alcoholic or something? What then?

He glanced back at her, already shaking his head. "Iced
tea. I don't drink."

"Oh," she said with perfect stupidity. She gave up and
shook her head. She just didn't get him. He was definitely
intelligent and honorable in his own way. He could be perfectly charming when he chose and he didn't seem slovenly
or drunken or even mean. In fact, he was better behaved
than most men she knew. What did that say about the freed
male population when they were put to shame by a convicted murderer?

She gave up on understanding life and attacked her pizza
instead.

Halfway through the second piece, her fingers smeared
with grease, her face beaming with a satisfied smile, she

mumbled through a mouthful of cheese, "Hey! This is your first meal as a free man. Or at least, a pseudo-free man."

He paused with his mouth poised around the end of his third piece of pizza. "I guess it is." He ravaged the end.

"Is there good pizza in prison?"

He shrugged. "Ever eat cafeteria food?"

She nodded, though it had been in a private school with its own in-house chef.

"Take that, make it three times worse, and that's prison food."

"Wow," she said, clearly impressed. "I'm surprised you didn't want to stop for food first thing."

His lips twisted dryly. "I had other things on my mind." His hands wrapped around the big glass bottle of iced tea and raised it to his lips. He drank gustily, his Adam's apple bobbing with each swallow, and Maggie stared, completely mesmerized by the act. He lowered the bottle, empty at last, and sighed. Belatedly, he became aware of her rapt attention.

"Did I spill something?" he asked immediately, gazing down at his shirtfront.

"No," she said and dropped her gaze hastily, focusing it on the carpet instead. Her stomach was all tight again. She took several deep breaths and searched for something normal to say. "Umm, going to have more pizza?" Oh, she was definitely a brilliant conversationalist.

Cain shook his head, already rising to his feet. "Eating too much makes you slow."

Maggie gazed at her hand already reaching for a third piece and promptly snatched it back. "Of course."

"We can take the rest with us."

"With us?"

He turned and from halfway across the room, his hands tucked in the back pockets of his jeans, he said steadily, "We'll sleep for four hours. That's it. Then I want to be on the road again."

"*Four hours?* But...but you look so tired."

He smiled wryly. "Worried about me, Maggie?"

She flushed instantly, flustered and not knowing what to say. She was, but she shouldn't be. He did look tired, but she shouldn't care...oh, darn! She just wasn't cut out for this hostage business.

"Why don't you go wash your hands, Maggie, and get ready for bed?"

She blanched immediately. He shook his head at her response, and for a minute looked genuinely haggard.

"Don't worry. Sex makes a man sluggish, too, and as we've already established, I can't afford to be slow. I did give you my word."

"I...well I... I'm going to go wash my hands," she announced at last.

"What a good idea."

She came out five minutes later, twisting her hands in front of her and looking more nervous than a sixteen-year-old on her first date. Cain had already closed the curtains and the room was swathed in darkness.

Dimly, her eyes made out his form. He was already in the other bed, the covers pulled up to his chin. She passed by the end of the bed with legs that trembled. He didn't say anything. He didn't try anything.

She felt as if her stomach had turned inside out and left her with nothing but a gaping hole. With her hands, she felt her way to her bed.

She pulled back the covers, she crawled in. She pulled the covers up to her shoulders, then lay perfectly still in the darkness. She could hear his breathing now. In and out, but not relaxed.

He was aware of her, she thought. As aware of her as she was aware of him. He still didn't move.

Finally, she whispered in the dark, "Did you love her a great deal?"

"Who?"

"Your girlfriend. Did you love her that much, and that's why her betrayal drove you to murder?"

A ponderous moment passed. Finally, his voice cut through the darkness. "How much can I blame her, Maggie? I introduced her to Ham. I helped bring them together."

"But—"

"Good night, Maggie."

And minutes later, she could tell from his breathing that he'd fallen asleep.

Chapter 7

"Maggie. Maggie, wake up."

From deep within the dark, comforting cocoon of sleep, she heard the voice calling to her. Wake up? The voice was nuts. She'd just fallen asleep.

"Maggie," it persisted.

She batted at it with her hand. "Go away. Tired."

"Maggie."

Her hand beat more emphatically. "Tired!"

The voice backed off. She snuggled back into the warm abyss.

"Meow."

Huh?

"Meow," the voice tried again, sounding like a cat with laryngitis. "I'm a three-legged cat," it insisted. "And I want to be fed."

One eye reluctantly cracked open, letting the light flood in. "Whuh?"

Cain smiled down at her, his expression wry. "Rise and shine."

Her other eye managed to crack open, then she blinked owlishly, blinded by the bedside light. A couple more blinks and Cain came into focus. "What time is—ah!" She bolted upright in the bed. "What did you do to your *hair?*"

He grimaced immediately. "I had a feeling it didn't come out right."

She could only stare at him. "Come out right? What were you even attempting?"

His shoulders hunched, he definitely looked chagrined now. "I thought I would shave it off."

"What in the world for?"

"Hair dye seemed very complicated...and obvious."

"I see. And a mohawk isn't?"

"It's not a mohawk." He sat a little straighter. "It's just not...anything."

"Cain, you shaved off the sides like...like bald laurels. Why don't you just shave off the rest?"

He looked very uncomfortable now. Finally, he squared his shoulders and peered at her steadily. He said quietly, "I forgot about my birthmark."

"Oh. Too distinguishing?"

"You could say that." He abruptly raised his hands and pulled back the golden locks still waving over his forehead, imitating baldness. "Who do I look like now?"

She couldn't help herself. She started to giggle. Then she just had to laugh. Then she held her belly and howled on the bed.

"It's not that funny!"

"But you're right. It's so true. You look just like Gorbachev!" She collapsed on the bed and laughed harder. He stood with an obvious sigh of disgust.

"Get ready. We leave in ten minutes. I'm sticking to baseball caps."

"You're going to go out in public like that?" She was still giggling over his haircut. She'd actually seen similar styles on teenage boys, the shorn sides leading up to longer, fuller hair on top. It suited a young surfer dude a bit more than a thirty-year-old man.

Cain shook his head, and clearly having had enough of the subject, turned on the TV.

For a moment, Maggie was too stunned to move. Then she whispered, "My God. Brandon..."

And it was. Brandon stood before the cameras, looking very serious and composed in a striking charcoal-gray suit. His face was lean, his eyes harder than she remembered, as if the past two years had erased even the memory of how to smile. Oh, Brandon...

"Turn it up, turn it up." She was on her knees immediately in front of the TV, though it wasn't necessary. With a concerned frown, Cain was cranking the volume.

"—a reward of one hundred thousand dollars," Brandon had just finished stating. "Of course, I am willing to work with you, Mr. Cannon, and act as a liaison between yourself and the authorities. I will even hire legal counsel to represent you if you desire. All I ask is for the safe return of my sister, Maggie. She's a gentle woman who's never harmed a soul, a warm, caring sister, daughter and grand-daughter—"

Maggie scowled unconsciously. As someone with a psychology background, she understood what Brandon was doing—humanizing her so that the psychotic would stop seeing her as just an object. Still, Brandon made her sound as interesting as Betty Crocker. It couldn't be any worse if they flashed her baby picture across the screen.

Or could it? As if reading her mind, the TV screen abruptly filled with an eight-year-old photo of Maggie sitting on the back of one of the Tillamook County Dairy Parade floats, a bamboo fishing rod dangling from her hands. C.J. and Brandon sat on either side of her, all of them wearing straw hats, rolled-up jeans and old T-shirts. Maggie was the centerpiece of the picture, however, her red hair in Pippi Longstocking pigtails and her face just plain ridiculous with its huge, delirious smile.

"Don't look at that!" she cried and flattened her hands over the incriminating photo. The picture was already vanishing, though. Now Brandon filled the screen once more, strong, dignified and powerful.

"As I have said," he repeated steadily into the camera, "return Maggie to us and no questions will be asked. I will do everything in my power to help you, my family will do everything to help you. We are well connected and well-to-do. Just give us back Maggie, safe and sound. One hundred thousand dollars, Mr. Cannon. One hundred thousand dollars."

The camera faded back to the newscaster, who recapped that Maggie had been missing since morning and was believed to be a prisoner of the escaped convict, Cain Cannon. Cain's black-and-white prison photo was flashed across the screen, his face grim and appropriately dangerous looking.

Maggie glanced at him surreptitiously. His green eyes remained riveted on the TV, sharp and wary. He turned at her gaze, his face perfectly expressionless.

"Well connected, well-to-do?" he quizzed.

She smiled weakly. "Maxmillian had a policy about only marrying rich women. He loved a poor one, but he only married the rich ones. My mother...Brandon's mother, too."

"Define rich, Maggie."

Her hands twisted on her lap. She didn't want to give away too much, but she wasn't a match for his hard green gaze either. "Well, my mother's family is remotely connected to the Duponts. Her father had a real gift for the stock market, too, I gather. My mom is an artist, a sculptor. She doesn't make a whole lot, but the trust fund is generous and well, so are her 'benefactors.'"

"And this Brandon? He could pay a hundred thousand dollars?"

Maggie nodded even more miserably. "His family had money as well, but then they fell into hard times. And the divorce—it was expensive to divorce Max. Brandon took

what was left and went to New York... He's a bit of a Wall
Street wizard," she confessed in a rush. "He worked so
hard, building the capital into enough to buy back the estate
for his mother, though it left him still wiped out. He figured
no problem, he'd just work a little harder. Two weeks later,
his wife died and the insurance policy paid him a million
dollars. It did something to him. Now, he does everything
he can to lose that money. Honest. But he has the Midas
touch. Every sure loss turns into a sure win and now...he
has *a lot* of money, the poor man."

Cain shook his head like a man trying to cast off a spell.
"Maggie, conversations with you start defying all reason."

She shrugged. "You asked."

"So I did," he muttered.

A new face filled the screen, a young man with pale face,
wayward brown hair and dark, burning eyes. "Joel," Cain
said softly and instantly stiffened.

"We're willing to pay fifty thousand dollars for any information leading to the capture of Cain Cannon," the
young man announced squarely, his dark eyes blazing.
"The reward is simply for information. As a police officer,
I must remind you that this man is armed and dangerous—
do *not* attempt to approach him on your own. And ladies,
please understand he can be very charming. Certainly my
sister..." The man's voice broke slightly. "My sister
thought he was very charming. But he is a cold-blooded
killer who committed an unspeakable act—"

Cain's lips twisted. "I knew him when he was just sixteen," he murmured, talking over the young man's laundry
list of Cain's sins. Maggie could only stare at him in word-
less horror. "Good kid, wanted to be a saxophone player
much to his father's chagrin. He was good, though. Kathy
and I used to go listen to him downtown at some of the
jazz clubs. I thought he should pursue it, and once as a
surprise he took one of the Knight's Tour formulas I had
written and translated it to music. Math really is music, or
music math, of course. Bright, bright kid." He stopped, the

pictures filling his mind all at once. The trial. Kathy's family sitting at the front pew, Ham right beside them. Joel, standing at the end during sentencing, those dark eyes so filled with fury. *How could you, how could you, how could you?*

Cain reached out, placing a hand on the top of the TV to steady himself. He was dizzy all of a sudden, and his heart beat fast and almost painfully against his ribs. "I understand he became a police officer in the end. He's sworn to rid the world of all the scumbags like myself."

His voice trailed off. He couldn't breathe anymore and he had to blink three times to get his eyes to focus. He could feel Maggie's gaze on him, wide-eyed and shocked and of course, filled once more with fear.

The newscaster reappeared on the TV screen. "The police have set up a special hotline number for any information you may have." The 1-800 number flashed across the screen. "Again, Cain Cannon was convicted six years ago for the brutal slaying of his girlfriend, Katherine Epstein. The man is considered extremely dangerous and is armed. He has an extensive background in weapons and survival training, is rumored to be well connected with various militia movements and should not be approached. Please contact the police immediately with any information you might have."

The news broke to a commercial. Maggie sat perfectly immobile on the floor. Cain's hands were still braced on the TV and his body felt slightly disjointed, as if it no longer belonged to him.

"Get ready," he said, his voice faint. He swallowed and forced himself to sound firmer, in control. "We're leaving now."

Maggie's mouth opened, then closed. Five minutes ago, she would have had something smart to say. Five minutes ago, she'd been laughing at his resemblance to a former world leader. Now, she was terrified of him. *Ladies, the man can be charming...but remember who he is.*

Oh God, oh God, she had forgotten. She looked at him and she just saw a man, a stoic, desperate man ready to take on the world and her heart bled for him and she wanted to help him.

He had her exactly where he wanted her. Ready to aid and abet a felon.

"Maggie, *move*."

"You can't outrun an entire state," she whispered abruptly. Her gaze lifted to his face. Her eyes pleaded with him.

"It will be a challenge."

"You could still turn yourself in. My brother is a man of his word. He'll help you, he'll hire you the best lawyer—"

"Do you think I'm stupid?" The question was abrupt, his voice louder, harsh.

Helplessly, she shook her head.

He took a deep breath. She saw for the first time that his hands were gripping the edge of the dresser so tightly his knuckles had gone white. Tension corded his neck and rippled down his back. He looked very, very, dangerously on edge.

He spoke, the words carefully enunciated. "For six years, Maggie, I've been using the legal system. I've reviewed my case, the trial transcripts. I've gone over similar cases with a fine-tooth comb. I've filed motion after motion, seeking some flaw in the testimonies, the evidence, police procedure, trial procedure, anything. There is none. I had a decent attorney, I had due process, and a jury of my peers found me guilty—all according to the book. There is *nothing* a lawyer can do for me."

"You could try to plead insanity," she suggested weakly.

"Do I look insane to you? *Do I?*"

Of course she shook her head. He didn't foam at the mouth, he didn't rant and rave. He was a computer programmer, a mathematician at heart, and he couldn't stop acting like one any more than he could stop breathing.

He picked up the backpack he'd purchased earlier and started stuffing all the supplies in it. Tentatively, hesitantly, Maggie rose.

"How does Brandon know you were kidnapped?" he asked abruptly.

She froze. "I...I imagine C.J. contacted him."

"So he is around as well?"

Wordlessly, she nodded.

"Do you think offering a reward is all that they will do?"

Her gaze fell. Miserably, she shook her head.

"They'll come after me," he stated. "I bet Joel will as well. As well as the rest of the police and any bounty hunter or get-rich-quick schemer who likes the sound of fifty thousand dollars. Then there's Ham. This state is getting very crowded, Maggie."

"Well what did you expect?" she fired back abruptly. "You murdered someone! Even if it was a rash act of passion, you're still planning on killing your own brother. You knocked out a guard. You took a hostage. You've...you've done bad things!"

He opened his mouth, and for a moment she saw something work in his eyes. He looked on the verge of protest, then he just looked disgusted. He shook his head, his eyes suddenly flat.

"Get ready to go. *Now.*"

Maggie couldn't take it anymore. She didn't know this man. She didn't know herself. She leaped to her feet and did as she was told. She didn't know what else to do.

Cain hefted the backpack over his shoulder and pulled the baseball cap low on his head. Without another word, he opened the door and gestured for her to lead.

It was now eleven o'clock. Rain had started to fall. There was no moon; the night was black.

She was scared.

* * *

The rain had picked up pace by the time they walked to the theater and reclaimed the truck. From a spring sprinkle, it turned into a thick torrent, solid sheets of water fired from the sky.

They both scrambled into the truck quickly, their shirts already soaked. Cain turned on the heater, flipping on the truck lights and the windshield wipers. Even then, visibility was poor.

Tough night for running, but it meant it was also a tough night for chasing.

Cain stopped on the outskirts of town and filled the tank, then hit the road.

The night was quiet, almost peaceful with the thunder of the rain, the steady rhythm of the windshield wipers, the thickness of the night. He'd expected something harsher. He'd open his door and encounter a posse. He'd make it to the highway and the entire state police force—led by burning-eyed Joel—would pounce.

His hands gripped the wheel too tightly. He felt the tension, raw and painful in his gut. His shoulders were beginning to cramp and knot from the unrelenting strain.

The world swirled around him, cops running, brothers chasing, bounty hunters... He stood in the eye of the storm, fighting for a way out. Justice for Kathy, justice for himself. And the great Cain, the brilliant computer programmer who'd once thought he held the world in his palm, didn't know the answer this time. He didn't know what to do, and he didn't know what would happen when he finally caught up with Abraham.

And he saw his brother, the last day of the sentencing hearing, sitting cool and composed at the front of the courtroom, not even blinking as they sentenced Cain to twenty years in prison, ineligible for parole for ten years.

Cain had stood at the end, his arms and legs shackled, and he'd stared into his brother's calm blue eyes. "Why?" Cain had whispered under his breath. "If you wanted re-

venge that badly, why not just kill me? Why her? Why her?"

And Ham had replied in a deep rich baritone, *"'If anyone kills Cain, he will suffer vengeance seven times over. Then the Lord put a mark on Cain so that no one who found him would kill him.'"*

That was it. Ham came, Ham plotted, and Ham won. Cain couldn't even say he'd put up a decent fight. At least, not until now.

He forced himself to take a deep breath and relax his death grip on the wheel.

He was in eastern Oregon now and there was nothing, absolutely *nothing* out there. The road was straight and lined with night. No homes, no cars, no streetlights. By day this land was red dust, sagebrush, and barbed-wire fencing. By night, it was simply a dark womb, protective, embracing and safe.

He relaxed by degrees. The rain banged on the roof, soothing and rhythmic. The inky-black well of night remained reassuringly unbroken. Dark and soft. Maggie curled up in a ball on the seat, clutching her locket, and seemed to fall immediately to sleep. He relaxed even more.

He could do this. If he remained calm, remained logical, he could do this. He'd already covered two hundred miles. He'd been careful to pay for things only with cash in Bend, he'd monitored the phone call between himself and his father. All the police—or this C.J., or Brandon, or Joel and Ham—knew was that he'd last been seen heading southbound outside of Portland. Maggie had withdrawn money in Tualatin, as bank records would show. After that... nothing.

Now, he was 250 miles from Boise, traveling through terrain where the sagebrush outnumbered the vehicles one hundred to one. He would need to stop one more time for gas, but they could be in Boise by morning.

He would head north then, up to the mountains that had raised him, and travel to the crest where he could still hear the sweet, fading echo of his mother's lilting voice singing, "Amazing grace, how sweet the sound..."

He pushed down on the accelerator and the truck picked up the pace. The night remained thick. The sound of the windshield wipers comforted him.

After another forty miles or so, Maggie finally roused herself. He glanced at her once, seeing her grimace as she stretched out her arms and rubbed her crooked neck. Her long red hair was tangled around her like a subdued mink and her features were flushed with sleep. Then she yawned, a cute little stretch that reminded him of a kitten.

At last, she leaned back in the seat, no longer looking as timid or stiff. She appeared to be an amazingly resilient woman and sleep had restored her. He had to force his gaze back to the rainy road.

"Are you hungry?" he asked at last. "We still have some pizza."

"I'm fine. Where are we?"

"About fifteen miles from Riley."

"Oh." Obviously, Riley didn't ring any bells for her. It wouldn't have rung any for him except that he'd just seen a green highway sign advertising its presence. "It's still raining," she observed after a few minutes of silence.

"Yes."

"Awful night."

"Yes."

"Is it hard to drive?"

"Road's too straight for the rain to make a difference."

"Oh." She knotted her fingers on her lap, tapping her index finger against one knuckle.

Silence resumed its reign and they stared out the windshield at the thundering night. She seemed lost in thought or maybe she was just half-asleep.

"Cain," she asked abruptly, "why didn't you kill the prison guard?"

He was so startled, he flinched. He stiffened his shoulders as quickly as he could, unconsciously clearing his face and erecting smooth, tough barriers all around himself. "Pardon?"

"You're the one who said there are economies of scale with crime. But even after escaping, you haven't hurt anyone else."

"It's only been fifteen hours."

"But you've had opportunity and motive," she replied shrewdly. "I mean, you have this militia background, everyone says you're dangerous. You grew up with a... different perspective on society and government and law enforcement. Yet when you escaped, you didn't shoot the prison guard, you knocked him unconscious. I would think you would've bought more time by...killing...him, and I would think you of all people know that. But you didn't do it. You didn't shoot him."

Cain was quiet, his finger tapping the steering wheel, his mind racing ahead to try and divine the point she was heading toward. "Do you want to believe I won't hurt anyone else?" he asked carefully. "Will that make you feel better, Maggie?"

"I'm just thinking out loud," she said and shrugged innocently. "I'm just thinking, here's this man who's supposed to be dangerous and I haven't seen you hit so much as a wall. By your own admission you don't drink. I've seen you angry, I've seen you desperate, but for crying out loud, you didn't even swear. You've threatened me, but you've never actually hit me. You've never thrown things, you've never had a rage-filled tantrum. For a man who allegedly committed a crime of passion, I have yet to see you so enraged that you couldn't control your own impulses. In fact, you appear to be an amazingly restrained and cerebral person."

"Maybe I've just matured over the past six years."

She looked at him quite seriously. "I don't think so. You know, Cain, you've never said you killed her. You said you allegedly killed her."

He didn't say anything. He wasn't sure he could. And suddenly, he didn't know anymore what he wanted.

"Tell me," she whispered softly. "Did you kill your girlfriend? Did you kill Katherine Epstein?"

He found he couldn't breathe. He found that the words wanted to escape from his throat without his permission, and he'd said them so many times before and it had never mattered. He realized abruptly that he just couldn't take it. He couldn't claim innocence and then survive the look of open doubt that would wash over her clear, expressive face.

He'd stood alone so long now. He wanted to just remain there, an island who could never be touched by another betrayal. He didn't need as other people needed, he reminded himself. He'd grown up alone, moved to the city alone, survived six years of solitary. Maybe he had become an island. He was simply untouchable.

"It doesn't matter," he murmured to his inquisitive companion. "It doesn't matter."

Maggie frowned, looking ready to contradict him, but suddenly headlights appeared up ahead. She perked up instantly, leaning forward. He glanced at the speedometer and forced himself to maintain a steady pace. The headlights before them appeared stationary in the rainy night, and the only car he could picture watching the road on a night like this was a police car.

Maggie leaned forward even more, her gaze peeled.

But it wasn't a police car. It appeared to be a hatchback of some kind, tilted off the road, its tires deep in the red mud. As they drove by, a young couple appeared, their hair plastered against their rain-soaked faces, their arms waving frantically for help.

Cain winced instantly. It was already too late. Maggie's gaze was on his face.

"There's no one else around," she said for her opening statement.

"Exactly. Including us."

"It's cold out, they're soaked to the skin. They could catch pneumonia and die."

"Only in a Brontë novel."

"Cain." She touched his arm and they both flinched. For a moment, his eyes abandoned the road and stared at her simple white fingers resting on his arm. She had short, sensibly cut nails. She had a small, sensible hand.

The truck tugged to the right. He yanked the wheel in the other direction and almost overcompensated them right into a ditch. Her fingers dug into his arm, and he straightened the truck quickly.

"Please," she whispered.

"I'm an escaped murderer," he said, but for some reason it sounded as if *he* were pleading with *her.*

"All right," she said earnestly, her shoulders assuming that determined look he knew too well. "I'll make a deal with you."

"You're a hostage. What kind of deal can you make?"

"I'll cooperate."

"Cooperate? Maggie, I have a gun. Of course, you'll cooperate."

"But it's only under duress, don't you see? You have to handcuff me to yourself, or to the bed. You have to plan when you sleep, you have to do all the driving and worry about my every move. You're the one who said you needed to be well rested to successfully pull this off. How are you ever going to be well rested if you're constantly having to worry about me?"

He blinked in the darkness. Her argument was amazingly lucid, which frankly scared him.

"So," she continued, sounding not at all cowed but actually quite brisk, "if you go back and just check on them, I'll cooperate. You might not even have to get out of the truck. Just pull up, you know. I'll roll down the window and ask them what they need, make sure it's no medical emergency or crisis, and the whole thing will be done in just five minutes. They'll be helped, and you'll have my unlimited cooperation for twenty-four hours. I could even do some of the driving and you could get more sleep. You must be very tired."

His eyes narrowed. He turned this scenario over in his head several times even as his foot was somehow slipping off the gas pedal of its own volition. "I let you drive and you can drive us straight to the authorities," he pointed out quietly.

She actually appeared indignant. "I beg your pardon! I'm a woman of my word!"

Well, he'd been put in his place, he thought dryly. "But you'd be helping a murderer," he persisted nevertheless. "Surely even a 'woman of her word' doesn't lose sleep over turning in a murderer."

Her fingers curled around his forearm again. He found himself staring at her once more and her strong, pale face was sober. "Listen to me. You've already said it yourself. You're going to get to Idaho one way or another. There doesn't seem to be much I can do about that. I wish I was like Brandon or C.J.," she said abruptly, and for a minute, her tone was wistful. "But I'm not. I never will be. I'm just me, and I'm telling you if you will stop and give five minutes to help those two poor abandoned people, I'll cooperate. Cain, it's such an awful night and they're all alone in the middle of nowhere. We can't just leave them like that."

"Maggie," he said quietly, "when you buy six-packs, you take off those plastic rings, don't you? You take off the rings and cut them with scissors so the dolphins won't get them stuck around their snouts and slowly starve to death."

"Of course! And everyone else should as well!"

"And those commercials to support a child overseas, paying for their food and shots and ABCs—you adopted one of those children, didn't you?"

"Well, two."

"And when you pass homeless people you buy them meals?"

"Everyone has hard luck sometimes."

"Of course." He knew he shouldn't do this. He knew turning around was the height of stupidity and he was not a man who could afford to be stupid. But she sat so regally at the edge of the bench seat, looking earnest and sincere and so well intentioned, he couldn't find the word *no.* Was it that she reminded him of his mother, and the natural grace and beauty she'd had? Or was it that she reminded him how it felt to be a man and not prisoner number 54276?

"You've given me your word," he reminded her quietly.

She nodded just as soberly. "My word."

"All right, Maggie. I accept your proposition."

He slowed the truck down and turned.

The couple appeared again as they drove up, looking soaked to the bone and unbearably happy that help had finally arrived. Cain pulled the truck alongside after instructing Maggie to lock her door. He was very conscious of the gun tucked against his skin as Maggie unrolled her window.

"What's wrong?" she shouted above the rain.

"Car's stuck," the young man shouted back. He didn't look a day over eighteen and the freckles stood out prominently on his cheeks. Maggie looked instantly at Cain.

"All right, all right," he surrendered, not even needing her to ask. "We've taken it this far."

He pulled the truck up ahead of the car, leaving it parked on the road since the sides did look thick and muddy. "Stay here," he said. "This should only take a minute."

"I can help, too," she replied and jumped out into the rain-soaked night as he was opening his mouth to protest. Cooperation? This was cooperation?

He shook his head and advanced, the rain slaking across his face and instantly molding his clothes to his body. He kept his arm crooked protectively over the spot where he'd tucked the gun.

"Thank God you stopped," the young man gushed instantly. "Me and my wife have been stuck here for two hours now. Damn, is it wet and cold. I was beginnin' to think that was just it—we're never gonna get out."

Cain eyed the car. Its wheels were deeply mired in the mud. Luckily, it was small and didn't look like it weighed much. "I'll get around back," he suggested. "You lift from the front."

The boy nodded, and Cain got to it. He didn't want to linger any more than he had to, especially with Maggie standing there getting soaked to the bone as she patted the young wife's hand and assured her everything was going to be all right.

Cain had just bent his knees to grasp the bumper of the old automobile when he realized the young man hadn't followed him. He looked up, already scowling through the sheets of rain.

And faster than he could blink, the young man reached beneath his sweatshirt, ripped out a gun and leveled it against Maggie's head. She froze instantly, her eyes turning into huge blue saucers.

"I'll take the keys to the truck," the young man announced. His body rocked side to side, his Adam's apple bobbed. His young face was a case study for desperation. Even then, Cain had to blink several times to register what was happening. Just how many gun-toting felons were running around this state anyway?

"The keys!" the young man barked, and pressed the gun against Maggie's forehead. She whimpered helplessly, her blue eyes rolling to Cain, begging for his assistance.

He still had his gun. He wasn't as brilliant a shot as Ham, but he'd trained with a firearm every day of his youth. He could take out the kid, though the boy might pull the trigger reflexively, hitting Maggie.

A man had to be prepared. A man had to be ready to make sacrifices. *War has casualties*, his father barked. *A man accepts those casualties! No pain, no remorse, no re-*

gret. You kill or be killed! That is the world today, my sons, that is how we live.

His gaze returned to Maggie's pale, rain-soaked face. Her red hair was plastered against her cheeks, already looking like blood. Her blue eyes beseeched him.

Slowly, he lifted his hands in the air. "All right," he said quietly, keeping his voice calm because the kid and his wife looked close to panic. "Take the truck. We won't try to stop you. Just lower the gun."

"The keys," the kid insisted.

"I don't have the keys," Cain confessed steadily. "I hot-wired the vehicle."

The kid stared at him incredulously. "You stole that truck?"

"Yes."

"You stole that truck and then came back in this kinda weather to help two strangers?"

"Yes."

The kid looked over at his female accomplice, a thin slip of a woman, and then started laughing. "Jesus, sir," the kid exclaimed. "You're stupider than anyone I ever met."

"That could be," Cain agreed dryly. Maggie, still wary of the gun, flushed, her eyes squeezing shut. "Take the truck," Cain repeated. "I won't try to stop you. Just lower your gun."

The kid looked at him one last time, then looked at Maggie, then at his wife. He shrugged and abruptly tucked the gun back into his jeans. Cain's hand twitched spasmodically, but he kept it fisted at his side. If he pulled out his gun now, Maggie might get caught in the cross fire.

A man accepts casualties. Not this man, Dad. I don't play that game. I will not live my life like that.

And I will find a way to triumph anyway.

Two minutes later, their big, blue, beautiful stolen truck with his supplies and her purse went tearing off into the night.

Cain strode forward and caught Maggie just as her knees gave out and she sank toward the rich red mud.

"Oops," she whispered, her soaked lashes fluttering against her rain-soaked cheeks.

"Oops," he agreed and cradled her wet, boneless body in his arms.

Chapter 8

"All right. Give it some gas."

Inside the relative warmth and shelter of the car, Maggie obediently pressed on the pedal. Behind her, Cain pushed against the tiny vehicle, his face contorted with fierce effort. The tires spun in the rich red mud. Cain pushed harder, his broad shoulder pressed against the muddy bumper, and Maggie could feel the vehicle rock and buck as if even it felt tired, wet, filthy and ready to get on with it.

But the greedy mud didn't release its grasping, sucking grip.

"Stop," Cain called out at last, his voice frustrated. Maggie's foot obediently slipped away. She studied him in the rearview mirror as she sat quietly, waiting for the next command. He was soaked to the bone now, his clothes molded to his solid frame and liberally streaked with mud. Rain dripped steadily off the black rim of his baseball cap, hammering against his cold white cheeks and running down his strong, corded neck. He didn't seem to notice the discomfort or chill. He simply stood there, his green eyes narrowed as he contemplated his options.

He looked strong and enduring against the dark night sky, calm and steady. The Rock of Gibraltar, Maggie thought. He spoke like that, too. He looked her in the eye and, even under the worst circumstances, maintained a low, rumbling baritone that soothed.

It was her fault they were in this mess, so to speak. But he hadn't yelled at her—as her mother would have. He hadn't turned away from her stonily—as her father would have. He didn't try to protect her from the consequences or tell her it wasn't really her fault—as Lydia, C.J., and Brandon would have.

He had simply looked at her levelly and said, "I guess we have a new vehicle now. Let's get it on the road."

Now, he crossed his arms over his chest, still analyzing the car speculatively, as if it were some riddle that would be easily solved if he could just deduce the key. Then abruptly, he scowled and raised his foot to kick the car, in the universal gesture of "logic be damned, let's kill the beast." Safely ensconced in the front seat, Maggie placed a hand over her mouth to hide her smile.

Finally, she popped open the door. He looked up immediately.

"I'll help push," she said, planting her first foot outside the car. The wind had picked up, and it slapped the rain against her bare calf like an angry, hissing woman.

"You don't have to do that," he said immediately. "Honestly, Maggie, I don't think it will make a difference."

"I'm stronger than I look," she said haughtily, bringing up her chin as she got out of the car anyway. The rain hit her hard, instantly molding her silk blouse against her arms and torso and chilling her to the bone. Despite her best intentions, she shivered, then crossed her arms across her chest for warmth.

Though he didn't say anything further, Cain still looked

skeptical, which aggravated her bruised pride. "I will have you know," she said as she took her first step into the squishy, sucking mud with her sandaled foot, "that I could build hay forts with the best of them, tossing and stacking straw bales into rebel hideaways just as well as C.J. and Brandon. They, of course, thought I should play Princess Leia to their Han Solo and Luke Skywalker. Princess Leia be damned. I always opted to be Chewbacca." Her foot disappeared completely into the mud, and with it, her favorite sling-back pumps. She stared down at the red ooze in shock while the rain raked over her back.

"Hay forts? What's a tiny rich girl doing building hay forts and playing 'Star Wars'?"

"Having fun," she said impatiently and experimented with raising her foot. The mud clung tight, pulling her foot down deeper like a gaping, gulping mouth. With a slight shiver, she pulled earnestly and was finally rewarded by the mud giving up with a popping, squishy gasp. Her foot came flying back to her, just in time for a next step. She proceeded with pigheaded determination and shivering fear. "We—C.J., Brandon and myself," she supplied, continuing to talk so she wouldn't have to think of the mud, or the rain, or the chill, "spent our summers on my grandmother's dairy farm in Tillamook. Have you ever been to Tillamook?"

Cain shook his head. "I've just eaten the cheese. It's very good cheese."

"The cheese, certainly. But Cain, you haven't lived until you've eaten the fudge. Oh my, that fudge..." She sighed wistfully, already tasting the white fudge with caramel strips melting creamy and rich on her tongue. She forced herself back to attention.

Cain still stood patiently behind the right rear wheel of the car, waiting for her to get around the vehicle. Once she'd made her intention clear, he hadn't tried to stop her but simply accepted her decision. She liked that about him. She liked that about him immensely. He respected her decisions, and for the first time in her life that made her feel strong.

"Well," she forced herself to continue briskly as she braved another cautious step and promptly watched her second Italian leather shoe sink into the red ooze, "you should go to Tillamook. It's nestled between the mountains and the coast like this tiny green emerald, shrouded in mist and filled with rolling green hills dotted with black-and-white heifers. You can hear the cows chewing their cud in rhythm with the crashing waves. My grandmother came to Tillamook in 1928, the year the Kellogg-Briand Pact outlawed war, Mickey Mouse was born and President Coolidge refused to aid our farmers mired in the agricultural depression. Her parents had set out from New Mexico to Oregon. My grandmother's youngest sister, Vivian, died during the first week from a scorpion sting. Her oldest brother, Joseph, died in Utah from an overdose of penicillin, given to him by an ignorant doctor. But they finally made it to Oregon and to Tillamook." Maggie arrived to the corner of the vehicle and stopped walking long enough to look at Cain proudly as she finished the story she'd been told more times than she could count. "My grandmother said she took one look at the tall, mist-shrouded mountains and lush, fertile fields, and knew she'd found home. And I will tell you there is no place on earth as beautiful as Tillamook, and you've never smelled sweetness until you stand in the middle of an alfalfa field in August as they bale the grass, and you've never seen stars until you sit on a patio and look up at the Tillamook night. Those were the best summers of my life. The...the best..."

Her voice trailed off with a longing she hadn't realized she'd felt. The summers of her youth, running around with Brandon and C.J. in a place where no one yelled or threw things and where she knew Brandon and C.J. would always help her. They had been magic moments. And then they'd grown up and gone their separate ways, and for the first time she was thinking how long it had been since the three of them were together. How long it had been since she'd felt happy and carefree and loved.

Belatedly, she realized both her feet had sunk deep into the mud, miring her into place. With a shake of her head, she planted her hands on the wet, slippery slant of the hatchback and worked on freeing her feet. Enough. Back to the matter at hand.

She made it the last two feet and looked at the small rear of the pathetic automobile with blatant determination. "All right," she said and squatted down, curling her hands beneath the bumper. "I'm ready."

"Lift with your legs, not your back."

She slanted him a narrow look. "I know that. Have you hefted a bale of straw lately? They're not that light. And the alfalfa—we didn't build with alfalfa much. Even C.J. could barely lift it."

"Of course," Cain murmured. "On the count of three."

"Right."

"One-two-three." With a mighty grunt, he heaved forward. She gritted her own teeth and lifted and pushed for all she was worth. The car groaned. The mud emitted a giant sucking sound.

"A little bit more," Cain gritted out.

"Right," she gasped back, and threw her entire 103 pounds behind it.

More sucking. More groaning. Then a slight tearing sound that might have been her muscles ripping or Cain's.

"Damn," he said weakly and abruptly let go. She released her grip as well, looking at him with genuine concern. Sure enough, his face was still contorted and his hand went to his back. "This really isn't my day."

"You've hurt yourself!"

"It's nothing serious."

"Of course it's nothing serious!" she snapped with genuine exasperation. "All men say that, it's instinctive and brutish. A bone could be protruding from the skin and you guys would still chirp, 'It's nothing serious.' The first caveman who got stepped on by a dinosaur probably un-peeled himself from the ground and grunted, 'Noth-ing…ugh, ugh…serious' right before dropping dead.''

She was already walking behind him, her ruined shoes making squishy, sucking sounds in the mud. Without hes-itation, she placed her hands on his rain-soaked back. He stiffened immediately.

"Upper or lower back?" she said in a brisk tone she thought her grandmother would be proud of. His back felt lean and strong, muscled and warm. She had a ridiculous urge to press her cheek against it and wrap her arms around his lean waist.

"Lower," he said in a strangely strangled voice.

"Okay." She prodded it gently with her fingers, secretly delighted by the feel of his lower back. The flesh was firm and toned, muscular and well-defined. Nothing squishy or soft here. No extra rolls of flesh or the classic doughnut rings she was used to seeing on men. Cain felt…powerful, raw, like stroking the flanks of a wild stallion. If she moved too fast, he might bolt, but if she stroked him just right, maybe the beast would stay, flesh quivering beneath her touch.

"Ah!" He winced, and she knew she'd found the spot. She remained standing there, her fingers pressed against soaked cotton, her belly lined up with his denim-molded buttocks. She wanted to start over again, stroking her fin-gers down from his broad shoulders to his tight butt over and over again, as if she were gentling a pawing mustang.

"Maggie?" he inquired. Was it just her, or was his voice breathless, too?

Maybe it was the pain. Her body, her touch, didn't in-spire much in men. She was a scrawny thing, she knew, definitely not cover model material. She could pump weights and eat her Wheaties forever and still not achieve the primal perfection of this man. This body…this was the kind of body Rodin had sculpted.

She wanted it.

Very carefully, she dug her fingers into the spot, slowly and surely rubbing tiny, tight circles. He stiffened. She could feel the apprehension and pain roll off him in waves. She held her breath unconsciously, continuing to rub the spot, wanting with every fiber of her being to feel him relax, to feel him respond to her. Maybe she would never inspire grand passion, but she could give comfort. She hoped, she wished, to do at least that much.

Slowly, bit by bit, his body relaxed beneath her ministrations. The muscle went from stiff to pliant, his shoulders abandoned their rigid stance and came down, rolling as the breath left him as a reluctant sigh nearly lost in the rain.

His body eased into her fingers, surrendered to her, and her blue eyes began to glow like magnificent, feral sapphires. It was a heady feeling, intoxicating and exhilarating. That she could affect him so, that her fingers could give him such a gift, make him sigh, make him relax against her. She wanted to touch more. She wanted to strip off his soaked clothes until he stood as naked and pale as marble in the night. Then she would lay him down in the rich red mud and stroke his entire body, learning every inch of him while gazing into his eyes so she could measure the impact of every touch and learn every nuance of his desire.

She'd never had a man. Never really gotten to touch one, never had one belong to her, sigh for her, want her. She'd watched her friends fall in love instead, listening to their stories about the new man, watching their gazes glaze over as they whispered of the first kiss, or the time *he* whispered in their ear. They never really talked about sex with her, though she didn't think any of her friends was a virgin. They just didn't associate her with sex or passion or desire.

She was a sexless woman, the kind, benevolent friend more akin to a dead saint than a flesh and blood woman. They talked to her of emotions and feelings, and when the time came, invited her to their weddings where they introduced her as "dear, sweet Maggie." So she bought wedding presents and attended the ceremonies solo. These days she was buying baby shower gifts, watching other people's radiance and wondering if it would ever be hers.

Maybe it wasn't inside her. Maybe she was too weak, too timid for a grand passion. Brandon had found it, but he was strong and fierce, even though he pretended not to be. C.J. fell in love every week, going through women like wine with an easy, beguiling charm.

Maggie couldn't seem to manage either method. She didn't have Brandon's strength, or C.J.'s gift at flirtation. Men spoke to her in bars and she simply stared at them with shell-shocked eyes, wondering why they were speaking to her. Or worse, after ten minutes of casual conversation, they abruptly poured out their entire life's story and adopted her as their new little sister.

She now had more "brothers" than any woman deserved, needed or desired. Not that she ever told any of these men that. She would never hurt them that way, and every one needed someone with whom to speak. If they were so comfortable talking to her about all their troubles with other women, maybe she should be satisfied that she could help them and bring them a degree of consolation.

But she was twenty-seven now. Twenty-seven and wondering if there was something wrong with her. She wanted marriage and children, white picket fences and that special, secret code of "us, our, we." She wanted a daughter to tell all the stories Lydia had told her. She wanted children to carry on Hathaway traditions, as she would carry on Lydia's, and invent new ones.

She wanted so much more than Friday nights with two cats, rented movies and low-fat microwave popcorn.

"Maggie. My...my back feels better now. Thank you."

His voice was so low it took her a minute to hear it. Then she stared at his back, where her small, pale fingers were still rubbing tiny little circles. I don't want to stop, she thought blankly. I don't want to.

"Maggie..."

Her fingers fell to her sides. Her eyes burned abruptly,

but she figured it was all right if she cried because she was already so soaked by the rain who would notice? She could cry and cry and cry and he'd never even know because the tears would just mix with the raindrops and it would all be the same. When she was younger, she'd thought that rain meant God was weeping. If so, God wept for Oregon an awful lot.

"We're not going to be able to get the car out," Cain said. His back was still to her, his arms braced on the hatchback. His voice didn't sound so steady anymore. "I...uh... I think we'll just have to wait for someone to come along."

"Do you think that couple will come back?"

He shook his head, his voice dry. "I don't think they're quite that stupid," he said.

"Not like me," she whispered.

He turned for the first time, his face curiously compassionate. "You're not stupid, Maggie. But you do have a generous heart, and in this day and age that's not easy." She wasn't comforted by that thought, which he seemed to understand. He added softly, "If you saw *another* stranded couple, would you stop?"

"Of course!" she exclaimed, bewildered by the question. "Those people might actually need help."

His lips curved. His green eyes softened for a moment, and she could only describe his look as gentle. "Exactly."

She looked away, not able to stand that expression on his face and all the turmoil it sparked inside her. Half of her was insanely pleased by the simple glance, the small, needy half of her that was no better than an insecure puppy granted a loving pat by her master. The other half, the half of her that longed to be something more, that didn't even completely understand why she hadn't become something more already, was irreconcilably hurt. She didn't want gentleness, she didn't want another adopted brother—not even an escaped-murderer adopted brother.

She wanted Cain to look at her and see a woman. A flesh and blood, desirable, passionate woman. And she was probably stupid to want such a thing from a man such as him. She did not know much about hostage protocol, but desiring a captor was probably self-defeating and sick.

She wanted him anyway. She wanted him, for her. Man to woman. Sparks, Fourth of July fireworks, the whole nine yards.

Cain turned and walked away from her. "Let's look inside the car and see what we have to work with."

He popped open the door, leaning inside. Maggie stood obediently in the rain, too soaked through to notice the raindrops anymore. Besides, she'd lived in Oregon on and off for twenty years now; this wasn't the first time she'd gotten wet.

"Nothing," Cain declared at last, beginning to look tired now. "Three unpaid parking tickets on the floor, umpteen gum wrappers and one empty can. Guess those guys traveled light."

"Do you think they were escaped felons, too?"

He stood and shrugged. "I don't know. They seemed too nervous to have much experience in this sort of thing. My guess is that they're just starting down the road of crime, but I don't know why. Maybe they're after the thrill, maybe just too lazy to work for things. Maybe they just robbed a liquor store and needed a getaway vehicle after theirs got stuck. I don't know."

Maggie looked down the empty stretch of road for a minute. She couldn't see much of it, the pavement disappearing quickly into an inky night. "I guess we just wait for the mud to dry out."

"Or someone else to come along."

She looked at him abruptly. "You're not going to hurt anyone, are you?"

He was silent for a minute, as if he were unwilling to commit either way. Finally, he said, "I don't want to cause any more trouble than I have to, Maggie. In chess, there is something called a quiet move. It's a move that neither checks nor captures, it doesn't contain any direct threats just helps improve your positioning for the final, last thrust of direct, decisive action. That's how I would like to pursue this game and locate Ham—quietly. If such a thing is possible with half the state after us."

"If you turned yourself in, my brother would help you. You heard what he said." A feeble, overused line but she had to offer it.

Cain didn't look impressed. "Let's get in the car, Maggie, and crank the heat. We're both soaked to the skin and if we stay out here much longer, we might fulfill your prophecy of catching pneumonia and dying."

His fingers began unbuttoning his shirt. She froze, though her gaze didn't leave his chest.

"You're taking off your clothes?" she whispered at last.

"Some of them."

"Your...your pants?"

His fingers stilled. "I don't want to make you uncomfortable."

"Oh." His fingers started moving again. His outer shirt opened up and fell limply, like an overused dishrag. He stripped it off casually and she saw the gun. He followed her gaze.

"You promised to cooperate, remember?"

"Yes."

He removed the gun from the waistband of his jeans, and with one quick move yanked the T-shirt up off his head.

She stared. She couldn't help herself. She'd wanted him naked and here he was, pale, sculpted and breathtaking. He didn't have chest hair, so nothing marred the smooth, defined lines of biceps, triceps and pectorals. His flesh was corrugated over his ribs and rippled like a washboard down his stomach. She would be delighted to scrub soap and cloth against that belly. She'd be delighted to press her lips there and taste his rain-streaked skin.

"I'm going to get into the car now," he said quietly. His gaze rested on her thin silk blouse, which was plastered against her arms and chest. "You do what you think is best."

He bent over and climbed awkwardly into the tiny car. She remained frozen with the rain battering against her. She licked her lips.

Strip it all off and straddle his lap with a sexy, husky smile, the way great-great-great-grandmother would've done.

He's an escaped murderer. He might seem very intelligent and even-tempered for a man who allegedly committed a crime of passion, I might even harbor the secret belief that he's innocent, but he's still an escaped murderer and I can't seduce a murderer. How would I explain it to my grandmother?

No, you know there's more to it than that. You've spent nearly twenty hours with this man. If he's a murderer, then your grandmother runs the gestapo. There is more to this than meets the eye, more to him. Besides, look at that chest!

Exactly. He's a Rodin sculpture and I'm a stick figure drawing. He'll take one look at me, pat me on the shoulder and start out with, "I always wanted a little sister...."

Stop it, Maggie. You know that's not true. You know he's attracted to you. His kiss was not a brotherly kiss, his gaze was not a brotherly gaze. He wants you, too. Why can't you accept that? What are you so afraid of?

I'm not strong enough, she thought abruptly, desperately. I want him, but I want all of him and he'll never be mine. I want to hold him and keep him. I want to wake up in his arms every morning. I want to see his face smiling and strong every night. But he won't stay. They never stay. Nobody ever stays and I can't bear the parting yet again. I can't stand the emptiness.

She was clutching her locket. She didn't know why, but she clutched her father's locket, containing the picture of some beautiful woman Maggie had never met. The locket was the last thing he'd given her. *Keep it for me, Maggie.*

But don't tell anyone about it. It's our secret, my secret with my little girl, he'd said.

You have to try this, the voice insisted. *You can be strong enough, you know you can be strong enough. Do you really want to be safe, sweet Maggie, forever? Think of your great-great-great-grandmother. Think of the legend of the Hathaway Reds.*

But I'm not like them. And abruptly, horribly, she knew it was true. She couldn't just seduce a man. She couldn't just crawl on his lap and say, Take me, I'm yours. Catch me on fire, Big Buddy. She wasn't that…adventurous. The other Hathaway Reds had been bold rebels, living outside the constraints of society. Herself…she could not even stand to cheat at solitaire.

Well, then, Maggie, it's a good thing he's not a deck of cards.

"Maggie," she heard him call softly. She blinked rapidly, then looked up. Cain had rolled down the window. "Sweetheart, you're getting soaked. Come inside the car, Maggie. Please."

"Okay," she whispered. Her feet moved forward. Her hand clutched her locket. Her eyes remained locked on his face.

And God, was he beautiful to her.

Chapter 9

"I'm...I'm ready." At the last minute, she realized she should have stated those words defiantly. Maybe with a come-hither toss of the hair. Instead, she sounded like a woman on the verge of strangling to death.

Cain nodded. As she watched, he seemed to take a deep breath. Moving very carefully, he opened the door and stepped outside.

He stood very close and felt very warm. She had an eyeful of pectoral and was wishing it could be a handful, but her fingers were fisted tightly at her sides, her knuckles clenched in sheer terror.

She could do this. She could do this. Taking a breath as deep and careful as Cain's had been, she ducked and climbed into the car. The front consisted of two bucket seats, separated by a gearshift. She dripped mud and water all over the vinyl, then slipped and nearly gutted herself on the stick shift as her hands went flailing one way, and her legs the other.

Instantly, Cain's hand was on her calf, his long, strong

fingers curling around her stockinged leg. She quietly stopped breathing, moving, thinking.

Was now the time to passionately exclaim, "Take me, I'm yours!"?

"Let me help you," Cain said quietly, his voice not as steady as it had once been.

She nodded, eyes wide and teeth digging into her lower lip as he slowly pushed her leg up onto the seat. He had such strong hands. Warm and rough. She let her eyelids fall shut, dewed lashes brushing her moist cheek, and concentrated on the sensation of his hand. That ridged callus, that vibrant heat, that slight friction of his palm cradling her calf—all that was being touched by a man.

She was beginning to understand the glazed look in her friends' eyes.

"Okay, now just lift your legs over the gearshift."

She nodded and managed the movement. Slowly, she righted herself, getting her feet on the floor where they belonged, her butt in the seat where it belonged, her hands on her lap where they belonged. Only her head remained out of her control, lost somewhere in the clouds, where she was now the great Margaret Hathaway, ready to perform the *lambada* in just a black lace shawl.

Cain resettled in his seat, closing the door. Small movements momentarily bridged their discomfort. His fingers turning the ignition on. Her fingers turning up the heat. His fingers adjusting the vents so that most of the warm air blew on her. Her fingers adjusting them back so he got equal share. His fingers playing with the radio dial until one lone AM country station provided a raspy, crooning cowboy singing about looking for love in all the wrong places.

The heat filled the tiny car and steamed the windows. The rain hammered against the roof and windows, still in full fury and competing ruthlessly with the radio. It sounded as if they lived in the middle of a cellophane wrapper being madly crinkled.

There was nothing more to do. Just sit here. Wait for the glow of headlights. Pray they didn't belong to a cop. Wait for the rain to end.

Maggie's fingers began to fidget on her lap. She took a deep breath, then another. Even with the heat pouring out of the air vents, she was chilly, water was still pouring from her hair down her shoulders and back in tiny, maddening rivers.

"My shirt is wet, but you could see if it makes a difference on your hair," Cain said at last.

"All right."

He handed her his crumpled shirt, then his hands returned quickly and quietly to his side of the car. She risked a glance at him. His gaze was still focused on the windshield, which had steamed over completely.

Her lips curved down a little. Finally, she leaned her head forward, spread out his shirt and used it as best she could to blot at her dripping hair. She accomplished nothing.

"If you..." His voice trailed off. She heard the sound of another deep breath. Then his hands were abruptly curling around her scalp. "May I?"

Maggie could only nod.

Oh those fingers, those glorious fingers. They wove into her hair, finding her sensitive, chilled scalp, making small, miraculous circles that brought the blood rushing to her head, her nerve endings tingling to defiant life. He didn't hesitate, he didn't go slow. He conquered her hair and she surrendered every strand to him, her eyes drifting shut, her neck arching to meet the soothing heat of broad palms cupping her head.

With relentless precision, he drove the water forward, pushing it along until his hands were tangled in the long, stringy ropes of rain-laden hair, pressing and massaging, working the moisture to the very ends. And then his hands began to wring, wrench, wring, and the water fled from her hair in a torrent, defeated and vanquished.

At last Maggie lifted her head and looked at Cain. His hands were still there, fingers woven into her long red hair.

"Thank you," she whispered, her blue eyes wide, her cheeks damp.

"I'm sorry I don't have a comb," he said hoarsely.

"Yes."

His hands slowly slid away. She wanted to tell him not to, but her throat was too tight to get out the words. Her Adam's apple bobbed, then bobbed again.

Belatedly, she turned her gaze to the dashboard, her fingers knitting together on her lap. She leaned against the seat, but the sensation of vinyl against her soaked blouse was unpleasant. More heat piped out the vents but it was feeble now. The car appeared on the edge of death, gasping and wheezing.

Finally, Cain reached out and shut off the ignition. "There's not much gas," he said. "We'll have to ration it."

She nodded. "Do you...do you think it will be long before someone arrives?"

"I don't know. It's a hell of a night to be on the road."

"Yes." Her gaze returned to the near-empty gas gauge. "Even if it stops raining, we can't go very far," she said softly.

"No. We can't."

"It's my fault."

"You think too much of yourself, Maggie." He glanced at her. "I accepted your proposition, I turned back and stopped this truck on my own volition. The choice, the risk, was mine as well. So don't accept responsibility for my actions. That belongs to me."

"Oh." She brought up her chin, and for a moment her eyes gleamed defiantly. "Then why did you escape from jail? That's escaping the consequences of your actions, isn't it?"

His lips twisted. "No, only the consequences for my alleged actions."

"What? Did—"

"Maggie, you ask too many questions."

Her gaze fell down to her lap at the softly spoken rebuke. He turned away from her, the small gesture putting even more distance between them. She shifted restlessly and uncomfortably in her bucket seat. There didn't seem to be anything more to say. There didn't seem to be anything more to do.

The heat escaped from the car too quickly. Soon she was shivering again. Goose bumps raced up her arms, prickling tiny hairs. She wrapped her arms around her middle and rubbed briskly. It didn't help much.

"You would warm up faster without the blouse on," Cain commented at last. His voice was level, but barely so.

"Yes…yes you're right."

Her fingers came up slowly to the first button. She struggled with a tiny pearl. Maybe because her fingers were cold and thick. Maybe because the silk ruffles that rimmed the neckline were plastered over the button. Maybe because she was scared out of her mind.

Either way, she couldn't quite claim that she nonchalantly shrugged off her blouse and casually flung it aside with a last, dramatic toss of her head. More like she wrestled with it. It clung to her skin and to her fingers and so she struggled and wriggled and writhed and contorted as if she were fighting a coiled serpent. At last, with a hissing sigh and victorious grimace, she ripped the clammy cloth from her torso, and promptly got it tangled around her wrists.

Cain wasn't watching. His gaze was steadfastly focused on the windshield as if it magically sported a mini TV and some important ball game were on. She would have been injured by his lack of attention, but her inept, uncoordinated efforts only made her relieved. Surely when the great Margaret Hathaway had strolled into a hacienda wearing only a black lace shawl and her flaming red hair, she'd done the deed with a bit more aplomb than her great-great-great-granddaughter.

Finally, Maggie wadded up her muddy blouse in her hand and sat tiny and hunch-shouldered. She wore a bra, of course, some sheer pink concoction that her mother had given her and Maggie wore only because it didn't show beneath the thin silk blouse. Looking down now, she realized just how sheer it was. And her chest indicated just how cold she was, too. Oh Lord.

She glanced up and found Cain's gaze upon her. Her pink lips slightly parted and her breath caught in her throat.

His green eyes were steady, dark like a forest green. He didn't blush, he didn't fidget. He didn't pretend he didn't see the hunger in her gaze and she could see in his eyes that he wouldn't pretend not to feel it. It was there between them, electric and rolling, a vibrant emotion barely restrained and just waiting to break free.

He didn't make any moves, he didn't attempt to free the beast. He sat there, as calm as ever. She understood then. He felt the attraction, he did not deny the attraction. But he would not act on it. Maybe he felt that would be improper, maybe he felt that would be taking advantage of "sweet little Maggie."

She would just have to show him otherwise.

She stole another surreptitious glance at his muscular torso and gnawed on her lower lip. How exactly did you go about cracking that man's control? Her skills were definitely lacking in the area of seduction.

Finally, she bent over and made a great show of unfastening her muddy sandals, wriggling around just enough for her skirt to hike up and show a little flesh. It didn't seem to make a difference and she broke a nail. With a small look of consternation, she sat back again and resumed worrying her lip.

Nylons, she thought abruptly. That was the ticket.

"My nylons are wet," she announced abruptly.

Cain blinked several times. "Yes. I imagine they are."

"I think I will take them off," she said loudly, the words only slightly stilted.

This time, he stiffened a little. "Off?"

"Yes. Off."

"Are these knee-highs?"

"No, they start all the way at the top."

"Oh." Blinking again. "Would you like me to turn away?" he offered in a strained voice.

No, you ninny! I want you to help! She scowled at him. She took a deep breath. "It's…it's okay. I mean…we're both adults." She thought her voice came out sounding quite reasonable, which was a miracle given the thundering of her heart against her rib cage.

"Ah…that's true."

"Yes, that's true." She took another deep breath, then worried her lower lip some more. Her mind began searching her mental files and finally settled on classic striptease music. Think of the daring, dashing Hathaway Reds. Think provocative. Sexy. Lust-ridden sex kitten.

I have legs that belong to a chicken.

Hastily, she banished that thought to a dusty corner of rotten memories. Everyone had to grow up sometime and this was her moment. She was seizing the day, or an escaped felon as the case might be.

Slowly, her fingertips found the hem of her knee-length plaid skirt. The wool was raspy and smelled as good as wet wool can smell. Don't rush, she reminded herself. No haste, no clumsiness. Smooth and languid.

She inched the scratchy material up her pale, mud-splattered thighs. She couldn't bring herself to look at Cain, because if he appeared the slightest bit bored her composure would leave and she would break down into tears. Instead she kept her gaze on her skirt, her teeth embedded in her lower lip, and her ears attuned to the sound of rain and slow, barely drawn breaths.

She reached the barrier of the seat. There was only one thing to do. She arched her hips up, a blatantly suggestive act and with a small rush, abandoned slow and yanked the damn wet skirt to her hips.

Was it her imagination, or did Cain's breath sound suddenly sharp and ragged beside her? She still couldn't bear to look.

Another deep breath and she hooked her thumbs in the waistband of her nylons. She didn't buy expensive nylons; she ran them too easily. These were thick, coarsely woven and, frankly, not something she would have chosen to flaunt in front of a man. Silk hosiery, now that was something to sinuously slide down her legs and toss aside. The grocery-store special, on the other hand…

Well, too late for that. She slid the dark brown tummy panel down, revealing sensible white cotton briefs. She'd forgotten about that, too. Why hadn't she worn the panties that matched the bra? Hadn't she realized she might get taken hostage and, after twenty-seven years, decide to finally seduce a man?

She was a horrible vamp. She would definitely have to listen to her mother's fashion advice more. Stephanie could probably seduce a granite statue.

Her legs had more goose bumps, her arms, too. If she didn't get this show on the road, she'd probably die of exposure. She began to peel down the dark, muddy nylons, revealing inch after inch of pale white skin. *Alabaster,* she corrected herself. *Think of your thighs as supple alabaster.*

She almost giggled hysterically. She reached her knees without incident. So far so good. Maybe for the finishing touch, she should raise her leg and support it on the dash as she rolled the panty hose down her calf. But the panty hose linked her legs, of course. She'd have to raise both of them. Surely a woman could not look sexy or dignified with her legs straight up in the air.

She leaned over instead, her small, sheer-clad breasts brushing her thighs as she rolled the nylon down her ankle, over heel and off her toes. With one leg free, she could raise the other slightly, pointing her toes to create a lovely arch in her foot as she slid the hideous panty hose off once and for all.

Her legs were bare now, bare and tingling from the cold and the moisture. She grazed her fingers up her calf briefly and was grateful to notice that at least she'd shaved. Not bad at all. She'd done it.

She raised her head to finally meet his gaze for a bold finish...and whopped her head against the dash.

"Ow!"

"Are you all right?"

His fingers slid into her hair immediately. Her eyes stung anyway. All right? Of course she wasn't all right. His voice was concerned and gentle, just like a damn brother's, and she didn't want another brother! The big, stupid oaf!

She rolled back, straightening at last and staring at him with big blue eyes that were slightly accusing.

"How is your head?" he asked gently.

"Hard as a rock," she snapped back.

His eyes widened some at her vehemence. "Okay." But his fingers were still in her hair, not pulling away. And they were making slow, rhythmic circles that sent a fresh rash of goose bumps down her spine.

"Umm...that helps," she murmured weakly. Her eyes were closing, she couldn't help herself. His fingers were very nice.

"Better?"

"A little bit more."

"Greedy, aren't you?" She heard the lazy smile in his voice.

"I'm trying," she muttered to herself.

But just as a fresh wave of goose bumps fluttered through her and tightened her belly, his hand drew back. She cracked open her eyes to find his fingers laced together safely on his lap. She looked at those fingers, she looked at the soaked denim sculpting his hard, muscled thighs.

And God, she was hungry. Just plain *hungry*.

For the first time, she understood her mother a little. She didn't forgive, but she began to understand.

She was shivering, shivering and shaking, and it had nothing to do with the cold. She wanted those hands back in her hair. She wanted to wrap her bare alabaster legs around his waist and press her high tiny breasts against his chest. She wanted to feel his skin, she wanted to taste it. She wanted to run her hands through his ridiculous haircut and feel the pale stubble on his cheek rasp across her neck.

She wanted to pounce on him and attack him like a fierce, ravenous feline. Her eyes darkened. Her flesh rippled with the goose bumps and she felt the interior of the car heat another five degrees.

"Maggie," Cain said, his voice faint, hoarse. "Maggie, you're covered in goose bumps."

"Yes."

"Are you cold?"

"Okay."

"Why...come sit on my lap," he said abruptly, his jaw tight, his gaze steady. "It will conserve body heat. It's the sensible thing to do."

"All right." She clambered up on the seat and fell obligingly onto his rain-soaked jeans.

Immediately his arms were around her, his skin still cold and damp, but unbelievably thrilling around her shoulders. Her fingers dug into his forearm, steadying herself as she leaned against the hard, unyielding wall of his chest. His thighs spread, cradling her on his lap, and though he didn't say a word, his hands began to briskly rub her arms.

She released her breath slowly, her eyes wide so she wouldn't miss a minute of what was happening. She was on his lap, in his arms, and she could smell soap and rain and a faint, masculine odor that was his alone. She wanted to sink her teeth in his neck and inhale him.

Instead, she carefully leaned her cheek against his chest, focusing on the feel of his bare skin. Smooth. Cool and yet warm, wet and yet vibrant. She could hear his heartbeat, thump thump, thump thump, fast and sure as a stallion's heart.

"I can hear it," she said without thinking. She raised her hand and splayed her fingers across his chest, marveling at the touch, the sound, the scent. "You sound like you're racing."

His hands began to rub her arms faster. "I suppose." He didn't sound composed anymore. She shifted on his lap.

"My hair must be wet against your chest," she said at last.

"It is."

"I'm sorry." She sat up instantly. He pushed her cheek back against him just as fast.

"You're fine."

She smiled at that, definitely beginning to make progress. If only she could get comfortable. She squirmed a bit more.

"Maggie." His voice sounded very strange. "What are you doing?"

"I'm trying to get comfortable." She sat up again, planting her hands on his chest and looking at him quizzically. "I think you have something in your pocket."

His face looked very strange, as if his lips were trying to do several motions at once. Finally, he said steadily, "I don't have anything in my pocket, Maggie."

"Yes, you do. Something hard and uncomfort— Oh." Her eyes got very wide. "*Oh!*"

"Yes. Oh."

"Did I do that?"

His lips finally curved and he granted her a wry smile. "You might have had something to do with it, yes."

Her face broke out into a brilliant smile. "It was the striptease act, wasn't it? At least until I hit my head."

"You didn't have to do any act, Maggie." His fingers cupped her head, his thumbs brushing her cheek. "Trust me, you didn't have to do an act."

"What...what do we do now?" she whispered earnestly, hopefully.

"I would suggest that you stop moving and hopefully the situation will resolve itself."

She complied immediately, sitting perfectly still with her hands frozen on his chest as she waited to see what would happen next. After another moment, he said, "You can still breathe, Maggie, just don't move."

"Oh." She expelled her held breath and drew in another ragged gulp. "I'm sorry."

"It's okay. It's a basic biological function, it happens. We're two adults, sitting half-naked in a tiny car, no one around, soft music, pitch-dark night, I haven't had sex in six years." His voice got definitely ragged and strangled. "Maggie, I'm sorry," he said abruptly and his hands wrapped around her waist. "You're going to have to sit on your side of the car. I can't do this."

She looked up at him, genuinely puzzled. She thought they were beyond all this and moving to the next step, the actual sex part. The part she'd never done before but read a lot about. "Why not?"

"Why not?" He drew in a deep, fierce breath. "*Why not?* Do I look like I'm made from stone to you? Do you think I'm so cold and remote that a half-naked woman can sit on my lap and I feel nothing, that I remain in total control?" The words held old anger. She recognized the sound immediately and leaned even closer to him, her breath whispering over his throat.

"I hope not," she whispered. "I really hope not." And then her arms curled around his neck, knocking off his baseball cap, and everything clicked for her. She was no longer thinking of her ancestors or her peer group or what kind of woman she wanted to be or what kind of woman she should be. She simply responded to him, woman to man, and recognized in herself that she'd been capable of this all along. With this man, at this moment.

Her lips settled on his and she thought he tasted sweet.

With a groan, his lips opened and succumbed. He suckled her lower lip hungrily and she opened her mouth for him, pressing against him and knowing what she wanted.

At the last minute, his hands gripped her face fiercely. He dragged back her head until he could find her eyes. She was dazed and hungry, already reaching for him. But his eyes were bright, deep and compelling.

"Do you understand what you are doing?"

"Yes."

"Do you understand I have nothing to give you?"

"Yes."

"I don't need like other people need, Maggie. You can't reform me, you can't save me, you can't own me. I will keep you hostage even after this moment, but I will also definitely let you go once we reach Idaho. You can go on your way. I will go on mine. But I am not one of your lost causes, Maggie, understand that. I've made my choices, taken my chances, and I'm willing to pay for them. Just don't ask me to pay for your choices—I don't do that.

"That's the way things are," he warned.

"All right."

"None of that is going to change because of one moment of passion," he continued.

"I know," she said, but she thought that he was lying. Because this *wasn't* just one moment and it would change everything.

His nostrils flared. Some of the composure seemed to leave him, and now she could see the sweat on his cheeks and the raw need burning in his eyes.

"I've never forced a woman, Maggie. I swear on my mother's grave I've never forced a woman. But it's been a long time and I want you...God, I want you like I haven't wanted anything. Once we start, I don't know if I can stop."

For the first time, she hesitated. She was afraid. She was an inexperienced virgin and he was a man who'd been around the block, a man convicted of murder.

Yet she trusted him. There was absolutely no rational

basis for it, and that should scare her because she knew she could be overly sentimental. But Cain wasn't emotional or rash. He was the first man—the first person—she'd met who was clear, concise and upfront. He didn't use guilt or badger or yell or any of the other games her parents had so excelled at. He accepted her as she was. He gave her options and respected her power of choice. He treated her like an intelligent woman. He trusted her word.

She took a deep breath. She looked him in the eye because he'd always granted her the same courtesy. And abruptly, her hands reached up and gripped his face. "Will you answer one question for me?" she whispered intensely, her eyes searching his gaze.

He hesitated only for a second. "Yes. For you."

"Did you kill Katherine Epstein?"

His gaze was so steady, so true. "No, Maggie, I didn't."

"I knew it," she whispered triumphantly and kissed him hard.

Chapter 10

Her mouth opened for his immediately. She'd tasted his tongue before and she wanted to taste it again. She wanted him to consume her, wanted to feel the softness of his lips, the warm, sure strokes of his tongue. He surprised her though. She thought he would be rough and eager, tearing at the few remains of her clothes and claiming her with a wild, reckless passion that would never give her time to think.

Instead, his hands remained on her face, his fingers tangled in her hair. He held her head steady, and instead of being frantic and clumsy, he explored her thoroughly, as if he'd just been granted a special gift and he wanted to know everything about it.

His lips were soft, soothing. He tasted her lips gently as if they had all the time in the world and at this moment he wanted to simply sip and savor her flavor. Next his mouth brushed her cool cheek, the corner of her eye. He kissed her lashes, and the feel of his lips against her eyelids made her smile. He touched her brow, her hairline, her chin.

Then his fingers moved slowly, splaying in her damp hair, rubbing her scalp luxuriously. They found the hot, swelling lump from her unfortunate encounter with the dashboard and lingered lightly.

"Does it hurt?"

"No," she whispered, her large blue eyes still mesmerized on his face. "Kiss me again."

He smiled. "Greedy, definitely."

"Yes."

His mouth moved deeper this time, his hands slanting her head so he could delve into her, explore the corner of her lips, the fullness of her lower lip, the moist recesses of her mouth. His tongue grazed over her teeth and she shivered at the new sensation. Then he stroked her, sure, strong, and knowing, and her fingers dug into his shoulders, holding him close.

His mouth left her, but before she could protest, he trailed warm kisses down her throat, tickling, quivering kisses that spiked goose bumps along her flesh. His hands moved, his broad palms curving around to support her lithe back. He bent her toward the steering wheel and she surrendered willingly, offering him her pale throat, delicate collarbone and gently rounded breasts.

The steering wheel was cold, her hair wet on her shoulders, the air damp and frigid. But his mouth was hot, hot and soft, and she felt it acutely, focusing on it as his lips moved across her chilly flesh.

His tongue nuzzled her pulse, which beat blue and rapid at the base of her neck. He nipped her throat and tasted the creamy expanse of her shoulder. And then his mouth trailed down to the rising swell of her petite breasts.

For a moment, she was self-conscious. She opened her eyes, looking at his bent head, the tousled mass of his golden hair, the look of rapt concentration on his face.

"It's not much," she whispered.

"What?" he murmured. His tongue traced the edge of her bra. Her whole body shuddered with the impact.

"I used to..." It was very hard to think. "I used to do that 'I must, I must, I must increase my bust.'" She rowed her arms weakly. "You know, from Judy Blume." She looked down at her ironing-board chest. "It didn't work."

For his response, he settled her back against the steering wheel and brought his hands around to cup the high, delicate crests. "Maggie," he said with complete, husky sincerity, "you are perfect."

"Oh," she said dumbly and felt her eyes suddenly fill with tears. "Don't stop," she whispered abruptly, her voice frantic and desperate and raw in the rain-filled hush of the car. "Please, just don't stop."

"I won't." And his hands moved suddenly, one slight twist and the frivolous material fell away. Her breasts were bare and beautiful, creamy white mounds topped with pale pink nipples. His mouth closed around her, sucking as gentle as a babe and the sensation ripped through her as fierce as a lion. She cried out his name shamelessly. She buried her fingers into his hair and held him against her breast. If he left her now, she knew she would just die.

Now she could feel the flame. It was inside her, low and bright in her belly, and with every tug of his mouth it grew bigger and fiercer, heating her veins, boiling her blood. She was a wanton, she was shameless. She *would* dance the *lambada* in only a black lace shawl to keep this man with her, to run her hands through his hair, to dig her fingers into his shoulders, to listen to his low, steady baritone.

"Please," she whimpered. Her head thrashed from side to side on the steering wheel and she no longer cared. His mouth increased its pace, laving her left breast, suckling hard and the darts of passion sparked hot and mad through her blood.

Her hips found the tempo on their own, her prim plaid skirt tangled around her waist, her bare feet digging into the seat beside his thighs as she arched herself against him. She heard his groan, she heard his ragged breath and then his hand slid abruptly between her thighs, cupping her mound.

"Maggie, you are so wet," he muttered, and his fingers slipped inside her plain white panties and plunged into her without further preamble.

She cried out. She arched her entire body, lifting off the steering wheel, her fingers digging into his scalp, her neck cording with unbelievable tension. The flame was so big now. So big it was consuming her and she'd never felt such heat, such fire. It was bigger than even she was, and when she lost her last grip on reason the conflagration would combust within her, annihilating her, reducing her to ash. And she was terrified and yet already inflamed and wanting the holocaust more than she'd ever wanted anything.

"Take it, Maggie," Cain whispered thickly. "It's all right. I've got you."

She fell apart. The desire burst within her and she fell into a million dazzling pieces, weeping, moaning and clinging to his sweat-streaked torso as if he was her last hope on earth.

Immediately his hands moved, curving around her shoulders and scooping her against his chest. He rocked her small shuddering form against his large, solid body, stroking her cheek and murmuring sweet words of nonsense as her senses blew away like confetti and her body disintegrated to ash.

I love you, she wanted to whisper, she wanted to weep. *I love you with my whole big, generous heart. Just hold me like this. Just hold me close to your heartbeat and never let me go.*

And then she began to cry in earnest, big, silent tears she couldn't explain. She'd just never realized how empty she'd been, how cold, how barren, how lonely until he'd wrapped his arms around her and told her she was perfect. It meant so much to her, this man, this moment, this feel of her cheek against his chest.

She wanted him as she'd never wanted anything. She

wanted to sleep curled in his arms, she wanted to wake up with his body already hard and earnest inside her. She wanted to scrub his back in the shower and she wanted to watch him eat breakfast. She wanted to know everything he feared and everything he hoped. She wanted to sit with him in front of winter fires and listen to his low, steady voice tell her about his dreams. She wanted to bear his children and suckle his son at her breast.

"Maggie, are you all right?"

No. How can I be all right when I want something I can't have? She'd been so careful not to want too much in her life. So careful not to dream too grand because she'd lived through her parents' marriage, and she knew what could happen to dreams.

And now she no longer cared. She was a Hathaway Red. She wanted it all.

She pushed herself up on his lap, wiping at her cheeks with her shaking hand. She couldn't meet his gaze. "I'm...I'm sorry. I...I bet, I—"

"Maggie." His fingers curled around her chin and raised it slowly. "Don't apologize."

"Okay," she said and felt her eyes well up again. His green gaze was so steady, so true, and his callused thumb brushed her cheek, as soothing as a kitten's lick.

He was shifting restlessly in the seat. She glanced at his lap, and realized belatedly that he was still hard, still hungry. She didn't ask and she didn't hesitate. She reached down her hand and found him through the wet, clinging fabric of his jeans.

His head fell back against the top of the seat. His green eyes narrowed to feral green slits and his breath grew ragged.

"I want you," she whispered fiercely, her hair wild and fiery around her pale face. "I want to feel you with my fingers, to hold you, to cup you. I want you inside me. I want...I want *everything.*" Her hands were already working the stubborn buttons.

"I want that, too," he murmured thickly. "Definitely."

Abruptly his hands gripped her face and he brought her lips to him fiercely. This was hard, this was earnest and primal. She wasn't glass anymore and he seemed to know it.

He split her lip. She liked the taste of blood. He bruised her shoulders with his grip. She wished he would hold her even tighter.

Her hands were fast and furious on his lap, tugging and pulling at the wet, unyielding denim. She could feel the straining desire of him, huge and hot. She should be afraid, because she was small and petite and he clearly wasn't, but she didn't care anymore.

He consumed her mouth, a huge biting kiss that she returned just as voraciously. The rain thundered around them. The tiny car rocked with the fury of their movements. The denim, however, continued to thwart her fingers and Cain struggled just as badly with her skirt and panties.

He drew back long enough for a gulping gasp of air. "The back seat," he suggested harshly. "More room."

"Okay." She tumbled between the front seats instantly, falling into the back seat and reaching for his hand.

He'd just risen, when he suddenly stiffened. He was no longer staring at her, but out the windshield.

"Cain!" she demanded without a single shred of pride.

"Headlights," he said. "Headlights."

Her mouth opened, her blue eyes widened and the slow sinking feeling in her stomach took her from high to low in one sickening lurch. "No," she whispered bleakly.

For one moment, he turned back. His jaw worked, his eyes softened. The headlights drew nearer. Big, high headlights, the kind that might belong to a semi.

Cain's shoulders squared. His face settled into the smooth, composed lines of resolve. And without his ever saying, Maggie knew the moment had come and gone.

He reached beside her and picked up the baseball cap

and his discarded T-shirt, which was still wrapped around the gun.

At the last minute, she grabbed his arm. "Don't you hurt anyone," she said harshly. "Don't do that."

He pulled his arm away without any effort. "You trust so little," he said quietly and popped open the door. "Get dressed."

He stood up in the rain, pulling the T-shirt over his bare chest and the gun tucked in the small of his back. He settled the cap over his forehead and began waving his arms.

She watched him for a moment and saw the headlights slow.

He looked strong in the night, relentless and ready to do what he had to do. He turned his emotions on and off so well. She just ached. Her body ached, her heart ached, her hands ached to reach for him. She didn't know how he pulled himself together so fast. Maybe women with foolish, generous hearts weren't meant to be able to do the same.

She reached for her silk blouse, drawing the damp fabric over her shivering shoulders with thick, trembling fingers. She didn't bother with tears and she didn't bother with regret.

She simply began buttoning the blouse and whispered, "Maggie, be strong."

Mike Jeffries was a big man. The I'm a Harley Hog Man print on his T-shirt was stretched to the point of near illegibility, and the navy tattoo on his upper forearm bulged to previously unknown dimensions. He sported a blond, handlebar mustache and sideburns Cain thought had gone out of fashion sometime in the seventies. All in all, he looked as if he could give Cain problems if he so chose.

Cain had pumped some iron in his time, sure. He was smart as well. But this truck driver appeared to consume a whole steer in a single sitting.

On the other hand, prison had been educational: It had taught Cain not to look at a man's biceps so much as look into a man's eyes. Mike Jeffries had clear eyes, smiling, benevolent eyes as he opened the passenger door and called out, "Looks like you could use some help, mister."

Cain eased his hand away from the gun nestled in the small of his back. "Yes, sir. Our car went off the road."

"Our?"

Cain looked at the man once more. Life didn't play fair. It routinely gave a man five seconds to size up friend or foe and make crucial decisions. And indecision was the worst choice of all.

"My wife," Cain supplied steadily.

Mike Jeffries simply nodded, no calculating look appearing on his face, no sudden flush of lust darkening his eyes. Of course, the giant hadn't seen Maggie yet. That long red hair of hers had probably broken more than a few hearts.

Or maybe it was simply the way she moved, the way she spoke. Every act earnest. She did nothing halfheartedly. She tried and she persevered, more than any person he'd ever known.

As if she were reading his mind, the back door of the car popped open and she stepped out. Both Cain and Jeffries turned toward her.

She stood straight in the pouring rain, the slashing drops instantly molding her deep red hair to her pale, oval face and slender shoulders. She was small and delicate, yet remote and ethereal in the dark storming night. It was as if the entire rage of nature didn't affect her, didn't touch her, because she willed it that way.

Cain had thought she might look hurt after his abrupt departure. He thought she might sulk. He'd forgotten just how resilient she was.

Instead, in a small endearing motion that impacted him far more than any tantrum would have, she carefully checked both ways of the empty road, and then crossed right toward him, her footsteps direct, even and without hesitation.

He found himself holding out his hand. He found himself wishing the semi had never arrived and he could have stayed with her in the back seat of the car, tasting her skin, listening to her soft cries, feeling her body contract around him.

And afterward, he would have liked to hold her a long time, listening to her soft voice proudly tell stories of her family while he stroked her long, red hair.

He forced himself to turn back to Jeffries and the matters at hand. The bigger man's eyes were still clear. That was a good thing, because maybe Cain was capable of murder after all.

"I'm heading to Burns," the driver said. "Then I gotta pull over and get some rest."

"How far is that?"

"Oh, 'bout another forty miles. Or I can drop you in Riley ten miles from here if you'd like."

"No, Burns would be great if it's not a problem."

"Nah, hop right in and get outta this rain. I got some towels in the back and a thermos of hot coffee if you'd like. Shoot, I've never seen two people so wet."

"Ugly night," Cain commented softly.

"Sure is. Sure as hel...heck—my apologies, ma'am—is."

Cain decided he liked Mike Jeffries then. Still, he positioned himself between the driver and Maggie on the seat, handing her the towel first as the semi lumbered to life and slowly eased forward into the rain.

"Could you tell me the time?" Cain asked, turning his torso to shield Maggie from the other man's gaze as she went to work drying her hair and her clinging blouse.

"Nearly 4:00 a.m. You in a hurry?"

"A little."

"No problem." Jeffries grinned. "No one can make up time like a trucker."

True to his word, Jeffries dropped them in Burns in just over half an hour, making good time on a straight, flat road that was being consumed by the storm. Ever helpful, the trucker pulled over at a bank in the middle of town so Maggie could use the ATM machine—she'd thankfully found the bank card in the pocket of her skirt, having tucked it there after the last withdrawal. Armed with cash, they requested that the driver leave them at a small, innocuous strip motel just outside the city limits. From there, they would be fine, Cain assured Jeffries.

They tried to offer him money for his assistance, but Jeffries wouldn't take anything. He shook their hands, blushing a little as Maggie thanked him in her sweet, soft voice, and wished them the best. Then he headed for the truck stop and Cain and Maggie stood under the porch trying to figure out what to do next.

Four-thirty in the morning. They'd now covered three hundred miles since leaving Portland and put one hundred miles between themselves and Bend. Their clothes were drenched and covered in mud.

Cain figured there was only one thing to do. He rang the buzzer in the motel lobby, waking the proprietor, and then with all the exhausted charm he could muster pleaded for a room.

The woman's gaze went from bedraggled Maggie to Cain to Maggie, her expression showing she was disgruntled at having been dragged out of bed. Then she reached beneath the counter, and just as Cain was beginning to hear alarms ring in his head, the woman whipped out a hair dryer, two boxed toothbrushes, a tiny tube of toothpaste and a room key.

"Thirty bucks for the night. Danish and coffee available in here at seven."

Maggie handed over the money. The woman fairly snatched it off the counter, then tightened the belt of her green velour robe and waddled away.

After exchanging startled glances, Maggie and Cain breathed easier.

"There are nice people in the world," Maggie said

softly, picking up the generously offered toiletries and looking at Cain pointedly.

"There definitely are," he concurred and picked up the
key. "Now let's find the room and get some sleep."

They had to go back out into the rain, but at this point,
they barely noticed. The storm appeared to be lessening,
which was a mixed blessing. Cain preferred clear weather
for faster driving time. On the other hand, the cops, Ham
and everyone else would also benefit from the break.

That was tomorrow's worry, though. He still had to get
through the night.

He opened the door of the room at the end of the strip
motel, and discovered the night wasn't going to get any
easier. The tiny room offered one bed—a queen-size mattress with just enough room for a cozy couple to sleep
tangled in each other's arms.

He swallowed thickly, feeling Maggie still beside him
and knowing she was thinking the same thing. His body
was already hard, his hormones insistent. His hostage was
a beautiful, passionate woman, and he already remembered
the taste of her mouth, the texture of her skin.

God help him, he wanted her. He wanted to slam the
door shut behind them, lock it so the world was held at bay
and strip off her clothes and consume her. Maybe he should
have been fast and furious in the car. Maybe he'd had his
opportunity and this unbelievable ache in his groin was his
penance for going so damn slow.

He hadn't wanted to rush, though. Even as a kid, he'd
hated to gorge. He and Ham had only gotten candy on the
rare occasions Zech had gone into town. Then, he'd bring
them back pieces of hardtack or sticks of butterscotch. Ham
always devoured his in a single sitting. Cain hoarded his
candy, however, stashing the pieces away in secret places
where he could pull them out and simply stare at them,
knowing they would taste sweet and delicious and deriving

as much pleasure from the anticipation as from the actual act.

He ate his candy slowly. One piece every few days, sucked and never chewed as he walked the mountain trails of his home, inhaling the fresh air and tasting the sugar melting on his tongue.

When he'd looked at Maggie, her pale skin, her delicate, supple body, he'd felt the same way. He wanted to take it bit by bit, dragging out each precious moment of delight, holding back until it hurt, because good things were few and far between, and perfect moments passed so quickly, leaving you with nothing afterward.

Now here was a hotel room with a single bath and a single bed. He could climb into the shower with her, a hot, steaming shower where he could strip off all her clothes with leisure and, starting at the widow's peak of her magnificent hair, soap her entire body. Her skin would be as supple and smooth as satin. Her nipples would be hard pebbles, grazing his palm, and her thighs would be soft and slender.

He would like to hear her moan through the steam. He would like her fingers digging into his shoulders once again, as she clung to him and begged him for release.

A moment of passion, sweetness melting in his mouth. And the aftermath?

He wasn't so big a fool that he thought a woman like Maggie could separate her heart from her body. He saw the way she looked at him now. He had recognized the shocked wonder of her first fulfillment. She didn't appear to be that experienced nor to understand the full depth of her sensuality. But now she was discovering it and the more Cain touched her, the more he bound her to him.

It was grossly unfair of him. Blatantly unjust. For the aftermath remained bitter. He was a wanted man with no good plan of escape. His next moves on the chessboard were full of so many assumptions and held such a huge margin of error he should be ashamed. He didn't have any better ideas, though. Ham had checkmated him with brutally simple efficiency the first time around, and Cain was still playing catch-up.

He took a deep breath and turned to Maggie. Her blue eyes were huge, slightly wary but also luminescent. She looked from the single bed to him to the bed. Her lips parted and he almost lost his resolve.

"Why don't you shower first?" he said, his voice uncommonly thick. He cleared his throat. "We don't have much time, Maggie. I want to be up again at seven."

Her eyes widened. "That's only two hours from now."

"I'm a wanted man," he said pointedly.

Her back stiffened. "It's not as if I've forgotten," she fired back.

Her spirited retort made him smile, made him ache. He brushed her cheek with his thumb without conscious intent. "Good." He hesitated, then was unable to stop himself from whispering softly, "Don't let me hurt you. Don't let me do that."

Her chin came up. "You think too much of yourself," she said haughtily, using his own words against him. "I take full responsibility for my actions, too, Cain."

"Then we understand each other."

Her nostrils flared sarcastically, a new look for her. "Sure, Cain. For all the good that does us."

She squared her shoulders. "I believe I'll shower first. Why don't you get some sleep? We only have two hours, you know."

He accepted her pointed jabs. She fought, that was good. Even women with generous hearts should know how to throw a few good punches.

She sauntered away from him, her shoulders straight, her head held high, her back graceful. She looked very different from the meek, hunch-shouldered woman he remembered kidnapping twenty hours ago.

He thought she'd never looked so beautiful.

* * *

Maggie showered for a long time, letting the steam soak into her chilled, shattered senses. Her nipples were tight, her breasts more sensitive than she ever remembered. She felt restless and wound up and more aware of her body than she'd ever been.

She shampooed her long hair and remembered Cain's fingers performing the same, massaging circles. She soaped her throat and remembered his soft lips nipping at her pulse. She soaped her breasts and gritted her teeth against sharp sensations that were near pain. Her body didn't seem hers anymore. Every place she touched reminded her of him.

And she knew from the tightly wound sensations that she wanted him again. And again. And again.

Was passion always like this? So unquenchable? So consuming?

There was so much more she wanted to know, so much more she wished he would show her. If only that darn semi hadn't shown up...

He was back to being removed again. Back to thinking too much, to trying to be honorable. The damn man thought way too much.

She scowled, turning off the water and stepping out of the shower at last. She dried off briskly, still feeling wound up, restless and disgruntled. At the last minute, she took the towel and wiped the steam from the mirror, staring at her naked reflection.

She still looked the same, she thought. Tiny, too thin. But then, maybe she was just slender. Her ankles were delicate, her calves nicely rounded, her thighs supple. Her waist was very narrow, her breasts small, but high and firm. And she had alabaster skin, she decided abruptly. Not pasty-white. *Alabaster.*

She perused the collection of bottled toiletries lined up around the sink and finally discovered a little bottle of lotion. With a spurt of resolution, she dumped out the rich cream and began massaging the carnation-scented lotion into her skin. Next, she plugged in the hair dryer and attacked her hair.

Fifteen minutes later, she stood still naked, but her skin glowed now, supple and satiny. And her fiery red hair cascaded down her body in rich ripples, falling from her widow's peak to her navel with warm, crackling life.

She spent five minutes washing out her clothes with shampoo and hanging them over a small radiator. Then she squared her shoulders, adjusted her hair over her shoulders and breasts as a flaming veil and decided if her great-great-great-grandmother could do it, so could she.

She stood in front of the door, took one last deep breath and strode naked into the tiny room.

Cain was sitting in a tiny, wicker chair by the window, his long legs stretched out in front of him and crossed at the ankle. He didn't look up as she entered; he didn't turn. She took another step toward him, her hair brushing her hips. Then another.

And realized that the object of her ardor had fallen asleep.

His chin was nestled on his chest, his face clearly lined with fatigue. In the past twenty hours, he'd slept only three and it showed.

She bent down beside him and simply watched him for a moment. He looked so unbelievably dear she didn't have the heart to wake him.

The new improved Maggie. More self-confident, still no audience.

She stroked his hand lightly, but he still didn't wake. There was only one thing left to do.

Half an hour later, after attacking her clothes with the hair dryer and pulling them on, she slid out the front door.

Cain's eyes cracked open at the sound of the door clicking shut. He stared at the closed door for a moment, blinking.

"Maggie?" he called out.

No answer. His head turned slowly to the bathroom.

Door open, lights off, room empty. The fatigue crashed down on him hard, his shoulders finally bowing beneath the strain.

He could only shake his head in the cool, silent room.

"You promised," he whispered. "Maggie, you promised."

Six-thirty a.m.

In Beaverton, Joel Epstein's phone started ringing and the junior officer fumbled for the receiver. He'd fallen asleep only an hour ago and he had too much on his mind to sleep well anyway.

"Officer Epstein?"

"Yes, sir."

"This is Captain James. We got a lead on the Cannon case. I thought you'd want to be the first to know."

"Yes, sir!"

Captain James was succinct. Two kids had been pulled over in Bend in a stolen vehicle and had been identified as suspects in a recent convenience store holdup. Looking for bargaining chips, the young couple claimed they hadn't really stolen the truck, but had taken it from another man and his tiny, red-haired companion. The police were pretty sure the second couple was Cain Cannon and his hostage, Maggie Ferringer.

The APB had just been updated in Bend with the license plate of a gray hatchback car the kids had abandoned in favor of Cain's truck. All police in the area were now on the lookout for that vehicle. When they found it, they would most likely find Cain.

"I would like to go to Bend, sir," Joel said immediately. His heart was pounding in his chest. Sometimes he remembered playing the saxophone in the smoky clubs with Cain and Kathy smiling at him from the audience, clapping their hands as the notes got high and sweet. But mostly he remembered the morgue, identifying his sister's body, and realizing for the first time what kind of man Cain truly was. And just what he'd done to Joel's sister.

Captain James hesitated. Joel understood that. The department would like to keep him uninvolved, given his emotional ties.

"Captain," Joel said in a steady voice, "we both know I have leave due to me."

The captain sighed, knowing at his age there was no point spitting in the wind. "Take your leave," he said. "Go to Bend, but not with your badge. And don't do anything stupid."

"Thank you, sir."

Joel hung up quickly. He hesitated one moment, then dialed a new number he'd been given just ten hours earlier. He should keep the information confidential, but then he knew too well what it was like to want to protect your sister. And he didn't want someone else to be too late for their sister, as he'd been too late for his.

"Brandon Ferringer, please." A two-second pause. "Brandon? This is Joel Epstein. I have a lead on Cannon. We're going to Bend."

Chapter 11

Maggie banged open the motel room with her hip, juggling three plastic grocery sacks and one bulky coat. Dawn was just beginning to lighten a lavender sky and triumph already stained her cheeks.

She stumbled over the slight step and half tumbled into the room, a crinkling blur of plastic bags and giddy smiles. The coat fell off her arm, but was embraced comfortably by the carpet. The rest of the bags she held out with a flourish.

Cain wasn't sleeping in the chair as she'd expected, but stood in the middle of the room with a single white towel wrapped around his lean flanks. His blond hair was damp from a recent shower and moisture still beaded his smooth chest. His face was curiously bland and guarded.

"I did it!" she declared and shook her bags of supplies. One fell open and a box of granola bars went tumbling to the floor.

Cain simply stared at her, his green eyes perfectly flat.

She decided more explanation was in order. "I wasn't

tired at all," she burst out in a rush. "So I thought, why not take care of everything now and save us a bit of time in the morning? I dialed the operator from the pay phone in the lobby and convinced her to hail a cab for poor stranded me. Then I got the driver—his name is Barney and he has three daughters, one of whom he swears looks just like me—to take me to a twenty-four-hour convenience store. Barney helped me pick out granola bars, orange juice, bananas and bagels. They didn't carry much in the way of clothes, but the man had some hunting supplies so I also got a thermos, a pocketknife, a canvas bag, two T-shirts saying Burns, Oregon—Been There, Done That. And then—" her smile grew huge "—my pièce de résistance— a hunting jacket."

She dropped the three bags in favor of the camouflage jacket, which she scooped up off the floor. "They only carried it in extra large, but Barney says the extra room is good so you can wear layers beneath it. Can you believe he didn't even charge me for the time in the store? He's such a nice man. I got his address so I can send him a thank-you card when this is all over."

She draped the jacket over the bed and surveyed her trophies once more with a satisfied nod of her head. Her cheeks remained flushed, and her blue eyes unbelievably brilliant. At last she settled her hands on her hips and declared in a very smug voice, "Not even C.J. could've done it better. Hah!"

She grinned at Cain, who still hadn't moved. His face hadn't changed, either.

"You shouldn't have done this," he said abruptly.

"What?" The roses faded from her cheeks. She stared at him, genuinely puzzled.

"You didn't need to do all this, Maggie," he said levelly. "I'm not one of your lost causes."

She scowled at him immediately, her hackles rising. "And you're welcome," she snapped back. "Now go back to bed and don't get up again until you've found your manners!'' Wow, she sounded just like Lydia when she said that. She resumed smiling, feeling ridiculously proud of herself.

Cain did not appear amused. ''I told you—''

She gave up, throwing her hands up in the air. ''What is wrong with you? I did a good thing here, I know I did. We have to have supplies. We'll save so much time now and—''

''What *we?*'' he gritted out abruptly, his voice uncharacteristically tight. ''There is no *we*. There is *me*, the escaped felon, and *you* the hostage, but there is no *we*.''

She looked at him, and for the first time some of the wind left her sails. She studied his face, searching for some sign to tell her where she'd gone awry. She'd been so sure he'd be delighted. She'd gone so far as to imagine him scooping her up in his arms and telling her she was so wonderful, so perfect, a true blessing/angel/godsend. She'd thought he might at least smile and say, ''Thank you, Maggie. That was very smart thinking.''

''I thought…'' Her voice sounded so weak, so faint. She took a deeper breath. ''I thought we were a little beyond that captor-hostage thing,'' she said at last.

''Why? Because of last night?''

''Last night? Cain, that was three hours ago.''

He didn't even look ashamed. He simply shook his head and said in a hard, relentless voice, ''I told you at the time, Maggie, that there were ground rules. I told you that you wouldn't own me, that you couldn't adopt me or save me, or any of that—''

''No!'' she cried, his words hurting her horribly. She didn't crumple, though; she jabbed her finger at him and fought back vehemently. ''You told me I couldn't own you, but now you're trying to own *me*. You're telling me how to think, how to feel. What I should expect, how I should act. Well, you can't do that. I'm helping you and you're just gonna have to suffer through it, mister. And I'm not leaving and you're going to have to suffer through that as well!''

"You don't even know anything about me!" he exclaimed sharply.

"I know what I need to know."

"And what is that, Maggie?"

Her face was more troubled. "That you're a good person, intelligent and levelheaded. That you don't usually yell at me. That *generally* you treat me like an intelligent human being who's capable of making her own decisions and strong enough to bear the consequences. That you respect me, that you think I have a big heart and that...that you find me attractive just as I am." Her voice faded away. She could no longer look at him. Instead she studied the rug, her hands knotted before her.

Cain was silent for a long time. Not moving, not speaking, just standing there. She finally risked a glance. His face was no longer blank, but troubled.

"I thought you'd left," he said abruptly.

"I did. I went to the store."

"No. I mean I thought you had *left*, as in you were never coming back."

Her eyes widened. "Cain," she said softly, "I gave you my word."

"I know." He looked at the ceiling. "I know. But I thought you had left anyway, and it bothered me, Maggie. It really...bothered me. I...I don't want to be bothered by such things." He peered at her through squinted eyes, his blond hair waving over his brow. "Can you understand that?"

"Yes," she whispered. "Cain, I—"

"Maggie, you've never asked about the murder."

"I don't need to."

"You can be that sure?"

"Yes," she told him honestly.

Her faith didn't seem to make him proud, though, or soften him, or touch him. Instead, he was abruptly shaking his head as if that proved she was a fool, and that hurt her tender feelings all over again.

"You think I'm so naive then?" she asked through an unbearably thick throat. "That it proves I'm stupid?"

"I wasn't going to s—"

"No, but you were thinking it. You were thinking, how can this tiny woman with her big ol' generous heart be so gullible? It's not like you're the first person who's thought that, Cain. And…and dammit, I refuse to apologize or defend or change. I trust people, all right? I go through life assuming the best about everyone, so there. Just sue me.

"And I've spent twenty-four hours in your company and I do *not* believe you are capable of murder. You didn't hurt the guard, you didn't hurt me. You are one of the most even-tempered people I know—the thought of you committing a rash crime of passion is frankly ludicrous. And then there's the simple matter that I asked you and you said no. You said *no*. I believe you, Cain. You can think I'm stupid if it makes you feel better, but I believe you anyway—"

"I don't think you're stupid."

"Are you so sure about that?" She refused to be so easily mollified. Instead, she stood five feet away from him, her fingers clenched into fists, her body stiff and her open face filled with hurt.

"Maggie…ah!" He seemed frustrated and distraught, and for the first time since she'd known him, at a loss for composure. His hand raked through his shorn hair once, then twice. "I'm mangling this."

"No kidding. And the clock is ticking, buster." She tapped her foot for emphasis. She was beginning to sense she had the upper hand and she had no intention of letting him off lightly. Let him squirm a bit; it was the least he deserved.

"I'm not used to people like you," he said abruptly.

"Oh?" She arched a fine brow. "You mean *nice* people? *Kind* people?"

His lips curved reluctantly. "Yes. Exactly." Then his face sobered. "I've been alone a long time, Maggie. I think sometimes...I'm better alone. Kathy used to say I was too remote, too self-contained, that no matter how much time she spent with me, she never knew what I was thinking, never thought that I needed her. I didn't really understand what she meant. But then she was dead and everyone agreed that I'd done it. My family betrayed me, my friends believed in the betrayal. Everyone, shaking their heads. 'Well, I never did feel like I knew him,' they all said, as if I'd been a stranger all along. As if none of it, none of the friendships, had been real.'' His voice broke. He forced himself to continue, his gaze planted on the wall. ''And then there's you, Maggie. You've known me less than a day, you've met me under the worst conditions, and you've already given me more, trusted me more, than anyone else. You believe in me. And by God, I didn't realize how much I needed that.''

He looked down, his voice too hoarse to continue.

Maggie gave up on distance. She strode toward him, not stopping until she was against his body, his damp towel against her damp skirt, her hands splayed lightly on his bare, freshly showered chest. Her fingertips massaged his collarbone, her gaze searched his eyes. ''Tell me, Cain. Tell me what happened that night, tell me everything. I promise to believe.''

''I introduced them,'' he whispered, and she could hear the underpinnings of guilt and remorse in his voice. ''Ham suddenly appeared in Portland, said he wanted to get to know me again as it had been five years, and without ever suspecting a thing, I invited him to dinner.''

''He wanted your girlfriend?''

''I don't think so. I think he just wanted to get back at me. He wanted to destroy his turncoat brother who'd spit on everything we were raised to believe. I'd just been appointed project manager to a new program we were developing for the government. I think that might have been the last straw for him.''

''I don't understand,'' she told him honestly.

"Our father...he believes the government is evil. Schools are corrupt, public water supplies, public services. Street signs and traffic lights contain secret codes that will one day be used to herd together all dissidents. The ZOG hates middle-aged white Christian males, and if Aryans don't stick together, we'll all hang separately."

"Do...do you believe it?"

"No. I'm the family heretic. I figured that if God asked Noah to save two of *all* the animals from the flood, then he must value the diversity of the creatures that he created, including mankind. It was an unpopular belief where I grew up. I moved to Portland instead. I met all the people I'd been told were evil—they weren't."

"Then Ham came."

"Yes." He said softly, "I was willing to believe he wanted a reconciliation. I don't know why. We'd always fought. There was no logical reason for me to think things had changed."

"He was your brother."

"He set me up. I let him in, introduced him to my co-workers, to Kathy, and he took it all in, and in one brutal stroke took it all away. It wasn't even difficult for him. He was handsome, charming, and Kathy liked men with a dangerous edge. We'd been dating for a while, but the flush was over. She wanted things I couldn't give her and we both knew it. She must have thought Ham was quite dashing.

"And he must have thought it was very easy to kill his brother's Jewish lover."

"Oh, my God," Maggie whispered and pressed against him. Her open face was filled with so much horror, so much compassion for him and Kathy both. "Oh, my God."

He found his hands buried in her thick red hair, he found himself pressing her body slightly closer. She felt tiny and delicate, but not breakable. She was too supple, bending like a willow when under pressure, while he knew only how to stand stiffly and snap.

It had been more than six years since that night, but it had changed too much to ever let go. He'd been so sure relationships could be simply and easily defined. How much could go wrong? Even when he'd begun to realize Kathy and Ham were involved, he hadn't wanted to dwell on it. Kathy was a free woman. He didn't own her, she didn't own him. She could make her own choices.

But he'd never told her about Ham's upbringing, about his hatred and bigotry. When Ham had arrived in Portland, he seemed to have left that behind as well, and Cain didn't push too hard or ask too many questions. Cain had been weak, after all, wanting to believe that his brother shared his enlightenment, that leopards could change their spots.

He'd made Ham's job so easy and Kathy had paid the price for Cain's naiveté. Life wasn't supposed to work like that. *His* life wasn't supposed to work like that.

"But you didn't do it," Maggie whispered softly. "Why didn't the jury believe you?"

"Ham used my own hunting knife, then testified as an eyewitness to my alleged enraged attack on Kathy. The case was open-and-shut."

"We'll have to change that," she declared immediately. Already, she was gnawing on her lower lip. "Now how are we going to prove that?"

Very gently he wrapped his hands around her waist and set her from him. "*We* aren't going to do anything," he said quietly. "I'm going to go to Idaho. In the meantime, I'm hoping Ham will arrive in Oregon. While he looks for me here, I'll try to find evidence against him at home."

"Do you think you'll find much?" Maggie asked, momentarily ignoring that silly *I-we* thing. She'd cross that bridge later.

"I doubt it. It's been six years. On the other hand, Ham likes to brag. His friends will never testify against him, but perhaps a bartender or cocktail waitress might. Or there are a lot of magazines and propaganda documents that circulate among militias. Generally, they include 'accounts of war,' generic anecdotes of local activities.''

Maggie's eyes grew huge and her face pale. "You mean...you mean he might have written up what he did and *published* it for others to read?''

"There are some people who think he performed a very noble act, Maggie.'' His lips twisted. "I'm sure my father is one of them.''

"Well! We're just going to find this account and bring it to a judge!''

"Maggie,'' he said calmly, "even if such a thing existed, Ham wouldn't be so stupid as to use real names. I don't think one story published in a propaganda publication will overturn a murder conviction.''

"Then we'll have to find something else!''

"I will.''

"Brandon and C.J. will help us,'' she continued unperturbed. "They're very capable.''

Cain couldn't take it anymore. He reached out, grabbed her hand and abruptly dragged her against him. His palms framed her face. He held her still and forced her to really look at him as he enunciated slowly, "Maggie, you *can't* help me. Don't you understand yet? There is a very strong chance that I may never be able to prove my innocence. There is a strong chance the police will return me to jail. There is a strong chance Ham will hunt me down, and I'm just not ready to kill my own brother. I don't have a lot of good options yet, and I *will not* let you pay for my mistakes. No more. I'm willing to stand alone and I'm willing to die alone if it comes to that. I pay for my choices, no one else. That's fair.''

He released her face. He took a resolute step back and pointed toward the door. "Please leave, Maggie. Now.''

"No.''

"Please leave, Maggie. Now.''

"No,'' she repeated.

His arm began to shake. "Dammit, I said, now!''

"And I said, no!" Her chest heaved, her eyes grew bright. She fisted her fingers at her sides and stared out at him with blazing defiance. "No, no, no!"

"Why are you doing this to me?"

"Because I can't help it!" she cried. "Because I want...I want to watch you *eat* in the morning, and...and shave over the bathroom sink and brush your teeth and put on your shoes. Because I want to hear more stories about your mother and listen to you sing along with the radio and...and I want you to hold me in your arms again and stroke my hair and tell me it's okay because you've got me, it will be all right. And I want to hold you, and I want to stroke your hair and tell you it will be all right. I'll introduce you to my brothers, I'll introduce you to my cats and my grandmother—you have to meet my grandmother.

"Because...because...because I want more out of life than a silly, stupid, damn locket!"

"A locket?"

"That's right," she declared fiercely, "a locket." And then her hand was wrapped tightly around the heart pendant dangling between her breasts. With a sharp tug, she snapped the chain. "I hate this thing," she said abruptly. "I hate it, I hate it. I wanted a father, I wanted a daddy to be there for me. And this is what I got instead—a cheap locket holding a picture of some woman I don't even know. But it was what I deserved, you see. Because I never asked him to stay. I never asked him to love me enough to be in my life and not keep running to someone else's. I just crept around the hallways like a little mouse, so convinced that if I was quiet enough, still enough, I could somehow hold it all together. If I just never made any demands, he would love me, my mother would love me...someone would love me."

She held out the locket and let it drop onto the floor. "What a bunch of hooey. You want something, you have to ask for it. You need something, you have to fight for it.

Well, I want you, buster, so I'm not going anywhere. You're stuck with me.''

His eyes widened, startled by her vehemence as she was startled by her vehemence. He opened his mouth as if to argue further, as if to demand that she leave. Instead, his mouth clamped shut. He looked at her with open, pleading eyes instead, and she could see her own need reflected there. "Maggie," he whispered. "You are killing me."

"I know," she said. "I know." And abruptly her fingers were on her tattered silk blouse and she was fumbling with the buttons. She wanted it off. She wanted her bare skin pressed against his, she wanted his lips on her cheek, her throat, her breast. She could see by the darkening of his eyes he wanted her, too.

"Stop!" he ordered hoarsely.

"Why?" she pressed fiercely.

"Because...because I want to do that! I...I want to do that."

He strode across the room. Two long steps and he was in front of her. Her fingers fell away without protest and his hands seized the silk.

"It won't change anything," he whispered feverishly, "it won't change anything." But his hands were fast, nimble and urgent on her buttons.

"Liar," she whispered and pressed her lips against his pounding pulse.

Her blouse fell away, battered silk floating down delicately to the carpet. She didn't wait for his fingers but attacked the buttons of her skirt while his fingers efficiently released her bra. She stood naked in just fifteen seconds. Cain joined her with a negligent flick of his wrist that sent the towel crumpling to the floor.

For a moment she couldn't breathe, couldn't move. She stood just inches from him, her eyes drinking in every detail. His strong, square-cut jaw was covered with soft, flaxen whiskers that reminded her of wheat lightened by an August sun. His chest was smooth, broad and sculpted, his neck corded, his collarbone creased, his nipples dark brown and hard. The pale coloring wasn't quite right for him, she thought. He should be lightly golden, not dark bronze but lightly tan from running along mountain streams with the sun deflecting off the water onto his skin. Prison had robbed him of that nourishment as it must have robbed him of so much else.

She raised a single hand and flattened it against his chest. "You're so beautiful," she whispered hoarsely. "I've never seen…never seen anything so lovely."

"Don't talk. Just let me touch you."

She nodded mutely.

Cain's hand reached out. He was surprised to see that it was trembling. He didn't touch her skin right away—it was so delicate, so translucent he was afraid he would mar it with his fingerprints. Instead he picked up a handful of her hair, feeling the thick, spongy mass, warm and vibrant in his hand. He opened his fist, and the silky strands wrapped sinuously around his fingers, his thumb, his wrist, his forearm. In the dawning light of morning, her hair glowed with an inner fire, like raw energy that was gathering, preparing and waiting to be unleashed.

He wanted that hair cascading over his lips, his throat, his chest. He wanted to bury his face in it, inhale the sweet scent of shampoo and drown in the vibrant life.

She stood so still, like a doe on the verge of flight, he wasn't even sure she understood just how beautiful, how extraordinarily strong she was.

He took one step forward, hooked his arm beneath her knees and swung her against his chest effortlessly. Two more strides and he tossed her onto the bed, listening to her breathless laugh of surprise and anticipation, following her quickly onto the sinking, queen-size mattress.

The bed dipped drastically beneath his weight, conveniently rolling Maggie into his body. He saw her eyes, heavy-lidded and luminescent. Her hands were half-fisted by her sides and he could tell she was slightly nervous, slightly afraid. It grounded him enough to slow him down.

"I would like to touch you," he whispered bluntly. "For a long time. May I?"

She nodded wordlessly, her eyes now wide.

He stretched out his body, supporting himself on his right elbow as his left hand reached out and lightly touched her cheek. She flinched and he frowned, beginning to realize just how wary and hesitant she had become. He was a large man and he knew she was inexperienced.

He could take it slow. For her.

He brushed back her hair, fanning it around her on the worn white pillow, combing his fingers through the strands until they gleamed a deep, golden red. Then he traced his thumb down her oval face, sliding his fingers down her throat, finally settling the base of his palm against her pounding pulse point. Her small, high breasts rose and fell rapidly. Her hips squirmed a bit against the bedspread.

His body began to truly ache. She was so warm, so generous, and it had been so long since he'd felt like anything other than stone. So long since he'd really let himself remember the simple pleasure of human touch.

He ducked his head and found her lips. Her neck arched instantly, her mouth opening, her arms curving around his neck. She pressed her lithe body against his lushly and he almost fell apart.

Suddenly he was raining kisses across her lip, her brow, her cheek. He nuzzled her throat, kissed her neck and drifted his lips even lower to the soft, tender flesh he had to taste. She sighed his name. She arched against him hopelessly, guiding his head to her breast, offering herself to him so sweetly it stung his eyes and thickened his throat.

His lips curved around her nipple. He tasted her, rose petal soft and dewy earnest. Her skin smelled of carnations and rain-swept skies. Her flesh filled him, consumed, drew him down into sweet places he'd never known.

He devoured her. He kneaded her breast, he suckled her

nipple as greedily as a child. She arched up, she cried out his name, and his lips pursed harder.

His pulse thundered in his ear. He couldn't think anymore. No more logic, no more chessboards or binary riddles. Maggie filled him, and for a dangerous, hovering minute, he thought he might need her as he'd never needed anyone. And a part of him wanted to plunge over the abyss and surrender to her completely.

"Please," she whimpered, "please."

He raised his head. Dimly he was aware of moisture staining his cheeks but he wasn't sure how it had gotten there. His hand moved down her body, his fingers splaying across her gently sloping belly, then curving down to the warm apex of her thighs. Her hair felt soft and coaxing. Her legs parted for him immediately, and she arched against his palm.

He cupped her. He moved his hand in stirring little circles, his dark gaze watching the sweat bead her upper lip. Her eyes were closed, her red-blond lashes glimmering like gold upon her flushed cheeks. Her neck had arched back and she had surrendered herself to his touch completely, with a fresh, guileless greed that squeezed his chest.

Her knees came up, her thighs spreading even farther, letting him in even deeper. He dipped in one finger, then two, feeling her unbelievably moist core. She contracted around him and it was too much.

He was a man, only a man and it had been so long.... He wanted her legs around his waist. He wanted himself impaled in her, moving in her, dying in her.

Too much sentiment. Not enough logic. What had happened to his control? To hell with it all.

He swept his body over hers, his mouth closing upon her lips, suckling her tongue. Her arms swept around his shoulders, her legs settled around his waist and he was lost.

One smooth thrust and he rent her asunder.

She stiffened immediately, her body suddenly rigid, her nails sinking into his back. She was tight, too tight.

"Relax," he whispered tightly and stroked her hip. "Relax, sweetheart. Trust me."

He heard her breath released as a sigh. Her body sank around him, becoming supple and pliable. He stroked her hip again and then again until he felt the last of the tension leave her and the pain washed from her face to be filled with slow wonder.

"Yes," he murmured. "Like that."

He moved slowly, gritting his teeth with the effort, fighting his own impulses and desperate, maniacal need. She was so tight and so moist. Hot and burning and she was killing him, absolutely killing him, and he was defenseless against it.

His eyes closed. He couldn't bear to look at her anymore, he couldn't bear to think. "You give me too much," he whispered and sank into her as deep as he could go.

She sighed his name and urged him deeper.

His hips rolled, small rocking motions that slowly built the tempo. Her breathing increased its pace and he heard her first gasp as the pleasure overrode reason. He arched his hips back and her legs tightened around him instinctively and thrust him back into her body.

His neck corded. His teeth bared and his biceps bulged and suddenly the pace was out of his control. It was fast and urgent and he wanted the release so badly that for a suspended beat of time, he couldn't find it. It was too much, too grand, too brilliant, too overwhelming for one man to take. It would shatter him and he hated being shattered. It would stand out forever in his mind and he resented the binds that memory forged.

None of that mattered. Maggie cried out his name, then screamed her release and he did shatter. Into a million sharp, glittering shards, his body combusted. His head fell forward. His hips collapsed into hers and he buried his lips against her throat and shuddered and shuddered and shuddered against her body.

He whispered her name. She held him even tighter and everything was all right.

Chapter 12

Seven-fifteen a.m.

The battered blue '79 pickup truck rumbled along the road, the fan belt held on by baling twine but the tires brand-new and bought just for this trip. It was a Chevrolet, of course—you should always buy American. On the left of the rear bumper a sticker proclaimed, My definition of gun control is hitting the target with every shot. On the right a second sticker emphasized, You can have my gun when you pry it out of my cold, dead hand.

Since Abraham Cannon had always believed talk was cheap, he backed up both stickers with a gun rack sporting two rifles in the cab of his truck. The gun rack was also new; he'd carved it with his own two hands from an oak that had been hit by lightning. The grain of the wood was fine and well polished. He'd already taken offers to build several more racks for others, which didn't surprise him. He was good with his hands and he took his work seriously. In this day and age, a man had to be prepared.

Abraham was prepared now. He wore his orange hunter's

vest over a khaki T-shirt and desert camouflage pants. His utility belt held an army knife, compass, waterproof matches and rudimentary first-aid kit complete with needle and thread should a man have to stitch up a wound—which he'd done twice, as one scar on his lower left calf and one scar across his chin proved. Above the stiff leather of his steel-toed combat boots he'd strapped his hunting knife.

In addition to the two rifles sitting in his gun rack, he carried a sawed-off shotgun beneath his seat and a cross-bow on the seat beside him. The crossbow was his weapon of choice and he was one of the best shots in Idaho. He'd the eyes of an eagle and steady hands guided by God him-self.

Abraham was not a person who harbored doubts.

Now he listened to the police scanner on his CB with half his attention, while the other half minded the road. Cool morning, damp morning, but the sun was coming out now and the water steaming off the pavement in a beautiful, misty display. It was too brown here, a little too stark for a man who loved mountains. But the red hills carried their own beauty and it was all God's land.

The scanner crackled to life.

Heading westbound on I-26, Abraham paused on the lonely highway and listened with full attention. His face didn't change. His lips never moved.

Finally, after two minutes of listening, he simply nodded to himself.

Seven-eighteen a.m.

He picked up the pace. He'd catch 395 south to I-20 and head to Bend. He didn't think he'd have to get that far. No doubt, he'd meet Cain somewhere in between.

A man had to do what a man had to do.

Especially in war.

"It's time to move."

Cain spoke softly, but his voice was firm. Lying beside him, Maggie nodded against the white pillow but didn't meet his gaze. Instead, she was staring at his hand with rapt attention. She'd splayed his fingers, turning his hand palm up. Now she pressed her own hand against him, her pale skin stunning against his dark complexion, her delicate fingers emphasized by his long, strong digits and thick ridges of yellow calluses. His hand dwarfed hers. It looked as if his grip should crush the fine structure of her bones or snap her wrist. But he wouldn't do something like that, which they both knew.

He wanted to touch her hair. He wanted to draw down her head and kiss her full, swollen lips once more. He wanted to feel her pulse begin to pound at the base of her graceful throat and listen to her sigh his name.

His gaze returned to her hand, so tiny and delicate and entwined so trustingly in his own. His chest tightened. His throat thickened.

And he felt it all over again, that primal urge to roll her onto her back, to slide into her body and make her his. It was crazy, but he wanted her as powerfully as a man could want a woman. He wanted her to be his in every blatantly chauvinistic sense of the word. He would walk down the streets with his arm around her shoulders so the world would know she was his girl. He would buy her dinner so he could watch the wine redden her cheeks and the food bring delight to her eyes. He would build her a home, give her anything she desired. He would protect her with his body and give his last breath to keep her from harm.

He would give her every part of him, body, heart and soul.

If he had been in the position to give her such things at all.

He repeated quietly, "It's time to move."

She looked up at last. "I love your body," she said simply.

He rolled out of the bed, his body already hard and his hands in fists at his sides. If he'd thought he was strong before, he realized now how weak he could be. And he wasn't a man who could afford weaknesses.

He stole a glance at the bedside clock. Big red numbers glowed 7:22 a.m. They were still nearly 150 miles from Idaho, with no immediate means of transportation. While Maggie's shopping venture had saved them prep time, they'd also stayed in bed twenty-two minutes longer than scheduled. They needed to get moving.

Once they were in Idaho, he could let Maggie go. She would be safe from Ham. Cain would return to the mountains he knew better than his own hands, and he would be safe for a bit, too. In the open, he was vulnerable. In the mountains, there was nothing he couldn't do.

"We leave in fifteen minutes," he said, not looking at her because the image of her lounging on the bed wearing only her tangled red hair was too potent. He picked up his mud-encrusted jeans.

Behind him, he heard the rustle of her finally sitting up on the bed.

"Do you want to have children?" she asked curiously.

His hand immediately froze with his jeans pulled halfway up. "Not today," he said at last, his voice surprisingly steady.

"I'd like to have four," she continued unperturbed, finally crawling out of bed and reaching for her underwear. "I used to think two, but really I would like to have four. One is too lonely. I hated being an only child. I wanted Stephanie to have other children, but she said she'd already sacrificed enough of her figure to have me. I thought I would be alone forever, then one day Maxmillian was gone, and Stephanie was telling me I had two brothers. Actually, she always refers to them as my half brothers. But how can you be half a brother? Are you the right half or the left half? The top half or the bottom half? They're just my brothers, and I'm their sister. I also have three step-siblings from Stephanie's later marriages, but they're still young children. I'm never sure what to call them. I mean the marriage made them my step-siblings, so does the divorce make them strangers? Or once you are a step-sibling are you always a step-sibling?''

"I don't know,'' Cain said slowly. He finished pulling on his jeans.

"I've never figured it out myself,'' Maggie confessed. From the corner of his eye, Cain saw her reach into one of her shopping bags and pull out two T-shirts. The larger of them she tossed to him, the other she yanked down over her head. It was ridiculously large on her petite frame, falling to the edge of her skirt. But even then, she still looked appealing.

Her hands went to work braiding her long hair. "When I was ten,'' she said conversationally as he belatedly returned to dressing himself, "I used to try and keep track of everyone. Stephanie had married Crandall then, and he had a baby girl from his first marriage named Charise. I got to hold her one weekend when her mother brought her. She was so beautiful and so adorable. I told Brandon and C.J. all about her, and they agreed we'd let her into our little group and when she was old enough she'd spend her summers on the farm as well. But next winter, Crandall had been kicked out and Charise was just gone. She and her mother lived in France and there was no reason for her mother to arrange for me to see her baby daughter. I sent gifts for a while on her birthday, but she never understood who I was and I didn't know how to explain it either. When Stephanie remarried the third time, I swore I'd be smarter but I wasn't. That man had twin boys, little five-year-old boys. Vincent and Brian. Cutest little kids. I'm not sure where they live now.''

"It's not easy to keep track of people,'' Cain said. He finished tucking in the T-shirt, looking at her warily and wishing he could follow her train of thought. She didn't appear sad, just matter-of-fact. "Why does this come to mind now?''

"I just wanted to tell you.''

He remained watching her silently. Her blue eyes finally swept up, peering at him through her shiny red hair.

"Family can be so confusing," she said quietly. "At least it is for me. So many stepparents, step-siblings, and half siblings passing through. It will never get easier, either. Marriage may not be forever, but divorce certainly is. One day I'll be a half aunt to children who will also have full aunts and maybe half aunts and full aunts on the other side of the family as well. That's a lot of aunts. Then there's the matter of grandparents. I have two sets, but my children would probably have three—four if my father was still alive. Three to four sets of grandmas and grandpas. On holidays, where do you go? Who do you visit?

"It's very complicated, you see. When I was little I got very anxious about it. I used to hold tea parties with my stuffed animals, each one named after one of my brothers or sisters who had moved away. And then I would cry because I thought that's the only contact I would ever have with all these children—stuffed animals bearing their names. But Lydia told me family was family and everything could be figured out. I want to figure it out, Cain. I want to get married someday even if my parents' marriages never worked out. I want to have children and give them a home and traditions like Lydia gave me. I want to unite all my step-siblings and introduce them to my half brothers. And maybe I'll start a tradition of Christmas week, and every two days will be spent with a new set of grandparents so everyone can see everyone because that's what the holidays are all about. And I'll get C.J. and Brandon to do it too, even if they grumble and pretend they're too tough for holidays.

"I want to do all these things. And I thought you should know about them because someday, I want to do them with you."

His body went very still. He thought he should say something but his mind remained perfectly blank. He could not think, he could not move. He just stood there in the middle of the room.

And he thought she was the most beautiful person he'd ever known. So many reasons to be bitter, yet there wasn't a bitter bone in her body. So many reasons to be tough and cynical, yet she remained warm and generous and determined to save everyone. She tried so hard and the world was running out of people who were willing to try.

"Cain?" she whispered after a moment, sounding vulnerable.

He forced himself to focus. "I…I hope someday you do all that you dream of, Maggie," he said at last. His voice was hoarse, so he cleared it and tried again. "But I don't think it will be with me," he finished quietly.

Her blue eyes grew luminescent. "You don't care about me?"

He opened his mouth to agree but found he couldn't look into those eyes and lie. "I have nothing to give you," he amended at last.

"I don't remember asking for anything."

"Love isn't free," he said levelly. "You of all people should know that. It requires commitment, time, care. I'm running from the law. I could be running a long time. I may never get free. I won't bind you to that, Maggie. That wouldn't be love."

She stared at him a suspended moment. "No," she agreed at last. "But the fact that you don't want to bind me to your problems—that's love."

He didn't deny it. He didn't agree with it. He just looked at her and she looked back at him, and it was simply there between them, something thick, nearly tangible, but too fragile for words.

He thought, Please, oh please, don't let Ham figure out what she means to me.

Cain picked up her locket where it lay in a gold puddle

on the floor. He placed it in her palm and wrapped her fingers around it. "You should keep it. Now gather your things. We need to leave."

"Good enough," she whispered, then added, "For now."

He didn't say anything. Instead he thought of the prison bars and the way they sounded as they closed, *kchink, kchink.*

The sound of regret, he thought now. The sound of someone who had made one too many mistakes.

Maggie looked over her shoulder once, then twice. There was still no one in sight.

"Okay," she whispered, though her tone still held a faint edge of mutiny. "Now."

One sharp downward blow and Cain popped open the ignition of stolen vehicle number three. He moved fast and quick beneath the canvas top of the Jeep, but Maggie was no longer impressed.

She'd wanted to buy an old junk car rather than steal another vehicle from some poor, innocent person. Cain, however, had pointed out that you generally needed ID to purchase automobiles, plus you had to fill out paperwork. All of that could be used to track them down.

So could a stolen vehicle, she'd countered.

Yes, he'd agreed. But stealing a vehicle was faster and a lot less bureaucratic.

So they were on the road again, this time in a Jeep.

Cain relaxed visibly once they were back on highway 20. It was just after eight and there wasn't much traffic. No sign of cops, no sign of pursuers. The pavement was still wet but drying fast beneath the warm embrace of a bright spring sun.

Maggie studied Cain for a while beneath the cover of her lashes. And then, because she couldn't help herself, she reached over, touched his cheek and smiled.

"You're ridiculously happy for a hostage." His lips were curving as well.

"Must be the company I'm keeping."

He grinned at her, and for a moment everything was all right.

She put back the top, letting in the cool spring air and scent of rain. The wind tangled through her braid. The sun caught her hair and lit it on fire. She leaned back against the seat, closing her eyes and tilting up her cheeks to the clear blue sky.

Big fluffy clouds looked like wads of fresh cotton. The distant tops of verdant mountains offered a beckoning horizon. Everything smelled spicy, fresh and green.

She thought it was a beautiful day.

Cain spotted the cop car first. It wasn't behind them. Actually, it was heading right toward them, barreling westbound in one hell of a hurry. Automatically Cain's grip tightened on the wheel.

"Remain calm," he muttered. Maggie wasn't sure if he was speaking to himself or to her. They were just coming up on signs for 395 north, and they were the only vehicle on the road.

She sat a little straighter, watching the police car take shape. As it grew on the horizon, dust and waves of heat shimmered behind it.

"Do you think he'll recognize us?" she whispered.

Cain glanced at her, then at the canvas top she'd pulled back. "Your hair," he said simply.

Her hands fingered the bright red strands self-consciously. Then with a belated flurry of movement, she grabbed the baseball cap from his head and stuck it on her own just as the cop car went flying by.

"What do you think?" she demanded to know, twisting in her seat to watch the brown vehicle whiz past.

She had her answer in less than five seconds. The brake lights lit up, the tires came to a screeching halt. Dust abruptly flew and rubber burned as the cop did a lumbering 180 and headed back toward them.

Cain wasted his breath on one succinct word, then the wail of sirens cut through the morning.

"Hang on," he called to Maggie, and pressed down hard on the gas.

She grabbed the roll bar above her head, her other hand holding the cap on her thick hair as the compact Jeep sprang forward like a well-trained beast.

Cain didn't fool around. The turnoff for 395 came and he took it, the cop car right on their heels. Its engine was more powerful. Cain was more desperate.

He watched the car come closer and closer, thought of all the buddies the cop must be calling on the radio. He wanted to swear more, he wanted to curse.

He had to remain focused.

"Maggie," he called above raging sirens, "do you trust me?"

"What?" she yelled back.

"I said, do you trust me?"

"Of course!"

"Good!" He cranked the wheel hard.

One minute they were burning up asphalt, the next minute they hit sagebrush and the little Jeep was airborne. They hit the dirt hard, moist earth and crackling brush cushioning the jarring blow and momentarily wrestling with the tires for traction. This time, the Jeep proved more stubborn than the mud and the vehicle leaped sluggishly forward.

The cop car followed, sirens growing louder as it, too, hit the air. It landed with a choking screech and the engine groaned loudly as the mud grabbed hard.

Maggie risked a look back. This close she could see the cop's face clearly, old and leathered beneath his brown hat as he leaned forward, putting his body behind his urging. The heavier vehicle remained stuck, though.

Maggie didn't have time to gloat. As the Jeep jostled and bounced her like a rubber toy, she saw the sheriff pop open his door and climb out of his vehicle. Then she saw him place the rifle against his shoulder and level it steadily.

"Cain, look out!" she screamed.

Gunshot cracked the sky, echoing in the vast sky and ringing in her ears. She flinched and ducked, losing her hold on the roll bar and almost getting bounced out of the vehicle. Cain simply tucked his head against his chest, not relinquishing his hold on the wheel even for gunfire. Another shot rang out, then another.

She heard the melodious tinkle of a rear light shattering, then the sharp thud of a bullet burying itself in the back fender.

"Faster!" she cried. "Faster!"

"No kidding!"

Then abruptly the ground opened up beneath them. One minute they were bouncing along, staring at flatland, the next they realized how much the horizon had fooled them. The ravine gaped open. They went sailing into the air.

Maggie had one moment to grab the dash. The Jeep plunged into the narrow ravine, burying its nose against the mud wall and ending with a whimper.

She went flying forward. The dashboard was very friendly.

Everything went black.

"Open your mouth for me, Maggie. That's it." Her cracked lips parted on command and sweet, thick juice trickled between them. Orange juice, she thought dimly, and drank deeply.

At the last minute, the liquid disappeared. She heard a faint groan of protest, then realized it was her own. Her eyes reluctantly cracked open.

She was sprawled out on the seat of the crumpled Jeep. Cain loomed above her, his face pale and grim as he looked down at her. She blinked a few more times and his body stopped wavering sickeningly.

"How do you feel?" he asked quietly, the concern obvious in his voice. He reached down and brushed back her hair once, then twice, then three times. Finally, he settled for keeping his hand on her cheek.

She turned her head into his palm, wincing a bit from the movement. "Like I've been in a car accident," she muttered against his fingertips. "And you?"

"The same."

Belatedly, she hefted herself to sitting. Her head hurt. She could feel a nice-sized lump growing on her forehead. But she still had two arms and two legs which functioned on command. She twisted at the waist, grimacing a bit.

"How long was I unconscious?"

"A few minutes."

"Is the cop coming?"

"I imagine we'll have all sorts of company shortly."

"Oh." She looked up at him miserably. "I'm sorry," she said automatically.

His lips curved, almost tenderly. "It's not your fault. I knew from the beginning that escape was a long shot. Do you think you can walk?"

"Yes, of course." She could walk. She could dance on a tightrope if he would just keep looking at her like that.

He hopped down from the Jeep, clutching the bag of their meager supplies in one hand. She followed more gingerly, but the wooziness was clearing rapidly. She must not have hit her head that hard after all.

Then she realized for the first time that he was limping.

"You hurt your leg!"

"Yes."

She scurried around to the left side of him, and her eyes widened. It was hard to tell, given the already disreputable shape of his jeans, but a wet stain appeared to be spreading along his thigh. "Cain, you're really injured!"

"I checked it out. It's not much."

She didn't believe him for a minute. He finally arched a single brow. "Do you know first aid, Maggie?"

She shook her head.

"If it is seriously injured, is there anything you can do about it?"

Once again she shook her head.

"Then its condition is moot. Even if it's serious, there's nothing we can do about it."

"We can sit here and rest!"

"I'm sure the police would appreciate that." He continued walking along the floor of the shallow ravine, looking around himself and assessing the situation with his cool gaze.

Maggie scowled at him, but she didn't know how to make him stop.

"I wonder how far this goes," Cain murmured out loud.

"What?"

"The ravine. My guess is that helicopters will be brought in shortly. The land here is fairly flat. So the ravine could come in handy, such as it is."

Maggie understood his point. The ravine was only about six feet deep and ten feet wide, more like a gully carved out by rushing water. But its top was obscured by thick, tangled brush, helping hide their progress, and it did appear to be long, snaking around so that they couldn't see the end, just rich red dirt where it twisted around another corner.

"Do you really think we can make it on foot?" she asked.

Cain didn't reply, but his lips got very tight.

And she knew it then, as he must have known it all along. He wasn't going to make it. They'd been spotted and they were now on foot. In probably less than thirty minutes the area would be crawling with state troopers, county sheriffs and miscellaneous bounty hunters. They'd bring in helicopters, they'd bring in dogs.

Cain was smart, probably as smart as Brandon. And he was strong, probably as strong as C.J. But he was still just a man.

The police would find them. She would be "liberated" and Cain...oh, Cain.

"You're not going to do anything rash, are you?"

He still didn't reply.

"Getting yourself shot rather than going back to jail would be pretty stupid," she said more vehemently.

"No one will know the truth if I'm dead," he said at last, his voice perfectly expressionless.

That scared her. Tucked away in the cool shadows of the ravine, she wrapped her arms around her waist.

"Keep walking, Maggie."

So she did.

They heard the first sound of helicopters after twenty minutes, the pounding beat of blades almost deafening. Cain didn't say anything. Instead, he halted and turned back to her long enough to brusquely tuck her red braid inside her T-shirt. The black baseball cap he pressed lower on her head, momentarily pushing loose tendrils behind her ears.

His face was expressionless, but she could see the strain etched in the corners of his eyes and the grim set of his mouth. His green eyes were determined, but she could see fatigue there as well and hints of pain. His steps had grown more labored.

She reached out her hand toward his chest, but he intercepted it in midair. His fingers closed around her wrist, gentle but firm. He replaced her hand at her side, his gaze level on hers.

Then he turned away from her, and without ever saying a word, raised the camouflaged hunting jacket over his own head to disguise his blond hair.

He resumed walking and, after a tortured moment, she followed.

The helicopters came and went. Once Maggie thought she heard barking, but the sound seemed very far away and things were distorted by the tunnel shape of the ravine. The barking never got closer, or the shouts of men. The ravine led them deeper and deeper around, until Maggie no longer knew which direction they were even headed, though they seemed to be headed up. She had the ridiculous thought that they would miraculously emerge in the courthouse in downtown Portland where all this madness had started.

Abruptly, she bumped into Cain. Only then did she become aware that he'd stopped walking.

Puzzled, she peered around his arm, and her eyes suddenly grew round.

They were on the top of a hill and beneath them, far enough away that the people looked like ants, an entire town had popped up in the middle of wild-running tumbleweeds. Even from this distance, Maggie could count four cop cars and a number of pickup trucks.

She turned to Cain. "Uh-oh," she said weakly.

His lips curved tightly. She realized for the first time that his face was dangerously pale. Her gaze flew down to his thigh. The stain had grown to unbelievable proportions.

"Oh, my God," she whispered. Her eyes bounced back up to his face. "Why didn't you tell me?"

"There's nothing you could do," he said, but then his bravado left him and he leaned heavily against the mud wall.

"Sit," she commanded, panic releasing her vocal cords and lending strength to her hands. "Now!"

He sagged down to the ground without further protest, and for a moment she was terrified that he'd passed out cold. But then his head tilted back drunkenly, his green eyes definitely worn. "Now what, Miss Nightingale?"

"A tourniquet," she determined.

"A tourniquet would cut off all circulation and I might lose my whole leg."

She blinked rapidly. She was a marriage counselor, for crying out loud, what did she know about these things? "Do you know what to do then?" she asked in an agonized voice. "Just tell me, Cain, and I'll do it."

"I want you to go down into that town."

"And get a doctor? I'll do it!"

The silence lengthened. "Sure," he said belatedly, too belatedly.

Her eyes narrowed. She sank back on her heels and regarded him warily. "What's going on, Cain?"

"Maggie, I know you'll disagree, but I think it's time for us to part company."

"You're damn right I disagree!"

"It's not your problem."

"Oh, don't give me that!"

His eyes abruptly fired to life. Color rose in his cheeks and his chin came up furiously. She'd thought he was weakened, but his hand snapped around her wrist with all the ferocity of a healthy, well-conditioned male.

"I'm in trouble, Maggie. We both know that. I'll go down, but I go down on my own. I don't take anyone with me. I don't take you with me."

"I'm not leaving you alone. Not injured and tired and—"

Her words were cut off as he abruptly dragged her forward. She fell across his lap, knowing she must be hurting his leg and trying to get a hand out to support herself. But he pinned her against his hard chest with his arms, his lips now just an inch from hers, his eyes blazing into her.

"This is the only thing I'll ever ask of you," he whispered fiercely.

"And I won't do it!" she cried back. Her eyes pleaded with him to understand, to realize just how much she loved him and that she couldn't abandon someone she loved.

For one moment, she saw the strain again. She saw his pain, she saw his fatigue. And then his spine stiffened and he became relentless.

"Swear to me you'll walk away and never look back."

"No!"

"Swear to me you'll walk away and never look back."

"No!"

"Swear to me, Maggie, that you will walk away and never look back."

"I can't do that! I can't leave you!"

"You have to, Maggie. It's the only thing I'll ever truly need you to do."

And those words hurt her. They lacerated her heart and filled her chest with a fiery red ache. The tears welled up. Her lower lip trembled when she wanted so badly to be composed.

"Don't do this to me," she whispered. "Don't hurt me like this when I love you so much. Cain..."

His composure snapped. The steadiness left his gaze and for one moment, he looked furious. And then his lips swooped down. He kissed her, he kissed her hard. And it was wild and raw and aching. It told her everything, how much he needed her, how much he wanted her. How much she'd managed to touch him in just twenty-four hours when he couldn't afford to be touched.

He consumed her mouth as he wanted to consume her, and her tears spilled over and ran down her cheeks. She kissed him back as savagely as he kissed her and wept against his face.

Just as suddenly his hands bracketed her cheeks and forced her head back harshly.

"*Go!*" he whispered fiercely. "Run away from me and live happily ever after. Find your brothers because they will keep you safe. Unite your step-siblings. Be happy."

He paused, then his green eyes grew brighter. Her breath died in her throat and she was pinned by those fiery eyes.

"Someday," he promised lowly, "someday, Maggie, if this is all behind me, I will find you. Wherever you are I will find you and I will throw myself at your feet and give you my life. I swear it!"

"I love you," she cried helplessly. "I love you, I love you, I love you."

And for his answer, he pushed her away from him so hard she stumbled and fell against the dirt. He pointed once more at the town, his whole arm shaking with the emotion. "*Go!*"

"All right!" she agreed at last. Her chest was laboring now, her hair red and tangled around her cheeks. She lurched drunkenly to her feet, swaying as she fought to breathe through the tightness in her chest. She knew what he was doing. Knew he was just trying to protect her, and dammit, she didn't need to be protected! Not anymore.

"I'll leave. But I'm coming back and you can't stop me. I'm going to trot right down into that town. I'm going to tell them all you're headed in the opposite direction. And then I'm grabbing a medical kit and coming right back up here. So don't you move. You want to talk about trust? Well, trust me to come back to you. Trust *me*, dammit!"

"Do what you have to do." His voice was tight, his hands clenched into fists at his sides.

"I will, thank you very much." She spared one glance at her watch. It read eleven-fifteen. "Give me one hour," she said curtly. "One hour and I'll be back."

Not waiting for his nod, she squared her shoulders, focused her gaze at that town and headed straight out into the blazing sun.

Cain remained seated on the floor of the ravine, watching her saunter down the hillside as proud and vibrant as Joan of Arc going to war. Two helicopters swooped down. The ant-sized officers rushed forward up the hill to meet her.

She kept walking, her gaze forward and her shoulders level as minutes passed until finally she, too, grew small and distant.

God, she was magnificent.

And his gaze swept over the growing crowd of men around her, trying hard to make out faces and identify the one face that still haunted his dreams. The cops closed in on her, accepted her, no doubt hammered the poor hostage with questions.

Still no Ham. Cain finally allowed himself to breathe.

The police had her now. She was the rescued hostage and there was nothing to indicate any other relationship.

Her brothers would probably be with her shortly. She'd spoken highly of them. Surely they would keep her safe.

Cain needed to know that she would be safe.

The crowd grew too thick. She disappeared at last from sight. Her twenty-four hours of adventure were over, and civilization had swallowed her up once more.

"Remember me, Maggie," he whispered as he sat in the red mud of the ravine. "Maybe that's the only other thing I'll ever need you to do. Remember me." *And I'll remember you. For all the days, weeks and months to come.*

He heaved himself awkwardly to his feet. His wound wasn't as bad as he'd made it out to be—he'd figured it would take near death to get Maggie to leave his side. But the gash was still tight. He could feel his thigh throb hot and angry with each step. He could walk; he had no other choice.

Maggie was safe, his first mission accomplished. And now he had other business to attend to.

Chapter 13

"Brandon! C.J.!"

Detective McDougal was in the middle of yet another of his "very important, downright critical questions," but Maggie didn't care. She bounded out of her seat as if it had been suddenly electrified and flew across the room.

Four steps and she leaped full-bodied into Brandon's open embrace, wrapping her arms around his neck and burying her cheek against his shoulder. Immediately his arms were around her, holding her as if she were the most precious person on earth, and as if simply she was eight again and he was twelve and together they could survive anything.

Her cheeks were suddenly damp. She thought she felt his shoulders shake. Oh, she felt bad that he'd been so worried about her, but it was good to see him again. Him and C.J. The three of them back together again. They could do anything.

She forced herself to pull back long enough to hurtle

herself into C.J.'s arms, hearing him grunt on impact. Then his well-toned arms caught her in a giant bear hug.

"Ah, kid," he murmured. "You scared the daylights outta me."

For her response, Maggie held him even tighter. Only slowly did she become aware of the third person discreetly clearing his throat.

She pulled back reluctantly, already wiping at her eyes. Brandon, impeccably clad in a charcoal-gray suit, was studying the floor and trying to pretend moisture didn't suddenly stain his sun-beaten cheeks. His face was grim and much leaner than she remembered. Wearing his usual faded jeans and loose cotton shirt, C.J. was grinning—he was always grinning—but his eyes appeared suspiciously moist as well.

Then her gaze came to rest on the new face that had appeared between her brother and cousin. Joel. Joel Epstein. She remembered those dark, burning eyes from the TV. How much he must have suffered. She wanted to grab his hands and tell him it would all be over soon. Cain would take care of everything.

Just as soon as she helped take care of Cain.

She summoned a smile to her face, shook Joel's hand as introductions were made and began guiding him toward the door. "So nice to meet you. Come back in ten minutes. Detective McDougal?" She began herding him briskly as well.

The men in the room exchanged startled glances.

"Miss Ferringer, we still have quest—"

"Of course you do. In a minute." The detective's mouth gaped, then he worked it a few times like a fish. Maggie gave up on benign smiles and stamped her foot.

"Excuse me," she declared in the most chastising voice possible, "but I have just been held prisoner by an escaped murderer for twenty-four hours. I'm exhausted, filthy, bruised and no doubt suffering from shock. All I want is ten minutes alone with my beloved brothers! Is that so much to ask for! *Is it?*"

Her voice rose to just the right fever pitch at the end. The room cleared in a hurry.

"Of course, ma'am."

"Sorry, ma'am."

"Let us know if you need anything, ma'am."

"Yes, yes, yes," she assured them and practically slammed the door of the room behind them. She turned immediately to C.J. and Brandon, both of whom were frowning.

"Are you all right?" Brandon asked immediately. His blue eyes skimmed down her intently, wanting to ensure that all was well with his baby sister.

She dismissed his concern with a wave of her hand. "Of course. How are you? And where have you been these days?"

"Indonesia. I'm fine." His gaze was still narrow and his brow furrowed. "Are you *sure* you're all right?"

"Indonesia?" She looked at him with genuine shock. "That's where Max's plane crashed. Brandon, what have you been up to?"

"Nothing." He turned to C.J. abruptly, but C.J. just shrugged.

"You're right," C.J. agreed. "She seems different. And what were you doing in Indonesia? I don't remember you saying you were going to Indonesia."

Brandon ignored C.J.'s question as well, returning his frowning expression to Maggie. "Are you *sure* you're all right? He didn't try...anything, did he? He didn't hurt you?"

"I'm fine," she said brusquely, then opened her mouth to launch her attack.

C.J. interrupted her at the pass. "If I didn't know better," C.J. said abruptly to Brandon, "I'd say she found a man."

"Hey!" She was flustered now. "What do you mean, 'if I didn't know better'? Why can't I find a man?" Then she gave up and decided this was as good an opening as she was going to get. "Fine then. I found the perfect man."

"Congratulations!" C.J. said immediately, clearly surprised, which didn't improve her mood. Abruptly, his eyes narrowed and she could see the pieces clicking into place as he realized what she had just said and whom she had spent the past twenty-four hours with. "Wait a second—"

"Maggie!" Brandon exclaimed. "What did he do? Why, that filthy—"

"Stop it!" she shouted at the top of her lungs. "Just stop it!"

And when their jaws quietly dropped to the floor at such a display of spirit from their meek little Maggie, she raised her chin haughtily and stared at them with all the blazing defiance of a Hathaway Red. "Cain's innocent," she declared in her most authoritative voice. "In fact, right now he's being pursued by his older brother, Abraham, who actually committed the crime. And if we don't help him, he'll never survive to tell the truth."

She leveled them with an impatient stare, waiting for them to hop to it.

Brandon said quietly, "You've been through a horrible ordeal, Maggie."

"I'm going to kill him," C.J. supplied, his tone a bit more succinct.

She stared at them both incredulously. "Haven't you heard a word I said?"

"Of course. But we know you have a soft heart," C.J. said soothingly. "It's something I've always admired about you. But we all know it can be too soft—"

"Not this time!"

"Maggie, you once stopped picking strawberries because you thought the pulling motion was too painful for the vines."

"I was nine!"

"And you won't enter the meat section of the grocery store."

"Well, that truly is barbaric!"

"You won't even buy a down comforter!"

"I don't want to have a bunch of geese running around naked because of me!"

"Maggie," Brandon interjected in an exasperated tone of voice, "if you ever met the devil wandering the streets, you'd take him home, fix him dinner and offer him his choice of rooms. Worse, you'd give him your soul for free the first time he wrung his hands and said 'pretty please.' And we all know it!"

"Cain is not the devil, Brandon. And how would you know anyway? You've never met the man."

C.J. and Brandon both took deep breaths. She surprised them, however, by regrouping quickly and launching a counterattack.

"Who said they would always be there for me?" she demanded.

"We're here!" they both exclaimed.

"Oh yes, and a nice job of saving me you did, too. You're here because I had you paged!" They both looked immediately abashed and C.J.'s grin had slipped into a dark scowl. "And now I am asking you for help and instead of listening to me you're treating me to a walloping dose of patronizing anecdotes. I won't stand for it!" She wagged her finger at them in a fine impersonation of their grandmother. "I have always been there for you, I have always trusted you. I put up with you, Brandon, though you jet around the globe, are impossible to find and are scaring the living daylights out of all of us with your strange, Max-like behavior. I put up with you, C.J., though I know perfectly well you do more than just run a bar in Sedona and your weakness for troubled women and lost causes will probably keep you from living to a ripe old age. Now I'm asking you two to do the same for me. And you can either sit down, shut up and listen, or turn around and walk out that door. But one way or another, I'm going to help Cain.

"*And* you're going to be very nice to him when you

finally meet him or I'll leak to the press how the brilliant millionaire Brandon Ferringer once got sprayed down by a skunk as you tried to sneak up on it because you'd read somewhere that you could catch and sell them. I believe we even have a lovely picture of you standing buck naked on the patio while Grandma dumped tomato juice over your head." She whirled on C.J. "Then I'll describe how a big strong Marine like you used to run screaming from butterflies because Brandon told you they were genetically engineered vampire bats. I'm sure photos can be arranged."

Brandon and C.J. remained suspended for a moment, exchanging cornered glances.

"I liked her better when she was my little sister," Brandon murmured.

"I think she's gone and grown up on us," C.J. agreed.

"If he hurts her, you know what we'll have to do to him."

"Oh, yeah." C.J. shrugged philosophically. "But I think now we have to let her have the first crack at him. She's not too bad, you know. When she scowls, she looks just like you."

Brandon blinked startled eyes at that. Maggie beamed proudly. "So you're in?"

"Of course," Brandon grumbled. He gave her another once-over, then submitted with a sigh. "You know we worry about you."

"I know," she said quietly. "Maybe I've let you worry too much. Maybe it's time for me to stop letting you fight my wars."

"Maggie, you know we don't see it like that—"

She held up a silencing hand, then gave up and stepped forward enough to catch her brother's hand. "But I saw it like that, Brandon. *I* did. And now I'm twenty-seven years old and I want to stand on my own two feet. I know you still don't believe me, but Cain is innocent. Once you've spoken to him, once you realize what kind of man he is, you'll know he couldn't have committed murder. You'll like him, Brandon. He's so much like you.''

"You've only known him for twenty-four hours," Brandon warned softly.

Her expression settled. She looked at him levelly. "And how long did you know Julia before you realized she was the one?"

His face tightened spasmodically, that ache slashing through his eyes and hurting her because she knew she'd inflicted the pain by mentioning Julia's name. Maggie had never seen Brandon happier than the day he'd stood at the altar with the sassy, irreverent Julia at his side. And she'd never seen him so lost as the day he stood shell-shocked beside his lovely wife's grave.

He didn't say anything now. She hadn't thought that he would. But his fingers squeezed hers and that was enough.

She turned enough for her gaze to include C.J. "All right," she said quietly. "We need a plan."

The sky was growing dark when Maggie and C.J. crept back up the hillside. It was only two o'clock, but storm clouds were gathering and another spring downpour seemed imminent. They'd sent Brandon into town to purchase supplies, including any surveillance equipment possible. In the meantime, Maggie and C.J. had retrieved the field first-aid kit C.J. had brought with him from the trunk of the rental car and they were off to find Cain. Of course, C.J. had suggested he go alone and Maggie attend to some vague duty such as "keeping others occupied." She'd set him straight in a hurry—she was going up that hill to help Cain.

There weren't many officers to keep busy anymore anyway. Most were merrily encircling Bend after Maggie had told them Cain planned backtracking and holing up for a spell. Only Joel and Detective McDougal remained, and that was because ostensibly they had more questions for Maggie. She'd informed them she needed a nap first and she would come find them when she woke up. Really, these covert activities weren't as difficult as she would have guessed.

Now, the stark red hillside was barren and quiet. The wind whipped at her cheeks, pressing the light cotton of her new khaki pants against her legs. The black baseball cap covered her hair and she still wore the too-big T-shirt, though Brandon had brought fresh clothes for her. The cap and T-shirt tied her to Cain, and she didn't want to lose those ties.

C.J. paused in front of her, finally twisting his flattened body enough to peer back at her.

"I think I see the ravine. Is he armed?"

"Yes."

"Is he going to shoot me?"

"Oh." She hadn't thought of that. "Maybe I should go first."

C.J.'s expression clearly stated what he thought of that idea. She ignored him and scurried forward impatiently.

"If he was going to shoot me," she informed her distrusting brother sourly, "he would've done it already."

"I don't like this," C.J. stated for the record.

"Just keep moving, MacNamara," she retorted defiantly and crept stealthily forward.

She could see the ravine now, as well. Her footsteps quickened and she would have clambered up to run if not for C.J.'s hissed warnings to keep her butt down. She kept her eyes on the ravine and slithered forward as rapidly as possible.

"Hang in there, Cain," she murmured. "I'm coming, I'm coming."

Had he passed out by now? Was he delirious from blood loss and pain? Would he forgive her for taking so long to return?

She wanted so desperately to see his face again so she'd know for herself that he was all right.

The ravine cracked open, its depths protected by an inky blackness. She glanced back one last time. C.J. was on her heels, Beretta in hand, but other than that the hillside was clear. They'd made it.

"Put the gun away," she commanded her overactive brother.

"Like hell," he informed her. "Locked, cocked and ready is the only way a Marine makes an entrance."

"Rambo," she muttered.

He grinned charmingly. "Rambo was a wimp, Maggie—an army man."

Maggie gave up on him and rolled her eyes. "Cain?" she whispered instead. "Cain?"

She thought she heard the soft echo of her voice bounce through the snaking ravine. Other than that, she heard nothing. She took another step forward, then another. C.J. was pressed to her side, his ribs against her shoulder. She could feel the tension radiate from him and see the dark shadow of the gun held poised against his chest.

"You're making me nervous," she whispered, and true to her words, her voice held an unsteady warble.

"Call his name again," C.J. ordered. Compared to her he sounded like steel.

She did. She called Cain's name again and again. She walked deeper into the ravine. She searched the shadows. She reached out her hands as if that would make him materialize once more in her arms.

But he was nowhere to be found. Nowhere at all.

"I don't understand!" she cried at last, and C.J. finally lowered his gun, wrapping his arms around her trembling shoulders instead.

"You only knew him twenty-four hours," he said softly.

She beat her fists against his hard belly. "It's not like that!" she insisted. "It's not like that at all! You don't understand. He's a good man. He's not like…"

"He's not like Max," C.J. said quietly. "At least you hoped not."

He cradled her head and she began to cry. She couldn't believe he'd left her. She'd been so sure he wouldn't do something like that. He was supposed to trust her as she trusted him.

At last, she forced herself to stand away, stubbornly wiping the tears from her cheek. "He had a good reason," she insisted tremulously. "Maybe the dogs were on his tail, or the helicopters got too close...." She looked at C.J. for confirmation. "Do you think?"

"We should go back to town, now," C.J. said quietly. "How long has it been since you've slept, Maggie?"

"I'm not leaving the area."

"Maggie—"

"I'm not leaving."

C.J. took a deep breath. "Listen, the town is just at the bottom of the hillside. We'll check into the hotel, you can get some rest, Brandon and I will continue looking for Cain." C.J. held up a hand against her automatic protest. "I swear to you Brandon and I will behave ourselves. No rampant death and destruction. We'll be perfectly nice vengeful relatives. I promise."

Maggie thought she should argue more, but suddenly the trauma and exhaustion caught up to her and she would have fallen if not for C.J.'s arm suddenly gripping her shoulder. He looked at her with so much compassion, she almost burst into tears again.

"We'll help you," he whispered and his fingers rubbed her neck lightly. "You know we'd give our eyeteeth to make you happy."

"I want to fight," she whispered soggily.

"In a few hours," he assured her. "Even G.I. Joe requires rest."

He took her hand and led her out of the ravine. The wind slapped them immediately, ripping through the stubby brush and howling its growing rage. Night seemed to have descended in just five minutes, the storm clouds reaching full boil.

C.J. shook his head once more, and when he looked at

her his eyes were knowing. "Ugly night, Maggie," he murmured. "Ugly night."

Joel paced the tiny room three more times, then gave up. He scowled at Detective McDougal, but the older man could only shrug. Maggie had said she'd ring them when she woke up, but that had been two hours ago. Of course, the poor woman was exhausted so who knew how long she'd sleep.

Joel felt more frustrated than ever before. "I'm going to Bend," he snapped at last.

Once again, McDougal shrugged. Joel was on personal time; he could go wherever the hell he chose. Still disgruntled and restless, Joel finally stalked out to his four-by-four and started up the engine.

He'd just put it in gear when the gun was pressed against his ear.

"Joel," Cain said quietly.

The young man's eyes widened in the rearview mirror, then just as abruptly his face split into a snarl.

"No!" Cain pressed the gun hard to remind the rash young man of all the things at stake. "Don't do anything stupid now. That won't help Kathy."

"Don't you say her name. You haven't the right to say her name!"

"I have more right than you think," Cain said softly. He risked a glance around the parking lot. The first fat raindrops plastered the windshield, providing him with more cover. Still, his thigh felt as if it were on fire and he was growing woozier. His original plan of running to Idaho to search for evidence had already come and gone.

Now he was down to hours and minutes. Now he was making it up as he went along and hoping he didn't pass out before it was over. He didn't want a confrontation. He didn't want to shoot his brother or any more violence. He just wanted the truth.

Heaven help him.

"Shoot me," Joel snarled from the front seat, his nostrils flared impressively with his rage. "Shoot me or get the hell out of my vehicle!"

And Cain felt the weariness press down against him. He wanted to slap this young man silly and tell him to stop being so stupid. Life was more precious than that. Survival more important. As long as you were alive, you always had a chance.

Maggie.

He kept his voice steady, though his vision was starting to swim. "I know you don't believe me, Joel, but I didn't kill Kathy. I know who did, though, and you're going to help me catch him. I'll give you justice, Joel. Grant me two hours and I will give you justice."

Joel still gnashed his teeth, but when Cain finally demanded the CB, he complied. At Cain's instructions, he issued the call code for Ham, broadcasting it over several frequencies.

Abruptly there was a click across the crackling airwaves as one of the frequencies finally found their target and Abraham responded.

"Hello, Ham," Cain said simply. "We need to talk."

"I won't talk about that bi—"

"We're not going to talk about her," Cain overrode steadily. He looked at Joel, taking in the young man's dark gaze, filled with so much rage. He thought of Ham and just how lethal his older brother could be. Knight to rook two. Winner takes all.

It was the last gambit he had. "I want to meet," he repeated. "No guns, no outsiders. Just you and me."

"I've got nothing to say—"

"Yes, you do. We're going to talk about Dad, Abraham. Dad. Because it may have taken me a bit, but I finally know everything."

Maggie left C.J. in the small lobby and walked to her room on shaking legs. The thought of sinking down into the black void of sleep was suddenly so appealing she could barely get her key into the lock.

She'd just finally slipped it in when she heard the footsteps behind.

"I'm fine, C.J.," she said reflexively and half turned to throw her overprotective brother a reassuring glance.

And for one moment, she thought the man was Cain and her gaze had already begun to melt.

But he wasn't Cain. Her gaze picked up too many discrepancies. His face was too dark and weather-beaten. His blue eyes were not calm, but glowed with a bone-deep purpose that made her shake. He was outfitted for the hunt, and in less than five seconds she realized that made her the prey.

Abraham. He had to be Abraham.

"The hostage woman," he murmured. "The police told me your hair was on fire."

He took one step forward and with a rapid move she couldn't even follow, he grabbed her arm and twisted it cruelly behind her back.

"We got an appointment," he said simply in her ear, and slapped his other hand over her mouth before she could scream. "No noise and maybe I'll let you live. Don't know yet."

He dragged her effortlessly down the hall and held her too tightly to even struggle.

C.J.'s feet popped off the coffee table in the motel lobby and hit the floor with a dull thud. "What the hell?"

His gaze peered out into the dark, dense rainfall and the two figures moving toward an old pickup truck. Visibility was shot, but there was no mistaking that red hair.

"Damn!"

He was up out of the chair and already pulling out his gun while the lobby receptionist gasped and dove for cover. Brandon picked that minute to walk down the hallway from his room, saving C.J. the inconvenience of having to break down his door.

"Move," C.J. commanded and Brandon didn't blink. He recognized the grim edge of his brother's voice and he moved.

"Cain?" Brandon yelled above the rainfall as they bolted from the lobby toward C.J.'s rental car. Both of their gazes had picked up the blue truck that was already pulling out of the parking lot.

"Who else?"

C.J. hopped into the car, gunned the engine and barely gave Brandon time to close his door. One second later and they were peeling off in pursuit, the rain hammering against their vehicle.

"I'm going to kill him," C.J. promised simply.

"Me first," Brandon murmured.

"You never used to be so bloodthirsty, Brandon."

Brandon didn't reply.

The world was spinning. Sometimes it righted itself enough for him to pinpoint the brown carpet and gold bedspread of a truly hideous motel room. But mostly the world spun and Cain was beginning to realize that his venture was truly just a pipe dream. He was going to pass out cold and that would be the end of it.

He struggled for lucidity, forcing himself to sit up in the threadbare wingback chair. He couldn't feel his left leg anymore. No more pain, just a curious numbness and pinpricks of coldness he figured were bad signs.

He'd made it here, though. He had the room registered in Ham's name so his brother would be sure to find it. He even had Joel handcuffed in the bathroom, serving as a living tape recorder of the events about to unfold since Cain didn't have the time or money for electronic devices. No doubt the junior officer was digging through the complimentary toiletry items with his toes, searching for tools to pick the handcuff lock while inventing new ways of killing Cain once he was free.

At least the pieces were assembled on the board. Cain had made it that far.

It had been two hours since he'd contacted Ham by radio. Ham had said he would need that long to get to the chosen hotel. Cain didn't know where his brother was at the time of the call to confirm that one way or the other. The two-hour delay had been painful, though, putting him at a further disadvantage. He was growing weaker and weaker. If Ham didn't get here soon, the end would be very anticlimactic. Ham breaking down the door, Cain already passed out cold.

Fight the pain. Dammit, Cain, fight it!

He placed his gun in the bedside drawer, not completely out of reach, but not conspicuous. He'd told Ham to come unarmed but didn't believe for a minute that that would be the case. Still, Cain wanted to avoid a standoff or shoot-out as long as possible. In his opinion, a hail of bullets was definitely a worst-case scenario. Whether he died or Ham died, the effect would be the same—the truth would never be told. Cain needed the truth.

But what about Ham's point of view on the subject? Cain had always done a poor job of anticipating Ham's actions. Did his older brother hate him enough to kill him? As a child, Cain had never understood why Ham seemed to resent him. After all, Ham had been the oldest son and their father's favorite. Of course, the Old Testament didn't put much stock in oldest sons, and in fact seemed to favor younger siblings. Thus Abel was chosen above Cain, Jacob over Esau, Joseph above his brothers.

But even if Ham was worried about Cain someday usurping his place, surely when Cain left the state that would have quieted such fears. Instead, Ham had come after him. Ham had hunted him down even though Cain had not spoken to him in five years. And when Ham had appeared, he'd known so much about Cain's life.

That should have been Cain's first clue.

He heard footsteps in the hallway. With a deep breath, he fought back the darkness once more and dimly managed to grasp a last hold on reality. Just a little bit longer. Just a little bit longer.

Sharp rapping on the door.

He sat up and dug his teeth into his lower lip as the pain lanced through him sharply. "It's open," he called out, his fingers squeezing the armrests for support. "Come in."

The door opened slowly. Cain was already holding himself stiffly, gritting his teeth through the swirling madness and preparing himself for Ham's lean, lanky form.

He wasn't ready at all for a pale, stumbling woman with glowing red hair.

"No," he whispered hoarsely. "Oh no."

Maggie stumbled into the room, her face drawn and frightened, her shoulders slumped. His first thought was to pretend ignorance. To dismiss Maggie out of hand as nothing more than a pawn he'd already discarded, as if he couldn't care less what happened to her.

But he took one look at her and knew Ham would never believe him. Already her face was transforming. She had simply to see him and suddenly she blossomed. Her spine stiffened, her shoulders straightened. She rose in the dimly lit room and her face took on the glowing radiance of a woman in love. This was his Maggie, the fighter, the rebel. She was probably thinking she'd dance the *lambada* in a black lace scarf to rescue him.

God, did he love her.

She did not touch him. She was not close enough to reach him. But from across the room her gaze caressed him tenderly, brushing his cheek, his lips, his throat. And his breath left him and his composure left him and he knew he must be gazing at her as intently as she stared at him, for suddenly Ham looked shocked, uncomfortable and then for a brief moment almost ashamed.

Ham recovered first, pushing her forward with sudden

savagery so that she stumbled once more, falling to her knees against the bed.

Logic fled from Cain's mind. He roared to his feet, the pain blanching his face, the sweat streaking down his fevered brow. He didn't notice anymore. He didn't care anymore. He had to protect Maggie. He had to protect her from Ham.

"Don't," Ham said quietly and suddenly he had a rifle pointed at Maggie. She froze, still leaning against the bed, her gaze going from Ham to Cain to Ham again. Her face was expressionless and still, waiting but not beaten.

The tension in the room ratcheted up another notch.

"Cain?" she questioned quietly.

"It's okay," he said, more instinctively than honestly. Belatedly he steadied himself with two hands planted on the TV beside him. His leg wouldn't support his weight and he couldn't afford for Ham to see the weakness.

"You shouldn't have brought her," he told Ham stiffly. "I said this was between you and me, yet once again you turn to the woman. Why can't you face just me, Abraham? Why can't you just stand up to me?"

Abraham's face darkened, a clear sign the barb had struck home. "A good soldier exploits weakness. You got a lotta weakness, Cain. Always did."

"Let her go."

"You're wastin' your breath," Ham said flatly.

Cain swayed dangerously, feeling rage, then an icy coldness that scared him even more, for it carried him dangerously close to the brink of unconsciousness. He had to keep talking, keep functioning and reclaim control. "It's over now, Ham," he forced himself to say. His lips didn't feel like his own. He stood at the end of a very long tunnel, seeing his lips move, hearing himself talk and unable to connect the two. After another shaky moment he squared his shoulders. "I know Dad planned everything." And after a ponderous moment, "I even know we're only half brothers."

He'd caught Ham off guard and the rifle momentarily wavered. Then the other man checked himself and leveled the weapon once more. "What're you talking about?"

"The truth," Cain ground out. "After all these years I'm finally talking about the truth. Mom's trip to Boise all those years ago. The trip to the 'city' she spoke of with such wistfulness only when Zechariah wasn't in the room. The fact Zech always hated me too much just as Mom loved me too much. And my name. He named me Cain not because of my shame, didn't he, but because of Mom's? Because she'd met someone else who had loved her and borne his child."

Ham's eyes grew dark. "Love her? She was in the city for only two weeks. It wasn't love, brother. She was a whore, a sinful woman, and if Daddy hadn't gone and saved her, she would have drowned in her sin."

"Dragged her back kicking and screaming," Cain filled in. And he could see his mother again, staring outside the window at the rainfall with such longing. As if the house was her prison. As if she would never be free. He'd always known that she was sad, but then he'd never been happy in that cabin either so he hadn't questioned it. Not until Maggie started asking him questions about his family, not until she started talking about her half siblings, did Cain suddenly begin to understand. Zechariah had known the truth of Cain's parentage. Abraham had known the truth. Only Cain had been ignorant, leaving his mother isolated with her shame. Sometimes, a man could be very blind.

"Zechariah planned everything, didn't he?" Cain continued, relentlessly. He was very conscious of Maggie's trusting gaze on his face. "I was the devil's pawn in his eyes and he'd named me so. Then I did everything he feared. I went to civilization, embraced society, made friends. Heaven help me, I paid taxes."

"You betrayed the mov—"

"I lived my life! I left behind your hatred, your fanaticism. I realized being a man isn't about hate and it isn't about war. It's not about pulling a trigger and it sure as hell isn't about slaughtering women. It's knowing who you are, Abraham. It's standing for your convictions even when no one else believes you. It's giving something of yourself to the people around you.''

"You are a traitor!"

"No. No, I am *not*. It's not your call anyway. God is judge and jury—look it up sometime, Ham. Only you and Zechariah can be so arrogant as to decide life and death of an innocent woman and then say it's justice.''

Ham's face darkened to a mottled shade, then just as abruptly smoothed over. "No," he said tightly. "I won't tell you that easy. You got a tape recorder, right? You want me to 'fess it all, so you can wrap it up nice and neat and give it to some atheist judge." He shook his head stubbornly. "Nope. No way. I'm no computer programmer like you, but I'm not stupid. You won't get me that easy.''

"I'm not trying to get you," Cain said just as calmly. "I'm going to get Zechariah."

For the first time, Ham appeared uncertain. "What?"

"I know you didn't act alone. I'm sure the phone records will show numerous calls between my apartment and Zech's cell phone. I'm sure the police will find at least one person willing to state that he heard Zechariah tell someone it was okay to kill the girl, even just—"

"I'll deny everything," Ham interrupted harshly. "You can't prove it."

"But I can," Cain countered quietly. "Because I can say I was the one on the other end of the phone. I was the one he commanded to kill Kathy." He looked at his brother levelly. "You set me up for the crime, Ham. You're the one who convinced the jury I was guilty. So now I'll play the guilty party. And I'll tell them all about my accessory, my father who masterminded the hate crime. No more crimes of passion, no more second-degree murder. When I'm done, it'll be a hate crime, a premeditated hate crime—

a federal offense. They'll lock Zechariah so deep into the concrete, Pine-Sol is the closest he'll ever get to fresh air.

"And it'll be forever, Ham. Last of your father's days, sitting in a six-by-eight maximum-security cell, allowed out for only one hour a day and then he can shower or lift weights. That's it. He'll listen to the rain and never feel it on his face. He'll see the sun and never have it warm his skin. He'll dream of the mountains night after night after night, and awake in a cold, gray tomb without even a phone call for comfort. I know, Ham. I know all about it because I was there, and I'll tell you now, he'll never make it.

"You got Kathy. But I've figured out the perfect way to murder Zechariah. I got it from you."

"You son of a bitch." Ham's voice was so low it was guttural and the look that filled his face was pure, animalistic rage. He tilted the rifle toward Cain's chest. Cain didn't mind.

"You can't," he said. "You can't kill Cain, remember?"

The rifle began to shake. The hatred and confusion warred in Ham's face, a volatile mix.

"It's your own fault," Cain whispered relentlessly. "You've never been able to stand on your own, Abraham. You never fought your own wars. You're just Daddy's lapdog doing whatever he asks. Ignore Cain, torture Cain. Kill his woman. You've never had an original thought in your head. You're just a slave, a thirty-three-year-old white-boy slave doing whatever you're told."

"I'm gonna kill you," Ham said.

"Then do it!" Cain exploded. He leaned forward, his arms trembling with the strain, but he was too far gone now, too filled with adrenaline to notice. "Come on, Ham, stand up and shoot that rifle, don't just hold it. But you can't, can you? You can't take me on, you can't stand up to someone as big as you or as strong as you. You're not a man, you know *nothing* about how to be a man. You're

Zechariah's shadow, Zechariah's passive, unquestioning lapdog.''

"It's not like that!"

"Like hell it's not. You're nothing!"

"I am not nothing!" Ham screamed. "I did it! Damn you, damn you. I don't need Zechariah to act. You think I need Zechariah to act? I don't need Zechariah. I killed her and it was me, my idea, my plan. You ain't the only clever boy in the family, you miserable SOB. I got brains too, dammit. And I fixed you, dammit, I fixed you better than you've ever been fixed, and it was all me and my idea and my hand that held your knife and slit her throat. And you want to know what, Cain? It wasn't even hard. It was really damn easy.''

"You son of a bitch," Cain whispered softly. "You are insane.''

And he stopped thinking, he stopped feeling. He just saw Kathy, poor trusting Kathy, who died because of Cain's ignorance. And he saw Maggie, beautiful, trusting Maggie, crouched on the floor waiting for him to save her.

Ham tilted the rifle toward Maggie and smiled.

Cain staggered forward, the pain ripped up his leg, savage and agonizing.

Maggie opened her mouth to scream.

And the world was spinning and the darkness clutched him. There was pain and blood, numbness and cold rage.

Ham settled the rifle comfortably against his shoulder and took aim.

And Cain lunged between them with his last burst of strength, his arm catching Maggie's shoulder, flattening her to the floor as his leg gave out and his body fell heavily on top of her. Down they went to the carpet, his arms curling around her, his fevered frame preparing for the bullet.

"Don't move." C.J.'s voice was cool, calm and collected as he pressed his Beretta against Ham's forehead. The other man twisted reflexively and C.J. didn't wait. He knew the stance of a professional when he saw it. Two swift chops of his left arm, and the rifle tumbled from Ham's suddenly nerveless hands.

Brandon swooped to pick it up. "Maggie," he called immediately. "Are you all right?"

There was a two-second delay, then he heard her muffled voice. She sounded as if she was crying. Immediately he was at her side. "Maggie, Maggie, what's wrong?"

But then he saw the other man, the man whose port-wine stain marked him as Cain. Brandon touched his shoulder. The limp body rolled lifelessly aside, the face dangerously pale.

Maggie looked up at Brandon, her expression tearing him in half as the tears streaked down her face.

"I think he's dead," she whispered. "Brandon, I think he's dead!"

Epilogue

The man moved slowly.

Strong, sinewy forearms were exposed by the rolled-up sleeves of his work shirt, tendons clenching as he wrapped callused hands around the saw and began the smooth, relentless motion. Sweat trickled down from his forehead, staining sun-bronzed cheeks and dampening his blond hair. He didn't stop to wipe it away and slowly the trickle built to stain his blue chambray shirt.

He didn't mind the sweat. He didn't mind the burn of his muscles as he moved the saw. He didn't mind the warm August day, or the bright sunlight that made his eyes squint.

Sometimes he did stop, but when he did it was just to inhale a huge gulp of the fresh, pine-scented air, hold it in his lungs like a fine perfume, then exhale it slowly as if he was still learning how to breathe.

When the two-by-four was cut to the right length, he set it aside, picked up another and resumed sawing.

Behind him, the log cabin had already taken shape. It was built by hand, his hand, and the process had been painstaking. He'd chosen the site himself, cleared it with a Cat tractor that he'd rented. He'd picked out the logs, good thick logs, and scoured building plans to come up with what he wanted. Every now and then, C.J. or Brandon would stop by and lend a hand. They moved faster than he, always in some sort of hurry. He preferred to take it slower. He had time now, and time was precious and should be savored.

There were nights he wanted to sleep with his eyes open so he wouldn't have to relinquish his view of the stars.

He finished with the last board. He picked up the ones he'd cut, wincing a bit as the movement pulled on his still-healing thigh, and began his rolling gait toward the house.

The external structure was done. Built into a hillside, the cabin was two stories high, really a main floor with a loft. The ceiling was vaulted at forty feet, with a wall of sheer windows so that daylight drenched every inch of the interior and a man could always feel as if he had one foot outdoors. The view extolled snowcapped mountains and endless green horizon. When he died, he wanted his ashes scattered here so he would never have to leave that view.

He'd broken ground of the cabin five months back. The day they'd released him from the hospital with his stitched-up thigh and governor's pardon. He didn't remember much about what happened before that. They said he'd been unconscious for ten days, and in those ten days the Ferringer clan had moved in and closed ranks around him. Phone calls had been made. Testimony from Joel, Maggie, C.J. and Brandon had been filed. A lawyer had been hired. A call had gone in to the governor's office, presumably from Brandon.

Cain had just floated, weightless, bodiless, and sometimes in the void he thought he could feel his mother's embrace. And so he'd floated, feeling her hand around his once again and beginning to realize that he was no longer alone.

When he'd finally regained consciousness, Maggie had

been there at the bedside and she had smiled at him and he'd known everything would be all right.

Later, there'd been a flurry of activity. Ham's arrest and his subsequent outpouring of racial diatribes had made national news. His location was now kept secret and the police watched him around the clock, fearing assassination. Zechariah had yet to be charged but was under investigation. Ham would not comment on Zech's involvement one way or the other. Nor would Ham comment on his own, using the opportunity instead to spout off his white supremacist rhetoric instead.

The Klan had flown in a high-powered attorney from Louisiana to take his case. The Epsteins had countered by hiring an even bigger-name attorney, who specialized in bankrupting white supremacist leaders, to file a civil suit against not only Ham, but the two white supremacist groups he belonged to.

Justice was now in the hands of the court and the media were already playing out the trial.

Cain stayed away from it. He needed the trees now. He needed the feel of tools beneath his hands. He needed to create something, slowly and painstakingly. He needed to watch it grow and take shape and know that he could do that.

He supposed he needed some time to heal.

His old employers had called him up the day after his release. They were interested in hiring him back. He countered by saying maybe he'd like to do some freelance projects. He had some ideas for a new generation of games. He wanted to start programming one called "Great Escapes," where the objective was to break out of jail.

They were amused. They were interested. They sent him a top-of-the-line PC and 28.8 baud modem in the mail, plus an advance. He worked on the game at night now, after the sun went down. It was good to be programming again; he liked the complexity. He had a feeling this game could really be something.

"Hey, this is where you've been hiding."

Cain turned, the smile already on his face.

She stood before the wall of windows, having entered without making a sound. The trees framed her luminescent face lushly, giving a wild, fey aura to her features. She glowed these days. Truly glowed.

"How are you feeling?" he asked immediately. He didn't have a chance to cross toward her; she was already crossing toward him.

"Like I swallowed a beach ball." She grimaced, rubbing her hands over her swollen stomach.

"Lucky beach ball," he whispered and replaced her hands with his.

"Did you feel that?" Little junior had learned how to kick.

"He's going to be a fighter," Cain agreed. He tweaked her nose. "Like his mother."

Maggie crinkled her nose, but smiled. Finally, she gave up on restraint and came fully into his arms. They never made it longer than two minutes without touching, and now they drifted into the embrace as naturally as a ship slipping into port. Her arms went around his waist, her head nestled into the curve of his shoulder. His hand stroked her hair. They let the silence linger and savored it.

"Don't forget," Maggie said at last, drawing slightly back, "tonight you finally have to bite the bullet and meet my grandmother."

"Uh-oh," Cain said.

"Exactly."

"She'll probably take down her shotgun and demand that I make an honest woman out of you," Cain said.

"No. C.J. has dibs on that."

"Ah."

"Lydia just wants to mess with your mind. She thinks anyone who builds a log cabin by hand must be a little crazy."

"She may have a point."

Maggie smiled at him. Then she snuggled back into his arms.

"So what about next month?" he asked at last. He picked up a heavy coil of her long red hair, held it up to the dappled forest light, then let it stream like silk through his fingertips.

"What about next month?"

"For the wedding," he said.

Maggie stilled in his arms. "What wedding?"

"Ours."

She finally pulled back, looking at him intently. "Cain Cannon, are you proposing to me?"

"I've been proposing to you," he said, "for five months now." He gestured to the house.

She looked puzzled for a moment and then her eyes widened. "You mean this cabin? You mean you've been building this for me?"

He took her hand. "Here, let me show you something."

He led her to the front door and gestured down. "You've never noticed."

"Never noticed what?"

"Look down on the door. What do you see?"

"A flap."

"Not a flap. Who puts a flap on a door? It's—"

"A cat door," she finished and then her eyes widened again. "Oh my God, you put in a cat door! It is for me!"

Now he grinned, relaxed and ridiculously pleased with himself. "You'll have to help me with the interior, though," he said softly. "I don't know exactly what you want."

"Oh," she said. "Oh."

He brushed his thumb down her cheek. "I love you, Maggie," he whispered. "Did you think I was going to risk you slipping away? A true Hathaway Red is hard to find."

"I...I don't know," she babbled. "I wanted you to ask, thought you would ask, but you did just get out of prison and you have a lot to figure out and I didn't want to pressure you or rush—"

He silenced her with a fingertip over her lips. "I'm not pressured. I'm not rushed. I'm in love. So what do you say, Maggie? Will you take one ex-convict, slightly used?"

"Okay," she said immediately. And then her face softened beautifully. "Oh, Cain, I love you so much."

Cain drew her back against him and it was good and it was right.

He held her with his cheek against her fiery hair. And through the windows of his new house, he could see the sun brighten the blue sky and dapple the endless flowing trees.

*   *   *   *   *

For an *EXTRA*-special treat, pick up

THE PERFECT COUPLE
by
Maura Seger

In April of 1997, Intimate Moments proudly
features Maura Seger's *The Perfect Couple,* #775.

Everyone always said that Shane Dutton and
Brenna O'Hare were the perfect couple. But they
weren't convinced...not until a plane crash
separated them, leaving Brenna at home to
agonize and Shane to fight for his life in the frigid
Alaskan tundra. Suddenly they began to realize
just how perfect for each other they were. And
they prayed...for a second chance.

In future months, look for titles with the
EXTRA flash for more excitement, more
romance—simply *more....*

COMING NEXT MONTH

NIGHTHAWK
by Rachel Lee

Come back to Conard County in May 1997 with Rachel Lee's NIGHTHAWK, IM #781.

Craig Nighthawk was a loner. After being wrongly accused of a crime he hadn't committed, the reclusive Native American just wanted some peace and a chance to rebuild his ranch. But then he met Esther Jackson. She was on the run and stumbling badly, and of all the places on earth, this determined lady just happened to stop to catch her breath in his neck of the woods. What happened next was irresistible.

If you missed any of the other Conard County tales, here's your chance to have them sent to your door!

At last the wait is over...
In March
New York Times bestselling author

NORA ROBERTS

will bring us the latest from the Stanislaskis as
Natasha's now very grown-up stepdaughter,
Freddie, and Rachel's very sexy brother-in-law
Nick discover that love is worth waiting for in

WAITING FOR NICK

Silhouette Special Edition #1088

and in April
visit Natasha and Rachel again—or meet them
for the first time—in

The
Stanislaski
Sisters

containing TAMING NATASHA
and FALLING FOR RACHEL

Available wherever Silhouette books are sold.

Silhouette®

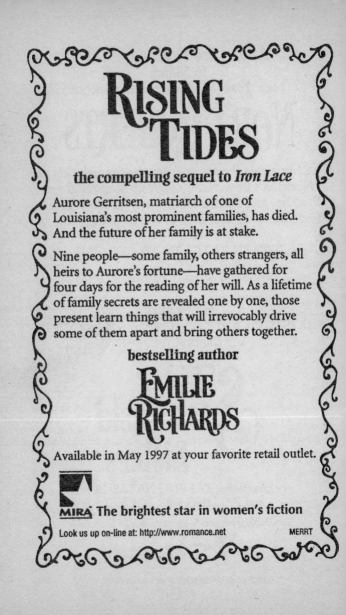